ALSO BY KELLY YANG

**FRONT DESK**

*THREE KEYS*

ROOM TO DREAM

**KEY PLAYER**

TOP STORY

# TOP STORY

# TOP STORY

A **FRONT DESK** NOVEL

## KELLY YANG

SCHOLASTIC PRESS / NEW YORK

Library of Congress Cataloging-in-Publication Data available
ISBN 978-1-338-85839-6

10 9 8 7 6 5 4 3 2 1                                           23 24 25 26 27

Printed in Italy     183

First edition, September 2023

Book design by Maeve Norton and Maithili Joshi

TO THE CHILDREN OF
CHINATOWN, SAN FRANCISCO:

MAY YOUR DREAMS SHINE AS
BRIGHTLY AS YOUR LANTERNS!

# CHAPTER 1

The crisp winter Bay Area wind hugged us as we got out of the car. Our old Chevy had heaved like an elephant all through California's Central Valley, but somehow, we made it, all the way from Anaheim to Chinatown, San Francisco!

I'd never been to Northern California before. I thanked my lucky stars for this dream opportunity wrapped in a Christmas vacation! I was here for journalism camp at one of the most prestigious papers in the country: the *San Francisco Tribune*!

"C'mon, Lupe!" I cried to my best friend as I climbed out of the Chevy and turned in a circle, trying to see all of Chinatown at once. "I want to check out how far it is from here to the newsroom!"

"Trying! This backpack won't budge," Lupe called from the trunk, where she was clenching her teeth and pulling on the thin straps of her bag.

Lupe had come with us so she could compete in the Math Cup state championships in Berkeley, a few cities farther up the coast. Our teachers had let us each take an extra week off school to pursue our passions.

I chuckled. "Every math book in the Anaheim Public Library is crying *ow!*" I teased, helping her heave the bag onto the sidewalk. She'd brought along so many books, her backpack was the size of a sofa.

I pulled my own suitcase out and we gazed up at the Golden Inn. Solid brick, with tall windows, it sat on the corner of Jackson Street. It looked like the Calivista back home, except more vertical. Like if you took all of our motel's rooms and stacked them on top of one another, like a Toblerone chocolate bar shooting straight up into the fog, with a thin, zigzagging fire escape running down its side.

It faced a building with a pagoda tower roof, and up and down the block, streetlamps with steel dragons twirled below red lanterns.

*"Whooooaaa,"* I breathed. "What *is* this place?"

"It's like a whole other country!" Lupe agreed.

"Isn't it amazing?" Mom asked, walking back from the parking meter she'd just fed with a handful of coins. "It's the oldest Chinatown in the United States! Proud home to Chinese immigrants since the Gold Rush!"

My eyes feasted on the Chinese characters on the street signs, and on the dancing red lanterns swinging side by side with Christmas lights. I smiled and waved at all the aunties and uncles walking past, buying groceries in tiny shops and carrying wrapped gifts.

I inhaled deeply, welcoming the scents of winter melon, oolong tea, and the hopes and dreams of a thousand immigrants.

I couldn't *wait* to write about this place! I grinned, thinking of the stories I'd uncover, and hopefully get the *Tribune* to publish!

That was my mission for journalism camp: to convince a national paper that Asian American stories were worth covering *all the time*, not just during special occasions, like the Women's World Cup.

My *other* mission was for me and Lupe to finally have some fun! We'd both worked so hard to get to where we were. But we rarely had time to kick back and relax. On the last day of school before break, I was excitedly talking about camp, and my classmate Stuart rolled his eyes.

"Geez, Mia, don't you ever just chill?" he'd asked.

"No, Stu," I'd snapped. "I don't *just chill*.'"

I'd been a little angry and offended by the comment, but a part of me was also curious. What was it like to chill? Could we finally try it in these city streets? It sure *felt* chilly in San Francisco.

"Can you believe these twenty-four square blocks were all the early Chinese immigrants had?" Mom asked us. "They had to do everything here. Their banking, buying their groceries, finding a job, raising their kids." She put her arms around me and Lupe. "All in this tiny slice of San Francisco."

"At one point, all *we* had was a tiny maid cart and the front office," I reminded her.

"And some cable tools in an old pickup truck," Lupe added with a smile.

I bumped my fist with hers. Now look at us! With that truck, Lupe's dad had built a successful business. He and Lupe's mom were on a cruise right now—their first vacation in forever—off the Gulf of Mexico. They'd booked it ages ago, before Lupe found out she was going to be in the Math Cup championships. Lupe didn't want them to waste their tickets, and since my mom would be with the Math Cup team the whole time, the Garcias decided to go, just the two of them.

My dad was back home, minding our motel and painting our new house, which we bought with our hard-earned savings. Mom was pursuing her dream of teaching math in a high school, and I was going to show a national newsroom what immigrant dreams were made out of!

*Not bad for a bike, huh?* I almost said to Mom. It was a million years ago when she first remarked that my English language skills made me a bike—while all the white kids were cars.

That comment had hurt my feelings.

A lot.

But I'd kept writing, and I kept fighting for my dream. And now I was walking, living proof that you don't have to be born with a language to write at a national level.

Mom turned to us. "I'm so proud of you two. You've both broken barriers to get to where you are. When you get to your competition and your camp tomorrow, I want you to think of all the immigrants who walked before you and were told their dream was too big, their value too small. And you *show them*, you hear?"

I felt myself stand even taller, my heart swelling with pride.

"Yes, ma'am!" Lupe and I shouted.

"There might be people who don't believe you can do it," Mom added gently. She rested a soft hand on Lupe's shoulder and added, "And memories that distract you."

I bit my lip, gazing at my friend.

Something had happened to Lupe right before we left. Something so horrible, she never wanted to talk about it again.

Right before we left for San Francisco, Lupe had finally mustered the courage to tell her friend and Math Cup teammate, Allie, that she liked her. *Like*-liked her.

Lupe knew that Allie might not feel the same way, but she had to be honest about her feelings. But Allie's response was worse than anything we could've expected: She said that Lupe couldn't possibly know she was gay, because a thirteen-year-old was too young to know that kind of thing.

Lupe was mortified. As if that wasn't bad enough, Allie then announced that she and Ethan were dating! Ethan is on the Math Cup team too, so Lupe won't be able to avoid seeing them together.

It will take every ounce of willpower for Lupe to stay focused throughout the competition. At least she gets to stay with us in Chinatown, while the rest of the team and their parents stay in Berkeley. Mom said she chose the Golden Inn because it's much cheaper, but I know she also wanted to give Lupe some space.

Now, Lupe was staring straight ahead, a determined look on her face.

"Nothing's going to distract me," she said quietly. "I'll show her."

"That's the spirit!" Mom turned to me. "And you, Mia—there might be some difficult bigwigs in that newsroom."

I put a hand to my hip and gave her my best Simba I-laugh-in-the-face-of-danger "Ha!"

Mom smiled but insisted, "I'm serious! Big organization like that? There's bound to be one or two thorns. And what are we going to say to those folks?"

"We're going to say *bring it!*" I gazed up at the towering green-and-red roof across the street. "It's going to take a pagoda tower to knock us off our game!"

"Yes it will!" Mom chuckled. "Now come on, let's go check out our rooms!"

Lupe and I grinned at each other. We were finally going to see what it was like to stay in a motel as *guests*!

# CHAPTER 2

An elderly couple sat at the front desk of the Golden Inn, chatting quietly. I stared at all the things that reminded me of home. There was a bell, just like at the Calivista. Shimmering keys hung on the wall, and a little sign said:

*welcome to your home away from home!*
*—Mr. and Mrs. Luk*

How cool and strange to be on the other side of the desk!

Another sign announced *Furry Pets Welcome*, and I immediately imagined the beagle puppy of my dreams, whom I planned to name Comma. I'd wanted a dog for what felt like forever. Now that we finally had our own house back in Anaheim, I hoped to get him as soon as we got back. I could not think of a better chill buddy!

Lupe reached for one of the feedback cards on the desk and wrote *wonderful service*, even though we hadn't been served yet. But we knew from experience how much nice reviews meant to motel owners and workers.

Lupe handed the card to Mrs. Luk, who chuckled.

"Thank you," she said. "We certainly try. At our age, it's getting harder and harder to compete!"

"We run a motel in Anaheim. Your rooms are more affordable than most in our area!" Mom said. "And good thing too, because my school's budget for travel is as small as a lychee. We had to raise the money for this trip through car washes at the motel!"

"Welcome!" Mr. Luk said warmly. "What are you in town for?"

"*This* talented girl here is in a statewide math competition," Mom said, smiling at Lupe. Then she turned and nodded proudly toward me. "And my daughter has a spot in a prestigious writing camp!"

"A writing camp! Wow!" Mrs. Luk gushed. "Chinese calligraphy?"

"No, *English* writing," Mom said.

Yep, I was definitely not a bike anymore!

"Zheng qi!" Mr. and Mrs. Luk praised me.

*Zheng qi* is Chinese for making your family proud—literally translated, it means you'd earned better air in your house, by way of accomplishments. I guess they didn't have windows back in the old days.

"Thanks," I replied, blushing. "I also work at the front desk of our motel."

"Wow, a kid who's actually interested in the family business!" Mr. Luk said. "I wish I could say the same for my kids. They're both in New York City."

"One's a fashion designer!" Mrs. Luk said. "The other works in a bank."

"We raised them to go after the American dream! And now here we are, trying to hang on to our small business all by ourselves," Mr. Luk added with a sigh. "For how much longer?"

His shoulders rose and fell in a dramatic shrug.

"With all the dot-com tech companies moving in . . ." Mrs. Luk matched her husband's sigh and shrug.

Mom nodded sympathetically. "This city is becoming a tech magnet!"

"It's not just the tech companies, it's all the people who work for them," Mrs. Luk said. "They all want to live in fancy condos with bay views. Everyone's rent is going through the roof!"

Mom gasped. "You're not thinking of selling, are you? Your location is fantastic! Right in the middle of this gleaming city!"

"*San Francisco* is gleaming, but Chinatown is struggling," Mr. Luk said.

I reached for my reporter's notebook. Chinatown was struggling? This small, beautiful paradise, full of history and wonder? This sounded like something I should write an article about!

"The tourists just aren't coming," he went on. "And when they do, they stay at the Four Seasons, and they go out and have tapas in Pacific Heights. They don't want to walk around Chinatown anymore."

"What about the ABCs?" Mom asked, meaning "American-Born Chinese"—the second generation of Chinese immigrants, who were born here in the US.

"The second and third generation, they only come to Chinatown for dim sum, maybe once or twice a year. That's not enough to sustain us."

Mrs. Luk slapped the desk defiantly. "We must sustain! This place has been in my family for over one hundred years. Think of all the banquets, and weddings, and family reunions!" Her husband put a sympathetic hand on her shoulder.

"Banquets?" I asked.

"Oh, you should see our banquet hall!" Mr. Luk said. "It's how we get by during the seasons when we don't have a lot of guests, like now. There's nothing like a Chinatown banquet! People come together, we eat, celebrate! There are speeches! Singing! Lion dancing!"

My eyebrows jumped. "Lion dancing?? What's that?"

"You've never seen lion dancing?" Mr. Luk cried. "It's a traditional Asian dance! Performers jump and dance inside a lion costume to bring good luck and fortune. Oh, sweet child, you must come!"

"Sunday night!" Mrs. Luk said. "The whole community will be here. Our cook makes the most delicious Peking duck you've ever had!"

*Peking duck?!* I licked my lips. I could just picture my friend Jason's face lighting up at the mention of his favorite Chinese dish. As the chef at the Calivista restaurant, he'd recently transformed Peking duck in a new and magical way that only he could.

I felt a tug at my heart, missing the rest of my crew. Dad would have loved to see the lion dancers, and Hank could sure give a good speech! I missed everyone, but most of all . . .

Jason.

# CHAPTER 3

"Do you miss Jason?" I asked Lupe as we threw our stuff down in our shared room. I started jumping on my bed immediately; I'd *always* wanted to jump on the guests' beds back at the Calivista!

Lupe laughed. "You mean from six hours ago, when we last saw him?" she asked.

I stopped jumping and blushed. Six hours felt like a long time, especially when you factored in the roast duck! And dim sum! And the pagoda tower and all the other things I was dying to tell him!

"You know what I mean," I said. "Jason would *love* this place. Let's call him!" I glanced around the room, looking for a telephone. "What? Is there really not a phone in here?"

I lay back on the bed and started calculating how many days we'd be here. How I was going to get through all that time without talking to Jason?!

Suddenly, I had to face a fact that had been slowly developing: Jason and I had become inseparable. Admittedly, we had . . . an *unusual* history, going from stone-cold enemies when we first met to business partners at the Calivista. But now we were best friends, and with Jason working at the motel's restaurant, East Meets West, we'd gotten even closer. Especially this year, with Lupe so busy studying for the Math Cup after school, Jason has been my steady partner in crime.

Not having him here was like missing my right big toe. I mean, sure, I could walk without it. But it'd be *a lot* better to have it with me.

Lupe shook her head. "We can live without a phone. Besides, this is *so* much better than staying at the DoubleTree with Allie and Ethan!" She sighed, then buried her face in the plush pillows on her bed.

I reached over and stroked my best friend's hair with my hand. "You've got to stop thinking about it. What she said was totally mean! And not true!"

Lupe peered up at me.

"I can't. It hurt so much, Mia. She was the first girl I've *ever* told my feelings to. And the way she reacted . . ." Lupe's voice took on a sneering tone as she imitated Allie. "'You're too young to *know*, Lupe.'" She shuddered. "It made me feel like a tiny pebble!"

I wrapped my arms around her. "I'm so sorry."

"I should never have told her," she whispered. "Should never have given her an opportunity to hurt me like that."

"You were honest!" I protested, sitting back so I could look her in the eye. "How were you supposed to know she would react so cruelly? Too young to know how you feel? PUH-*LEASE*. You're thirteen! Jason knew when he was *ten* that he liked me."

That got a giggle out of Lupe.

"And if I'm being honest, I've known since I was eleven that I liked boys," I added. "Way before Da-Shawn."

"You had a crush on someone before Da-Shawn?" Lupe yelped. "Who?"

I pressed my lips together, shaking my head. It was way too embarrassing.

Lupe got a wicked look on her face, and suddenly she was tickling me and crying, "Spill the beans, Mia Tang!"

"Okay, okay!" I squealed. "It was Macaulay Culkin!"

She instantly stopped tickling and stared at me. "The *Home Alone* kid??"

"Hey!" I said. "He did the best he could in a dangerous situation!"

We were still giggling when the door between our room and Mom's creaked open and Mom poked her head in.

"You girls settling in okay?" she asked.

"Uh-huh!" I said, turning beet red, hoping Mom couldn't hear us through the wall. I didn't really want to talk to Mom about boys—I knew that the minute I did, she would start going on and on about *not getting distracted* while I was still in school. And I *wasn't* distracted. I just . . . daydreamed sometimes.

"We're super, Mrs. Tang!" Lupe agreed.

Mom nodded. "I checked with the DoubleTree Hotel and the rest of the team got in fine. They're all going out to dinner." She handed me a piece of paper, adding excitedly, "Speaking of which! Here's a map of Chinatown! Why don't you girls pick out where you want to eat tonight?"

"Great!"

I waited until Mom went to her room before turning back to Lupe.

"Seriously, Mia? *Kevin McCallister?*"

"He was perfectly calm and organized throughout the whole robbery attempt, which was very impressive," I insisted.

"So you have a thing for boys who can *calmly* blowtorch a criminal's head?" Lupe asked, giggling again.

No, I didn't actually. I knew for a fact that the boy I liked would never torch anyone—and definitely not calmly.

But I wasn't ready to tell Lupe any more secrets just then. So I pointed to the map.

"Let's go find a good place to chill."

Lupe gave me an amused look. *"Chill?"*

I nodded.

"Mia, we don't know the first thing about chilling!"

*True.* But I was intent on changing that. Starting now. I unfolded the map. "Look, there's a fortune cookie factory just up the block!"

Lupe's eyebrows rose.

"It's open till six o'clock! We still got time! C'mon!" I jumped up again, grabbing my notebook.

"I *could* use some good fortune," Lupe said, her face falling.

I found my wallet. Time to bust out the tip money! I was determined to wrestle a smile back onto my best friend's face, no matter how many fortune cookies it took!

# CHAPTER 4

Walking through Chinatown, Lupe and I oohed and aahed over all the shiny souvenirs in the curio shops that lined the streets. Mom told us that Chinatown was shaped like a trapezoid, sandwiched between Nob Hill on one end and the bustling Financial District, where the *Tribune* was headquartered, on the other.

The streets were like mazes, home to a million tiny shops in tiny alleys. The thick blanket of fog, which Mom said the locals lovingly called Karl the Fog, made the whole place seem even more mysterious. I wanted to touch and buy everything. Intricately patterned ceramic bowls and gold Buddha figurines sat beside luminous jade necklaces and pearly mah-jong sets. After we'd window-shopped for a while, Mom took us to a small café and bought us each a huge milk tea with little squishy balls bobbing in it.

"They're called boba! From Taiwan!" she explained.

"Jason told me all about them!" I thanked Mom, taking my drink eagerly.

At my first sip of my boba, I missed Jason even more. It tasted even better than he had described—soft and bouncy, like biting into a jelly ball!

We sat on a bench with our treats. Next to us, three elderly Chinese women were watching the passersby. One pulled out a wok she'd just bought and held it so the others could see.

"That's a good handle!" the woman sitting in the middle said in Chinese. "How much you spend? Twenty dollars?"

A man a few benches away hollered, "That metal looks hollow! Very light! Good for flipping!"

Mom leaned closer to the women. "Say, you guys know where I can find a cute scarf for cheap?" she asked. "I've got a very important day tomorrow—first day of a big competition for the math team I'm coaching! I have to meet all the other coaches! Want to look nice!"

"Absolutely!" the elder with the wok said. All three women pointed across the street, at a clothing store next to the spice store. Mom thanked them, then told me and Lupe we could stay out on the benches while she shopped, if we wanted.

"You ready for tomorrow?" Lupe asked me.

I gulped down my boba and nodded. "Can't wait. Every morning, we learn and practice a different journalism skill, and we get to pitch our stories to the editor for our beat! I hope they assign me to the city section!"

"Not sports?" Lupe asked.

I shook my head. "I want to write about *all kinds* of topics. I'll bet they don't know half the things happening in Chinatown!" I told Lupe I had about fifteen ideas already.

Lupe chuckled. "I can't wait to read 'em!"

"What about you? How's Math Cup championship going to work?"

"Well, the competition's all this week, but only in the mornings. In the afternoons, we get to do workshops with all the coaches and explore Berkeley! Your mom says this is the university's way of supporting the top high school math kids in the state."

"Oooh! Sounds like they're trying to woo you!" I teased.

Lupe raised her boba tea cup in a toast. "Hope so!"

We finished our teas and got up to investigate the spice store across the street. Lupe picked up a star-shaped pod and held it up. "What's this?"

"I think that's anise?" I guessed.

"Should we buy some for Jason?"

"Good idea!" I started reaching for my wallet, then remembered that we were going to be here through New Year's. If we bought a bunch of herbs and spices now, our hotel room would probably smell like braised beef stew by the time we left. "Or wait—let's come back and get it later."

Lupe put the star back in its bin on the shelf. "You and Jason have been spending an awful lot of time together. Is it ever still awkward between you two?"

"No. Why?" I asked, trying not to blush. *What was she asking? Did she already know . . . ?*

"Because . . . last year?" Lupe said.

Suddenly, I realized what she was alluding to. "Oh! Because of what happened *last* Christmas?" I said, nearly laughing in relief. "Okay, yeah, that *was* awkward."

The *unusual* history that Jason and I shared included a really unfortunate chapter. Between hating each other and becoming best friends, there was . . . a kiss. That is, Jason kissed me. It was totally unexpected and strange and embarrassing and *boy* did I let Jason know that it was NOT cool.

"We're okay now," I told Lupe. "Just two best friends."

"But aren't you worried that deep down inside, he secretly still likes you?" she asked.

I shook my head. I was not worried.

Not about that, anyway.

Before she could ask anything else, Lupe turned toward the window of the spice store. It was getting dark outside, and a flashing sign glimmered from down the block.

"Mia, look! There it is. The fortune cookie factory!" She dashed out to the sidewalk and I followed—but first I stuck my head into the scarf shop, where my mom was chatting with another woman at the counter.

"Mom!" I hollered. "We're going over to that factory!"

She gave the shopkeeper a wave and scurried out, proudly draping a red scarf around her shoulders.

"How do I look?" she asked, posing as we followed a sign down a narrow alley to the factory. "Like I belong on the state Math Cup committee?"

I stopped walking. "Wait, you're trying to get on the *state* committee?"

"Go, Mrs. Tang!" Lupe said, high-fiving Mom. I gave her a big hug.

"Thank you," she said, "but first I have to impress all the committee members!" She rolled her eyes. "And the other coaches. It'll take some doing. I'm not exactly good at networking."

"But you're good at working!" I pointed out.

Mom laughed. We started down the alleyway again—though I was practically skipping with excitement. I couldn't believe what big plans my mom had!

Lupe reminded Mom, "Who else taught her team out of a motel room instead of letting her administration tell her she couldn't coach? Who *personally* washed eighty-five cars to raise the money it took to get her team up here from Anaheim?"

Mom beamed. "And that's why I want to be on the committee. So I can work to bring access to the Math Cup to more underfunded districts!" she said. "And to make sure we recruit more women math teachers to judge our competitions, especially women of color!"

"Yesssss!!!" Lupe and I cheered.

In my excitement, I almost didn't see the factory at first. It was a lot smaller than I'd expected, and looked more like a store than a factory. But the huge cast-iron machines we could see through the windows and the sweet, buttery smells of cookie batter wafting from the door were a dead giveaway.

As we walked inside, a girl about the same age as me and Lupe came striding over with a big grin.

"Welcome to Dragon Fortune Cookie Factory!" she said confidently. "I'm Emma Wong!"

Lupe and I gaped at her, then at each other. Could it be that the factory was run by . . . a kid?

# CHAPTER 5

Emma Wong was about my height. She had a splash of freckles on her fair nose and deep brown eyes. Her shiny, light brown hair bounced on her shoulders as she hopped around the factory.

"Want me to give you a tour?" she asked eagerly. "Then you can try a piece?"

Lupe, Mom, and I nodded gratefully.

"Great! I'm Dragon Fortune Cookie Factory's concierge!" she said, her bright eyes sparkling.

Lupe and I smiled at the word *concierge*—we'd been debating whether to call *ourselves* that at the motel.

Emma told us she was twelve years old and half Chinese. She switched effortlessly to speaking perfect Chinese when we passed the other workers. There were four women working at the machines, including her mom, Grace.

We waved at Auntie Grace through the thin partition, where she sat on a stool in front of the big steel machine. Every time the machine presented a cookie, Auntie Grace hand-folded it.

"The factory was established in the 1960s. It's family run!" Emma said, squeezing behind the thin partition to lead us over to her mom. She was nimble and fast, darting between the machines in her overalls.

We hurried after her and watched Auntie Grace and the three other women work. Freshly baked cookies rolled out on a circular conveyor belt, and as they came by, the workers reached out and hand-folded each still-soft piece of dough into its iconic triangular shape, stuck a fortune inside, and placed the cookies in a big bucket to harden and cool. It was fascinating—but what I really couldn't take my eyes off was the tower of fortunes. There must have been a million slim strips of paper peeking out of the plastic bag next to the women.

I pulled out my reporter's notebook.

"How long have you been working here, Emma?" I asked.

"My mom's been part-time here for years. She folds while I give tours," she said enthusiastically. "We live right over at Sacramento and Stockton—I was born at the Chinese Hospital, same as Bruce Lee!"

Wow! I wasn't sure whether to ask her more about Bruce Lee, the famous martial arts actor, or the fortunes! I quickly jotted down everything she'd told us so far. I was so busy writing that Lupe had to poke me repeatedly, then point at Emma, who was holding out a box. "Try a sample!" she said.

Mom, Lupe, and I reached in gratefully. The box was full of broken pieces, but they were still warm from the oven. One nibble of wafer and I was in heaven, crispy sugar melting on my tongue.

"These are *so* good!" I raved.

Emma beamed, exchanging a proud look with her mom. "That's because we make them all by hand. Most of the ones you get from Chinese restaurants are made by machine. But *these* are the real deal, right, Mom?"

Auntie Grace nodded from the other side of the partition.

"Do you get a lot of customers here at the factory?" I asked, getting back to my notes.

"Sometimes. But we're only here Mondays, Wednesdays, Thursdays, and Saturdays. When we're not here, we help out over at the flower shop, or at Mr. Chu's kite shop!"

My eyebrows shot up. "You work *three* different jobs?" *Dang, girl*, I thought. "You have even less time to chill than me!"

I was joking, but Emma looked a little sad.

"Well, we're trying to save up to get out of our SRO," she said.

"I'm sorry, I didn't mean it like that. I totally get it. My family saved up for years—at one point, we were living in our car."

Emma's face brightened. "Really?"

I nodded.

"What's an SRO?" Lupe asked.

"It stands for 'single-room occupancy.' Most everyone in Chinatown lives in one."

"Like a motel room?" Lupe asked. "We know a lot about motels."

"Yeah, kinda!" Emma said, cheerful again. "Except we don't have our own bathroom, we share one that's down the hall. More like dorms. Our building originally housed the workers who came to build the railroad in the 1800s! Did you know that twenty thousand Chinese immigrants helped build the transcontinental railroad? They blasted tunnels and laid hundreds of miles of track, even in freezing cold and scorching heat. Hundreds died. If it weren't for the Chinese workers, we would never be able to build it as fast as Congress wanted! Anyway, after they finished, many of them came to Chinatown and lived in the SROs."

Wow. We *had* to get this girl on *Jeopardy!* I marveled at her extensive knowledge of history. *And* her ability to keep her hair so shiny without a private shower.

Emma's mom took a break and joined us, leaning down to mutter to her daughter in Chinese, "Don't be talking about our room, it's embarrassing!"

Emma's face turned red. "Sorry, Mom."

I knew that wriggly feeling—all too well. My first year in Anaheim, Jason had made sure that our entire class knew that I wore clothes from thrift stores. Everyone had made fun of me.

In that moment, my fondness for Jason shrank a little.

"You should have seen *my* room in the apartment we used to live in," Lupe offered.

"Mine too," I added. "We've been living in a motel in Anaheim. This year, my mom didn't even sleep in the same room as my dad, because the manager's quarters is so small!"

Talking to Emma, it occurred to me that maybe chilling was kind of a privilege. One that not everybody had. At least not me, back then.

Emma smiled gratefully. She turned and grabbed a box of blank pieces of fortune-size paper. "Want to write a fortune?"

"Wait, we can write our own fortunes?" I asked.

"I do all the time!" Emma said. She grabbed a small tray of papers and showed us one that read:

Never shop retail! Find yourself a Chinatown grandma and get a senior discount at any major store!

I laughed. "Solid advice!"

"Thanks! The owner doesn't like me messing around with these, though." She sighed, pointing to the stack of printed fortunes. "These are the official ones. We print them all right here."

"Really?" I asked. I looked around. "Where?"

"In the back," Emma said, pointing to a room tucked behind the owner's office. "But *I* think it's fun to mix it up." She handed us pens. "Jot yours down and my mom will put them into the cookies for you!"

"How much?" I asked, searching for my wallet.

"Hmm. How about a dollar each?"

Lupe and I each gave Emma a single bill.

But when I held my empty piece of paper, I paused. How could I settle on just one fortune?

I'd been desperately wanting a computer. There were a few at school, and Da-Shawn got one for his birthday. I'd watched enviously as his words magically appeared on the screen.

And there was Comma, the beagle puppy of my dreams.

Plus making a good impression at camp, and decorating the new house with my dad, and everything back home . . .

But in the end, I decided to write:

Even when it feels like you don't have all the tools, you'll find the way to achieve your goals.

I smiled and turned to Lupe. She covered up her fortune. "Lemme see! What'd you write?"

But she shook her head shyly, and handed her fortune directly to Emma's mom. It wasn't until later, after she ate her cookie quietly by the window in our room, that I saw what her fortune said:

You'll never get your heart broken again.

# CHAPTER 6

On my first day of camp, I stood in front of the full-length mirror in our room. Hair in bun, secured with a pen? Check. Reporter's notebook in my pocket, check. Camera, check. Comfortable walking shoes, check. Earplugs, in case I needed to cover a rock and roll concert, check. Lip gloss, in case I got to interview a celebrity. And fortune cookies, in case I got . . . well, hungry.

I put everything into the unicorn backpack Lupe got me for my last birthday. Ready! Today I'd be a part of the newsroom of one of the most influential newspapers in the nation. I closed my eyes and imagined myself getting promoted from camper to *Staff Writer Mia Tang. Editor Mia Tang. Publisher Mia Tang.*

Okay, maybe not *publisher.* That was probably too ambitious. But I *was* determined to make my mark!

Mom, Lupe, and I hurried downstairs, eager to have a bowl of congee before hitting the road. Mom was dropping me off at the *Tribune* headquarters before taking rapid transit with Lupe to Berkeley.

Mr. and Mrs. Luk were already in the dining room, wearing aprons and bickering.

"He just *quit*? Did he say why he was leaving?" Mr. Luk asked his wife.

"Something about his kids in Chicago," she replied. "You know how much he wanted to be closer to them."

I looked around and noticed that the serving trays and congee bowls were all empty.

Mr. Luk threw up his hands. "Where are we going to find a chef over the Christmas holidays? What about our banquet?"

Mrs. Luk threw up her hands too. "We're just going to have to cancel," she said sadly.

"But we *need* that banquet to break even for December!" her husband argued.

"You don't need to remind *me*. I'm the one who booked it!" Mrs. Luk frowned at her wrinkled hands. "If it weren't for my arthritis, I'd do the cooking myself . . . But three hundred people . . ."

Mr. Luk's shoulders slumped as he put a hand on his wife's back. "Let's face it. We're just too old for this, both of us," he said. "Maybe it's time we called that realtor. See if that dot-com company still wants to buy—"

"WAIT!" I cried. They couldn't hang their coats up because of one missing cook! My mind was spinning.

Mr. and Mrs. Luk's eyes flashed at me, surprised.

"I know who can cook for your banquet!" I cried.

# CHAPTER 7

Mom and Lupe both leaned in, trying to hear the other end of the phone call as I explained Mr. and Mrs. Luk's situation to the two best chefs in California.

"I've always wanted to go to San Francisco!" Jason cried.

"This is perfect! I got family up there!" Hank said.

"You do?" I blurted. That was news to me!

"Yep," said Hank. "My brother Darrius. It's . . . complicated. We'll talk about all that later, when I see you. Jason and I will hit the road as soon as possible!"

"YAY!!!" I cried. "But what about East Meets West?"

"It's the holiday slump down here," Hank said. "This'll give our staff a few hard-earned days off. Come back refreshed for the new year!"

"And it'll give my mom a chance to go to Vegas with my dad! She's been trying to get him to go with her to a Celine Dion concert!" Jason added.

I tried to imagine Mr. Yao at a Celine Dion concert, singing along to "The Power of Love." It was really hard. But hey, if it meant Jason could come to San Francisco, I was all for it! I gave my friends the Golden Inn's address.

"We'll see you soon!" Jason said, and they hung up.

The Luks clapped and hugged. Lupe gave me a high five.

I thought of Hank and Jason jumping in the car and driving up the coast, and I could hardly breathe with excitement. And not just because I'd saved the banquet. . . .

. . .

The glittering *Tribune* tower shot up straight into the sky. I gazed at the high-rise for so long, the pen in my bun practically drew a smiley face on my neck.

The sleek, imposing newsroom sat right on the corner of bustling Montgomery and Sutter Streets. Just blocks away from Chinatown, it somehow felt like a different planet. There were no red lanterns or playful dragons. There were just suits—lots and lots of them. This was the big leagues, all right. Writers who walked into this building were *career writers*.

"Nervous?" Mom asked me as we walked up the steps to the main entrance.

I put my arm around my tummy to calm the butterflies and reminded myself I had nothing to be scared of. It was just writing. One word at a time! I could do this—I'd done it before!

All around me, the other campers were saying good-bye to their families.

A weeping mother hugged a girl dressed in an argyle sweater. "First day of work! Can't believe it! My baby's all grown up!" the mother wailed.

"Mom! Get ahold of yourself," the girl said. "It's just camp, I'll be done by three o'clock. And I'm fifteen years old!"

I sucked in a breath as I turned and scanned the other

campers. They all looked so much older. Some were even carrying briefcases. Was I the youngest one here?

I looked down at my shoes.

"Mia!" Mom said excitedly. "You're the youngest writer here! And the only Chinese girl! Oh, your ancestors will be so proud." Her eyes widened. "You know what that means?"

*That I need to call Hank before he leaves and ask if he has a briefcase I can borrow?*

Mom didn't wait for my answer before gushing, "They *see* something in you, honey! Even though you're only in middle school! You got your foot in the door—now you gotta kick it down for everyone else!"

A boy standing nearby swung around and blurted, "You're only in middle school?"

The girl in the argyle sweater looked over. "No way!"

Now everybody was looking at me. I shrank under my backpack straps, feeling like a unicorn. And not in a good way.

"You should see her writing!" Lupe announced. Then she gave me a hug and whispered, "You'll be fire!"

"Thanks," I whispered back. We held each other's hands as I said, "Have a great time at Berkeley! I'm rooting for you! Remember—just focus on the math!"

We gave each other reassuring smiles, then Lupe's fingers pulled away.

And it was just me.

As the older kids continued to stare, I reminded myself that this itchy, scratchy feeling of folks questioning whether I'd earned something? I'd felt it before. And what did I do? I proved I belonged—starting with the first sign I made at the front desk.

So let 'em look. Let 'em stare. Then let 'em read my words—they wouldn't know what hit them.

Bravely and boldly, I lifted my head and walked up the steps into the *Tribune*.

# CHAPTER 8

High up on the thirty-eighth floor, I fidgeted next to my new camp-mates, trying to look as polished and sharp as everyone around me at the big, dark wood table in the conference room. I kept staring out the floor-to-ceiling windows to the San Francisco skyline. On the opposite wall, more glass let us see the sea of desks that made up the main newsroom. Phones rang and men and women scurried around carrying papers and coffee. Some looked like they'd been here all night. It was all so exciting and terrifying and grown-up. I was getting goose bumps just watching.

At the front of the conference room stood Ed Walters, who intro-duced himself as the city beat editor and the director of the camp.

When I heard "city beat," I sat up straighter and crossed my fin-gers. *Please let me be on his beat!*

Mr. Walters was a clean-cut white man in his late forties. He wore a white shirt with the sleeves rolled up, a small bow tie, and suspend-ers. Exactly how I'd pictured a big editor.

"We are so glad you are able to join us here in San Francisco for the seventh annual *Tribune* Journalism Boot Camp," he boomed, pushing up his small, round-rimmed glasses. "You've all been selected for your talent in journalism, and we hope that our camp will push those talents to even higher heights! Allow me to introduce the teachers of the camp this year, my fellow editors!"

He gestured for his colleagues to come in. We all glanced over to the door. Two other men and a woman walked in. Mr. Walters introduced them as Phyllis Hart, the editor of the business section, Ben Axel from sports, and Alexander Owen, the opinion editor. They were all white, like most of the reporters I could see answering phones and filing papers.

I was encouraged that the business section editor was a woman. Still, this paper, overall, seemed a lot less diverse than the *Anaheim Times* back home. I wondered how they managed to tell the stories of this huge multilingual and multicultural city. Could they even report on Chinatown, where so many aunties and uncles spoke only Chinese? Maybe that was what I could bring to the table. I sat up even taller.

Mr. Walters explained that once we get our section assignments, we'd stay with our group.

"Each morning," he went on, "you'll have workshops teaching journalism skills. Then a catered sandwich lunch, then Newsroom, where you'll put your skills to use and pitch stories."

The girl with the argyle sweater raised her hand. "Will we all get published?"

"That depends on the quality of your pitch. Keep in mind, we're *very* selective." Mr. Walters took off his glasses and leaned forward on the table. "We're at a critical time in our industry. With the rapid development of the internet, soon every grandma with a laptop will be publishing articles. News, as we understand it now, will cease to mean anything."

Everyone gasped.

"*If* we as a paper, as an industry, and as a nation, are to survive," he continued, "we must have strict standards. Only the highest quality stories will be accepted. *But* if your piece is accepted for publication, you'll receive seventy-five dollars!"

My eyes turned into saucers. Seventy-five dollars was a fortune! That was way more than my editor in China paid me for my columns about life in America!

An Asian boy in a bright yellow sweatshirt started clapping. A smiling girl with braided hair and a turquoise beaded necklace joined him. I started clapping too. I was going to make *bank*!

Then another man poked his head in. He wore a tan sports jacket and jeans and looked much younger than Mr. Walters.

"Just popping in to say hi!" he said. "I'm John Miles, the editor in chief! My great-grandfather started this paper over a hundred years ago. I'm so happy you could join us."

A photographer followed Mr. Miles in and started snapping photos.

Mr. Miles smiled brightly for the camera, then back at us. "We're especially proud this year to expand access to our program by offering full scholarships to some very talented young writers." He and Mr. Walters gave each other a nod. Then, to my horror, Mr. Miles held out an arm and announced, "Introducing our first class of Golden Scribes! Mia Tang, Lucas Perez, Jadyn Johnson, Tamara Miller, Haru Tanaka, and Amne Sullik, will you please stand up?"

I slid my chair back and stood, looking around at the other full-scholarship recipients. Sitting down, I could get away with looking like everyone else, but standing, I was clearly much shorter than my peers. The Asian boy and the Indigenous girl with braids stood too, plus a Latinx kid wearing a newsboy cap and a Black boy with glasses. A white girl with a beaded headband waved to everyone from her pink wheelchair.

Mr. Miles waved us all over to stand behind the girl in the wheelchair. As we smiled awkwardly for the photographer, the editor in chief boasted about all our accomplishments. I managed to hear that Amne had written an article about the forest fire in the Bay Area last year for her high school paper; Haru, a freshman, published a piece on the heroic tale of a Japanese boy who sailed alone across the Pacific; and Tamara had interviewed a legendary filmmaker about her documentary on the disabilities rights movement.

I was definitely the youngest, but supremely honored to be included in this crew!

Finally, we sat back down. Mr. Walters got out a piece of paper from an envelope with a flourish.

"Now, the moment of truth—your beat assignments!" he said. "Mia, Amne, Timothy, Jenna, Zoe, and Haru, you're with me. Welcome to the city beat!"

I couldn't help letting out a little squeal.

After the other editors announced their campers, Mr. Walters handed out our staff cards.

"These will allow you to get in and out of the building every day. But more importantly, flash this downstairs at Jenni's Smoothies for ten free smoothies!"

Smoothies cost five dollars! Mom almost never let me buy them! Ten was mind-blowingly generous! I held my card carefully, but noticed the other campers stuck theirs into their pockets with a muted "Thanks." Clearly, not everyone had the same appreciation for this bonus.

I decided not to worry about it as I followed Mr. Walters over to his office. The other campers and I might come from different worlds, but we were in the same place now. We all had the same chance at getting published.

With that, I grabbed my pen from my hair, *ready for my shot!*

# CHAPTER 9

We sat around a smaller oak table in the city section conference room and Mr. Walters explained the city beat.

"To me, this section is all about *people*. Stories that move readers at the deepest level. They're everywhere, but they're often hidden. To get these stories, you have to be curious. You have to dig, ask the hard questions. So for workshop today, we're going to work on your curiosity."

He pointed to the glass conference room wall. "I want you to imagine those elevator doors opening and your biggest idol stepping out. You have five minutes to come up with three *interesting* interview questions for them. Go!"

All around the table, a series of thumps sounded as my fellow campers pulled out their laptops. I told myself not to fret. I might not have a laptop, but I had plenty of ideas! My fingers twitched with adrenaline as I reached for a blank piece of paper. I noticed Amne and Haru writing on paper too.

Fifteen minutes later, I was proudly rereading the questions I'd written for Ann M. Martin, the author of my favorite book series, The Baby-Sitters Club. But as soon as I heard the other campers' idols and the questions they wanted to ask them, I started sweating.

Timothy Madison, a boy with extremely gelled blond hair,

announced, "I would want to ask Jay Madison: If Sam Goldwyn had not made such a terrible movie of *To Everleigh with Love*, would he have let others take a crack at adapting *The Ivory Mirror*?"

Wait, was this Timothy kid talking about *the* Jay Madison? The legendary icon? One of America's greatest writers of all time?

"WOWZERS! What a fabulous question!" Mr. Walters praised. "Any relation, may I ask?"

"He was my grandfather," Timothy admitted.

My jaw dropped. *Are you kidding me?* I was going to writing camp with the grandson of one of the most beloved writers of American literature?

Imagine the literary talent flowing through Timothy's veins! The stories he heard growing up! The respect he could command when he called someone up asking for an interview, just by uttering his name!

Mr. Walters looked like he was thinking the same thing.

"You know what would be fun?" he said. "To have you write a story on the bookstores in our city! What your grandfather would have thought . . ."

And just like that, Timothy got his first publishing assignment. He didn't even have to pitch it!

That's when I realized, it wasn't just laptops and gadgets I was up against. It was powerful last names too.

. . .

By the time it was my turn, I'd changed my interview subject five times.

I looked down at my crumpled-up paper. Jenna Sterling had *also* picked Ann, *and* announced that her mother had gone to Smith College with her.

"Well, Mia?" Mr. Walters asked.

I blew at my bangs in frustration. Then I had an idea.

"Hank Caleb," I said.

Mr. Walters pushed his glasses up, intrigued. "Hank Caleb, huh? Never heard of him. He a state senator? Assembly member? Radio host?"

"He's a small business owner and a chef," I said. "A very good one."

"How many Michelin stars does he have?" a girl named Zoe asked. Zoe's interview questions were for the manager of her dad's chain of celebrity nightclubs.

"Well, none, but—"

"Then why's he your idol?" she asked.

I forced myself to look her right in the eye as I explained, "Because he's wise, and he's kind. And he helps me make sense of the world." *Like right now.* If Hank were here, he'd know just what to say to make me feel like I deserved to be at this table.

I glanced at the clock, counting the hours until he and Jason got to San Francisco.

Mr. Walters sat back and nodded. "I think it's wonderful your idol is not someone famous. Remember, the city section is all about the news of the little people." I looked at him, thinking it was ironic, given he'd just offered a story to Timothy based on his famous grandfather. "Go on. So what would you ask Mr. Caleb?"

I took a deep breath.

"First I'd want to know how you keep the faith alive, when you realize not everyone's at the same starting place in a game," I said, peeking over at Timothy. I wasn't mad at him. He couldn't help who his grandfather was. But still, it gave him a briefcase of advantages.

"I'd ask Hank how he taps into his kindness every day." I paused, smiling a little just thinking about my friend. "And finally, I'd ask him what his greatest hope is for the future."

Mr. Walters's mouth twisted to one side. "That last question is a little weak." He looked around at the group. "Remember, always ask the unexpected. We're not interested in basic, canned answers. We want what's *not* been said. And in order to do that, we've got to *surprise*, ask the *tough* questions."

I nodded, trying not to let my disappointment show as I stared down at my pen. I'd been hoping to knock Mr. Walters's socks off with my questions. Instead I got . . .

*A little weak.*

*Basic.*

*Canned.*

As Mr. Walters went on to the next person, I sat very still, trying not to let any of my emotions show. *It's just the first workshop.* But all I could think about was Mom, and what she said about all the immigrants who walked before me. I imagined my ancestors looking down at me from the gold mountain-mining, railroad-laying heavens.

I could almost hear their collective *aiya* as they shook their heads at me.

# CHAPTER 10

I tried not to think of my poor workshop performance all during lunch. The free turkey sandwiches were actually really good. They'd ordered the fancy kind, with crusty bread and avocado. With every bite, I felt the guilt mount. The newspaper had spent so much money bringing me up here, giving me this incredible experience. And I couldn't even put three interesting questions together. I did not deserve avocado.

I thought my luck would turn around at Newsroom, but Mr. Walters said no pitches today. He wanted us to come up with interesting questions for the next city council meeting, on whether to let a developer build another luxury condo. I had a *ton* of interesting questions, thanks to Mr. and Mrs. Luk.

But I was paired up with Timothy, who shot down all my ideas.

"We should ask about the views," he said. "The stuff people will want to know."

After the way Mr. Walters fawned all over him, I kept thinking Timothy *must* know what he was doing. After all, he was much older than me. And he had more writing experience in his blood. So I let him take the lead.

And when we presented our questions to the staff reporters going to the meeting, they politely said, "The project hasn't been approved. So we can't ask about the view."

I was still kicking myself for listening to Timothy at 3:00 p.m., when Amne approached me at the elevator banks.

"Hey, want to stop by Jenni's to get our first free smoothie?" Her kind eyes peeked at me under her long lashes.

I smiled, surprised. I still had an hour before Mom and Lupe came and got me, and I'd been planning to start brainstorming for Newsroom tomorrow.

"Sure!" I said. "Oh, but I left my staff card at my desk. I'll meet you down there!"

"Great!" Amne beamed, revealing two dimples before she turned and hopped in the elevator.

I walked back into the office. Thankfully, Mr. Walters had assigned me a work desk next to Amne and Haru. I thought I would be stuck with Timothy the famous grandson forever. But he insisted on sitting by the window, because he said the light reminded him of Paris and inspired him to write better. I had to pretend I had a fly in my eyelash to cover up my eye rolling.

I reached for my staff card on my non-window desk.

As I was walking out, I spotted Mr. Walters in Mr. Miles's office. The two men were deep in conversation as I walked closer. The door was opened wide, and they were talking about *us*! I froze, leaning against the wall.

"So how was your group?" Mr. Miles asked. "Phyllis said she has a kid who can't report on Cisco because his family owns too much stock in it."

"Well, I have Jay Madison's grandson on board to write a piece on what his grandfather would think of San Francisco bookstores," Mr. Walters said.

Mr. Miles snapped his fingers. "Great idea! Good advertising hook too!" He paused. "How are the Golden Scribes doing?"

I sucked in a breath.

"They're nice. Eager and motivated," Mr. Walters said. "But are we going to get some juicy exposés out of them? Doubt it. They seem pretty soft."

*Soft?* My jaw dropped. I took a finger and stuck it to my collarbone. It was as hard as a rock! Or . . . was he talking about my writing? He hadn't read a single word yet! Then I had a terrible thought—what if he never accepted a pitch from me? What if I never got a chance to prove him wrong?

As I turned to slink away, I heard Mr. Miles say, "We can't make *any* editorial mistakes this Christmas. With the internet exploding, we've got to prove to the advertisers we're not walking dinosaurs."

"Yes, sir," Mr. Walters replied.

I lugged myself, one heavy foot in front of another, back to the elevators. Riding down, I tried to picture the delicious free smoothie at Jenni's. But all I kept tasting in my mouth was a smoothie of regret.

I should not have let Timothy bulldoze all my questions during Newsroom. I should not have been intimidated. I had a job to do at the newspaper, and I wasn't going to let Mr. Walters or my own insecurity stop me.

# CHAPTER 11

Amne and Haru had already gotten their smoothies by the time I walked into Jenni's. I pointed distractedly at the menu board, anger bubbling inside me.

If Mr. Walters didn't think the Golden Scribes could produce useful articles, what was even the point of bringing us to the camp?

As I waited for my free drink to finish blending, I glanced at the corkboard hanging on the wall near the counter. Notices about community events and advertisements were tacked up in a jumble of colorful paper.

I was reading an ad about learning guitar when the clerk called my name. After scanning my staff card, he handed me my drink.

"You have nine free smoothies left," he informed me.

"Thanks," I said. Rather than feeling like a proud member of the press corps, I shoved my card deep in my pocket.

"Over here!" Amne said, waving. "What flavor did you get?"

I sat down. "Raspberry?"

I must have looked pretty sad because Amne offered, "Hey. It's just our first day. I thought your question about the view was good!"

"That wasn't my question. That was Timothy's. I wanted to

ask about the impact on all the mom-and-pop businesses."

"So why didn't you?" Amne asked.

I fell quiet.

She exchanged a glance with Haru. Then, quietly, she pointed to my smoothie. "You know . . . I'm pretty sure that's actually thimbleberry! It kind of looks like raspberry, but the flavor's more intense. And you know the thing about thimbleberry?"

I shook my head and took a sip. The flavor was intense—tarter than a raspberry but sweeter than a lemon. I liked it!

"They're only ripe for one day in the summer. Sometimes you just gotta take your chance." She bumped my shoulder gently, and I realized she was talking about more than just the smoothie.

I smiled.

"Like the cherry blossoms in the Japanese Tea Garden in Golden Gate Park!" Haru said. "They only bloom once a year. It's so beautiful. My dad always brings me up to see them."

"Do they have Japanese gardens in Los Angeles?" Amne asked.

"You're from LA too?" I asked Haru. "Where?"

"Yeah, I live in Little Tokyo. It's near downtown. My dad works at the Japanese American National Museum—I help out there too," Haru said. "It's a wonderful museum. You should come check it out!"

"I will!" I told him, making a mental note. "We live in Anaheim, but I bet my dad will take me after we get back." I felt a pang, missing Dad.

"We're launching a new exhibit in January. It's called *Dear Miss Breed*," Haru said. "It'll showcase all these letters—two hundred and fifty of them—that were written by Japanese children during World War Two. After Pearl Harbor, they were forced from their homes and thrown in internment camps. But they wrote to Miss Breed almost every day, and now we can read all about what they went through, in their own words!"

I'd never heard anything about this! I had a million questions for Haru, but I started with, "Who was Miss Breed?"

"She was a children's librarian at the San Diego Public Library from 1929 to 1945. She loved all the kids who visited her branch," Haru told us. "She was heartbroken when she learned that the Japanese American families were being taken away from their homes for no reason. So she stuck penny stamps on envelopes, and on the day they were being sent away, she ran all the way down to the San Diego train station to give the envelopes to the children, so they could write to her."

"Wow," I said.

"And did they?" Amne asked.

"They sure did! She sent them books! The letters are heart-wrenching—they describe the conditions of the internment camps and how the children tried to hang on to hope," Haru said. I put a hand over my heart.

"And you have all those letters at your museum?" I said, amazed.

"Yep," he said proudly. "They're all going to be exhibited. It's one of the reasons I came to this camp—to write about it!"

"You totally should!" Amne said. "I'm so happy their stories are preserved in those letters! That's what I want for my people too."

She put her smoothie down and told us her story.

"I'm a member of the Muwekma Ohlone Tribe. My family's been living in the East Bay of the San Francisco Bay Area since before the United States was formed. This is our ancestral home. But we're still trying to regain our federal recognition. Even though the govern-ment first identified and recognized us back in 1906 as the Verona Band of Alameda County, to this day, we're unrecognized and landless . . . All because this one anthropologist, Alfred L. Kroeber, said that we were extinct and a Sacramento Bureau of Indian Affairs agent, Lafayette Dorrington, removed our tribe from the list of tribal communities awaiting land purchase. Even though, *hello!* We're totally still here!"

I stared at Amne, fury brewing in me as I tried to process the hurt and trauma of being labeled "extinct." I thought of all the aunt-ies and uncles walking around in Chinatown, and where we'd be if we didn't have a place to call home.

"How do you prove that you're not extinct when people just don't believe you?" Amne threw up her hands. "And why is it even our job to prove we're here? Anyway, that's what I want to write about."

Suddenly, I felt excited again, even more than I had before camp started that morning. We had all these groundbreaking, impor-tant stories that deserved to be told!

I remembered what I'd overheard Mr. Walters and Mr. Miles say-ing on my way out of the *Tribune* that afternoon and told my new friends.

"We're just going to have to prove him wrong!" Haru said, eyes shining.

"Yeah," Amne agreed. "We know the stories of this land better than anyone, and we can prove it!"

I nodded, feeling so much better. I wasn't all alone. I had allies here. Talented, amazing writers who treated me like an equal! "We'll explore every lead!"

"Every letter and detail," Haru continued.

"And we won't stop until we get our voices heard!" Amne concluded.

She raised her cup and the three of us Scribes clinked, determined not to give up until we struck gold.

# CHAPTER 12

Mom peppered me with so many questions when she picked me up, I could hardly get a word in.

"Was it amazing? What were the other kids like?" she asked as we speed-walked back to Chinatown. "How'd you feel, sitting and writing in that fancy building? Was it everything you thought it'd be?"

I *wanted* to tell her it was harder than I expected. A lot harder. But the look of pride on Mom's face made me swallow back the words. Instead, I muttered, "It was good," and turned to Lupe. "How was Berkeley?"

"Great!" she said. "We breezed through the competition in the morning, then one of the coaches taught a real calculus class!" She was nearly skipping down the sidewalk.

"He was magnificent," Mom said. "Not a tiny bit nervous. You should have heard him, cracking jokes. Walking around the lecture hall. I don't think he even looked at his notes once."

We stopped at a crosswalk and I saw her frown.

"When's it your turn to teach, Mom?" I asked.

"Friday," she said. "The day before the Final Cup. It was *supposed* to be tomorrow, but I begged the other coaches to trade with me—I need more time! Math is one thing, but public speaking . . . in *English*?" She grimaced.

I knew how hard this all was for her. She'd slept with flash cards with English pronunciations of math terms under her pillow for *years*.

"It's okay! We'll help you!" I said, looking over at Lupe.

"Totally!" Lupe nodded eagerly. "Oh, Mia, you should see the campus! It's amazing! There's a creek named Strawberry Creek that runs all along the campus! And a tall tower, called the Campanile! And they even have a little farm up the hill, called Tilden Park! Where you can feed goats and cows!"

"I want to feed goats and cows!" Talk about the perfect place to chill! "We should go!"

Lupe's grin faltered. "Yeah, maybe . . ."

"What's wrong?" I asked.

"I have a lot of studying to do."

Mom went to press the walk button.

"C'mon, Lupe," I urged. "You said you breezed through the competition in the morning." I lowered my voice. "Which is a lot better than how I did."

"Really?" she whispered.

But Mom was back, so I said, "It was fine! Great!"

"So have they assigned you any stories yet?" Mom asked.

I flushed. "The first day's just orientation." I dug in my pocket and pulled out my staff card. "But I did get to use my staff card to get a free smoothie!"

Mom gasped so loud, people walking on Montgomery stopped and stared.

"Just admiring my daughter's staff card!" she said loudly, grabbing it and waving it in the air. "At a *national* newspaper! She's the youngest writer there! Can you believe this immigrant girl came to this country without a single word of English? Now she's writing for the *Tribune* and getting *free smoothies!*"

"Mom!" I cried, dying of embarrassment.

But it was no use. Mom kept waving my card all the way home, lighting our path with her blinding pride.

# CHAPTER 13

*Come on . . . come on . . .*

I sat waiting on the stoop for Hank and Jason, craning my neck whenever a beige car turned the corner.

Lupe took a seat next to me. She was holding a big Berkeley course catalog.

"So what *really* happened?" she asked.

I sighed and told her all about how I'd botched Newsroom.

"Mia, if anything, this famous kid should be intimidated by *you*! What's *he* ever done? Has *he* saved a motel from a corporate takeover, or convinced a national soccer team to review a burger publicly?" she asked. "He may have watered-down stories from his grandfather, but you've got *real-life* stories from experience!"

I couldn't help but smile. "You're right," I said. "I guess I just got scared because I'm the youngest one there."

"Welcome to my life," Lupe said. "I gotta go to high school every day with stinky, swearing giants."

I laughed.

"So tell me more about this petting zoo," I said. "Do they have puppies?"

Lupe shrugged, opening her Berkeley catalog. "No, I think it's just goats and cows. Maybe some bunnies?"

"Bunnies!" I exclaimed. "We've *got* to go!"

"Maybe if we *win* the competition."

I crossed my arms. This whole idea that we only deserved to have fun when we won or achieved something was very familiar. But lately, I'd been thinking how none of our classmates had to win a statewide competition in order to have fun. They just *did*. Maybe the goal was not to keep moving the goalpost . . . but to actually enjoy the moment.

"You deserve it *now*," I told her. "We both do. Let's go this weekend."

She shook her head. "Nah, it sounds kinda babyish," she said. "I want to move on to bigger things." She pointed at the directory. "Like macroeconomics!"

I tried to hide how hurt I was that Lupe called the petting zoo babyish. I knew she hadn't meant it in a mean way. But what if I still wanted to do the babyish stuff . . . and I'd missed it, and now it was too late?

Lupe flipped the page. "And look at this one! The Politics of Sleep."

I screwed up my face. "You want to skip playing with baby goats for the Politics of Sleep?"

Now *that* was depressing.

"No . . ." Lupe sighed. "I just . . . I want to learn something exciting. I don't want to slog through high school for four more years."

I knew that she'd had a hard time fitting in, and now with the Allie drama, it would be even harder. "I'll be there too, remember?"

Lupe shook her head. "Don't you ever want to just . . . grow up?"

I shook my head. To be honest, I wanted to go to an Angels game and eat hot dogs and do the wave! And run around the mall, trying to get a stuffed animal from those claw machines that Stuart from my class was always complaining were a total rip-off. I wanted to get ripped off too!

But Lupe was miles ahead. "I met this girl at the Math Cup—she's only fifteen, but she's going to Berkeley next year. She says all we have to do is take a test. And we can take it right now!"

*Whoa.* This was worse than Lupe not wanting to go to the petting zoo. Now she wanted to leap ahead to college—and move all the way up to Berkeley?

"Can't you see us, roaming around the Bay? You're already working at a national paper! You really want to sit through four more years of high school English with a bunch of clowns screaming, 'Someone farted!'"

I stopped worrying for a second and burst out laughing. She had me there.

"But Lupe, aren't the stinky, swearing giants even more GIANT and STINKY in college?" I asked.

"Yeah, but they'll be sophisticated giants," Lupe said. "And they'll never even know we're younger."

Easy for her to say. She'd had a growth spurt this summer, and was now almost as tall as Jason. I, on the other hand, stuck out like a purple radish at camp.

"All we have to do is take the SATs, and it's not even that hard!" she went on. "I can teach you the math, it's easy!"

"No way." I shook my head again. Even if I *could* get through the math, there was zero chance I would jump ahead. "Besides, I can't leave Jason."

The words just slipped out. Lupe put her directory down and stared at me.

"*That's* the reason?"

I blushed hard. And then I heard Jason's voice—for real.

"Mia!!!" he screamed from down the street. He was hanging out the window of Hank's car, waving wildly, hair flying in a million directions.

I laughed. What a sight for sore eyes.

Hank pulled to the curb and Jason hopped out. We ran into each other's arms. As he held me tight, I felt his warmth cover me in a thousand layers of comfort. Then he pulled away and gave me a huge smile. "Couldn't live without me for two days, huh?"

I tousled his crazy hair.

"You wish!"

"Just when I thought I could have a nice quiet Christmas, relaxing by the pool," he said, shaking his head. "Just kidding, I'm so glad you called. I was starting to get seriously depressed."

"You *were*?"

"You and Lupe both gone? I was bored out of my brain! I even went to the library!" He turned and hugged Lupe.

"Well, good," she said. "You should! The library's awesome!"

Jason rubbed his hands together and blew into them to keep warm. "It sure is chilly up here! I should have packed more sweaters."

"There's a scarf shop around the corner," I said. "I'll go with you after you unpack!"

Hank parked and ran over. I was getting too big for him to spin in the air, so we hugged and bumped fists.

"My girl!" he cried. "Wow! Will you look at this place? My God, how San Francisco has changed. Haven't been back since my little brother's law school graduation!"

"What's up with this brother?" I asked. "How come you never told us about him?"

Hank pointed at me. "*That* is the million-dollar question, miss budding journalist!"

As I followed my friends up the motel steps, I looked down at my right big toe and smiled. It sure felt good to have it back.

# CHAPTER 14

We showed Jason and Hank to their room—they were sharing too, like me and Lupe. I was jealous that Jason and Hank's had a fireplace and ours didn't. But before I could dwell on it, Lupe pulled me toward our door.

"Is something going *on* with you and Jason?" she whispered.

"What do you mean?" I asked, all innocent.

Lupe glanced back down the hall and shrugged. "You seem different around him."

"I do not," I insisted, opening our door and hurrying inside.

She followed me, so focused on our discussion that she didn't bother to shut the door. "I saw you touch his *hair*."

I crossed my arms. "So?"

"So, it looks like he stuck his head out the window for the entire drive. There's probably tree bark and squirrel fur in his hair."

"No there wasn't!" I protested. "It was silky and smooth!"

Lupe's eyes lit up. "Mia Tang! You *like* him! You like Jason!"

"Shhhh!" I whisper-yelled, running over to close our door. "Say it a little louder, so all of Chinatown can hear, why don't you?"

Lupe giggled, but quietly. "Sorry! But Mia, whoa, when did this happen?" She sat down on her bed. "And why didn't you tell me?"

I sat down on mine, facing her. "Because you were going through a lot," I explained. "With Allie and everything. I didn't want to bring it up." I looked down at my hands and added, "Besides, it's embarrassing."

"Why?"

"Because it's *Jason*." I covered my face with my hands. "We're talking about the boy who *licked* my *pencil*. He got the whole fifth grade to make fun of my clothes!"

"I remember," Lupe said softly. "But he's changed so much. I mean, he's basically a normal human now!"

"*Basically.*"

Lupe giggled again, louder this time, and I started giggling too. The two of us rolled on our beds, laughing and kicking our feet in the air like two kids with a delicious secret. It felt so good to finally tell her about my crush—even if it was still kind of embarrassing.

And it was *just* a crush. There was no way I was ready for anything more. That was another reason why I was in no rush to grow up. I mean, I still closed my eyes during the swoony parts of *Little Women* (though I felt exploding happiness in my heart when the music soared)!

I'd been keeping my Jason feelings a secret ever since the day in PE when Bethany Brett was being a particular brat and Jason assured me my sneakers were cool. And later, we'd hung out at his house, and he confessed that before he met me, he was ashamed of what his dad did for a living—but that I made working in a motel look cool.

That was when I knew that Jason had really changed. He understood me on a level that no other boy possibly could.

Still. Was that enough for me to permanently get over his rotten behavior in fifth grade?

And if so, *should* I tell him how I felt?

Lupe finally stopped laughing and looked over at me, apparently reading my mind. "Are you going to tell him?"

I groaned. "I don't know! Should I? He's one of my best friends. I don't want anything to mess that up. I think I even wrote that in a letter to him once."

"Well . . . I have news for you," Lupe said, getting up and coming over to pull the pen from my hair. "You're a writer. You can start a new letter whenever you want."

With a smile, she handed me the pen.

I shook my head. What if he was ready to *not* close his eyes during *Little Women*? I just wanted to be his friend who had a crush on him. But that was way too hard to explain in a letter, even for me.

# CHAPTER 15

I left Lupe to study and went downstairs to find Jason. As I got closer to the kitchen, I heard him talking with Mr. and Mrs. Luk.

Or . . . arguing.

"We don't need you to come up with a menu!" Mr. Luk said. "We got it all right here!"

"But I like making the menu!" Jason insisted. "I have so many great ideas. It's going to be amazing! Hank and I will give you a banquet you've never had!"

I hurried inside and saw Mr. Luk shaking his head, frustrated.

"We don't *want* a banquet we've never had," he said. "This is a Chinese banquet—people come for the prawns with honey-glazed walnuts! For the beef with oyster sauce! It's *tradition*!"

Jason tugged on his hair, which hadn't gotten any less wild since he'd arrived. "Prawns with honey-glazed walnuts? That's something my dad would order! What about a coconut shrimp with red chili flakes? I can bake them with my new oven mitts!" He held up a pair of red silicone mitts. "My dad just bought them for me—they're from Japan!"

Just then, Hank walked in behind me. "Ooooh! Those look nice!" he said.

But Mr. and Mrs. Luk were still frowning. They turned to us, and

Mr. Luk pushed their big red binder of recipes into Hank's hands. "Please understand," he said. "We really need this banquet to work. We can't afford to take any chances."

I gave Jason a *be quiet for a second* look and said, "Don't worry, Mr. and Mrs. Luk, they're on it."

Jason opened his mouth to argue some more, but I just gave him a big smile and said, "Let's go for a walk! You have to see the neighborhood!"

His eyebrows shot up in surprise, but he followed me without another word.

. . .

As we walked through Chinatown, I tried to explain to Jason the shaky financial ground the Golden Inn was standing on.

"That's exactly my point, though!" he said. "That's why we have to try a new way. You're the one who taught me that! Think about what we did at the Calivista."

Jason paused in front of a fruit and vegetable stand.

"These cherries would go so *great* with the duck," he said. "Maybe like a roasted cherry and juniper berry glaze? Smell that!"

"Delish," I agreed, sniffing. "But it's not in the binder!"

"C'mon, Mia. You're never afraid to shake things up! It's what I love about you." Jason seemed to suddenly hear what he said, and rushed to add, "I mean, it's what I like about the Calivista. Like—it's just—you know what I mean."

He turned the same color as the cherries. We both fell quiet for a minute.

"But the whole point of Chinatown is honoring tradition," I reminded him. "Here, we don't have to worry about keeping up with the winds of change, because this is our own little pocket. We'll always be safe here."

"Will we, though?" Jason asked gently, glancing at the empty restaurants on the street. "If we can't keep up with the rent?"

The question hung in the air like a dark lantern.

"We have to protect this place," Jason said. "It's too special. I mean, look." He grabbed a round white onion. "Isn't this beautiful? I want to *live* inside this onion."

I laughed. "But you'd cry all the time."

"Kinda like that time you put Tiger Balm all over my eyes?" he joked.

My jaw dropped—I couldn't believe he was bringing up fifth grade! Jason almost *never* wanted to talk about our past.

"Hey," I said, trying to cover up my shock by lightly punching him in the arm. "I didn't put it all over your eyes, I put it on *my* pencil."

"I was such a donkey that year," Jason said, making a face as he put the onion back. "How can you even stand me? I can't even think about it, or I'll break out in post-cringe."

Wow.

For some reason, I'd always thought that when we finally talked about it, we'd both be old and gray in some senior folks' home. Maybe over a fine cup of Jell-O, I'd finally bring up the Pencil Incident (and Everything Else). And Jason would claim that, due to his old age, he couldn't remember what I was talking about.

But instead we were talking about it now, in Chinatown, under the witness of Karl the Fog. He *did* remember. And he was so mature . . . and eloquent.

"Every night I'd think, *Well, I can't possibly mess up tomorrow more than I did today,*" he went on. "Then the next day I'd put my foot in my mouth all over again."

I shook my head, still surprised, but relieved to get this all out in the open. "You definitely did!" I agreed, and we both laughed. Then I asked him a question that had been bugging me for years. "Why didn't you just stop?"

"Oh, Mia, I wish I had." Jason covered his face with his hands. "I'm so sorry. If there's a year I could erase from my life, believe me, it'd be that year. . . . Just press *delete*. But then . . ." He paused. "I wouldn't have met you."

My heart pounded as he dropped his hands and our eyes locked.

"Thanks to you," he said, "I've learned and I've grown. The next girl I like, I'm going to treat like a queen!"

Oh. That was . . . good?

I smiled awkwardly. "Actually . . . there's something I have to tell you."

"What is it?" Jason asked.

I paused, searching for the words that had been sitting under my tongue for months.

But then a voice shouted, "Mia!"

We turned—and saw a bright red lion pouncing toward us.

Jason grabbed my hand and we jumped out of the way. But the lion stopped right in front of us, took off its head, and there was Emma!

She grinned, her satiny light brown hair blowing in the wind, and held out a hand to Jason. "Hi! I'm Emma. I just met Mia yesterday! Who are you?"

I watched as Jason struggled to remember his own name. His eyes were the size of bowling balls. What was it with boys when they see a pretty lioness?

I felt myself shrink next to Emma.

And all my words sank to the bottom of my shoes.

# CHAPTER 16

Hank walked me to the *Tribune* the next morning, and I filled him in on everything at the camp.

As always, he knew exactly what to say.

"Remember, it's not who you know, but what you know," he said. "Anybody can just write a story. But you, Mia, you *see* people. You see what they're going through. You *care*. That's what sets you apart. That's what's going to get you the story *behind* the story."

How had I made it through even one day in San Francisco without him? I took a deep breath, determined to hang on to the surge of confidence I felt thanks to Hank's pep talk.

We got to Montgomery Street, and Hank stopped to gaze up at the gleaming steel-and-glass skyscrapers.

"Can't believe my baby brother works up in one of them sky-pokers," Hank said. Though he was shaking his head, he was also glowing with pride.

"Tell me about him," I said.

Hank checked both ways and we started across the intersection. "He was the pride and light of my mama's life when she was alive," he said, grinning. "Top of his class at Stanford Law. Can you believe it?"

"Of course I can believe it," I said. "He's your brother, isn't he?"

Hank beamed. "Oh, you're very kind. But I was never book smart like Darrius. All the teachers loved him. He could read a chapter, and five days later, he'd be able to tell you exactly what was in it, down to the last detail. Then he'd tell you which sentence had an error in it." Hank chuckled. "Probably why he's such a good lawyer!"

I thought about Mr. Walters's advice: *Be curious. Ask the hard questions.*

"So how come you didn't want to ask him for legal help with all the burger stuff?" I asked softly.

Hank had gotten into quite a pickle a few months ago, when a major restaurant ripped off his amazing Crunch Burger recipe.

He sighed. "I thought about it. We'd been out of touch for so long, guess I didn't want our first interaction to be me asking him for help."

I nodded. I thought of my own parents and how they'd rather gnaw off their arms than borrow money from their siblings.

We were stopped at another light, and this time we both looked up. The buildings looked less imposing when I thought about people like Hank's brother working inside.

"But I'd like to think he would have helped. He's a dang good lawyer," Hank went on. "Made enough money to move our mama out of Detroit and into Farmington Hills."

I pointed up. "Do you know which firm he works at?"

Hank shook his head. "We lost touch after our mama passed. All I know is it's one of the big ones in San Francisco. The kind of place where if you make partner . . ." Hank whistled.

"Partner?"

"'Making partner' means they value you so much, they share their profits with you. You're not an employee, you're a boss!"

I beamed at Hank. "Like you! You're a partner!"

Hank laughed. "Not sure Darrius will see it that way, but yes, I suppose I am!"

"You gonna tell him?" I asked as we stopped in front of the *Tribune* building.

Hank took a deep inhale of the brisk San Francisco air and rubbed his hands together. "We'll see," he said. "You go on and get to your camp now! I'll pick you up after!"

I gave him a quick hug and turned toward the doors.

"Oh, and Mia? Knock 'em dead!"

. . .

*Knock 'em dead. Get the story behind the story. It's* what *you know, not* who *you know.* I repeated Hank's words to myself as I rode the elevator all the way up to the thirty-eighth floor. I gripped my pen in my hand, my hair flowing free, as I pictured myself kicking butt in workshop today.

The elevator doors opened and I saw Mr. Walters was already in the city beat conference room talking to my fellow beat-mates. Timothy was typing away at his laptop like a mini-editor. Mr. Walters frowned at me.

*I was late!*

*How could it be?* I hurried down the hall and squeezed into the conference room, finding a seat next to Amne and Haru.

"Ms. Tang!" Mr. Walters said. "Didn't you check your email? Start time moved up to eight thirty today! We're taking a field trip to Symphony Hall this morning. The musicians are going on strike!"

"I don't have email," I said. "But that sounds really exciting!"

"I don't have email either," Amne whispered. "Me and Haru just got here too."

Mr. Walters frowned, and turned back to the room to continue, "At the press conference, your job is to listen. You want to think about what the impact of this strike is. Why should people care, not just in San Francisco but all over the nation? That's the key to our beat's success—a local story with national appeal!"

I raised my hand.

"Yes, Mia?" Mr. Walters said.

"Can we ask questions?"

He considered carefully. "Only if the question is *good*," he finally replied. "There will be television crews there."

My stomach did a little somersault. As laptops flew into backpacks, I turned to my friends and said, "When we get there, we have to get up to the front of the room!"

"It's just a press conference," Timothy said, rolling his eyes. "I've been to five million of them. They only call on reporters they know by their first name."

He was already walking away, so I had to raise my voice to call, "Well, it's *my* first press conference. And after my question, they'll know my name!"

# CHAPTER 17

Musicians lined the steps of the San Francisco Symphony, holding signs. There were at least twenty reporters there, including a television cameraman. Amne, Haru, and I squeezed to the front and got a good look at the head musician—a tall man with bright red hair, named Stephen Teller. The TV camera focused on Mr. Teller as he got up to the microphone and spoke about insufficient pay, canceled performances, and long bus travel times to out-of-town concerts.

"If you want us to play our hearts out, you gotta treat us with respect!" he said. "Until our pay and working conditions are improved, we'll be on strike!"

A hand shot up from a man standing next to me. Mr. Teller called on him.

"Joe Pierson from the *Chronicle*. How long will the strike last?" he asked.

"As long as it takes!" Mr. Teller said.

Five more hands shot up, including mine. My heart pounded. *Pick me, pick me!*

To my surprise, Mr. Teller did.

"Mia Tang, from the *Tribune*, sir," I said. "Have you gotten any response from the management to your demands?"

"No. But we don't want to cancel the Christmas concerts, and we hope they don't want that either," he answered.

I shot my hand in the air again, asking my follow-up question without waiting to be called on. "How many concerts would that be?"

"We have so many patrons flying in to hear us, we're doing *five* Christmas concerts!" he said proudly. "Which speaks to how popular we've grown nationally!"

I scribbled down *nationally popular*, then checked to see if Mr. Walters had heard. He smiled and I grinned back.

Then I caught Timothy's eye. *Take that!*

He shrugged like *big whoop*.

· · ·

Back at the office, Mr. Walters gathered us for a recap.

"Great job, Mia," he said. "Thanks to your question, our city beat reporters have a great quote on the national impact!"

Amne and Haru cheered loudly. I glanced over at the city reporters, cranking out the story just outside the conference room. I was on cloud nine.

"Mia, why don't you pick your partners for Newsroom today?" Mr. Walters said. "You'll be working in teams of three."

"Amne and Haru," I said without hesitation.

"Wonderful! And Timothy, Jenna, and Zoe are the other team." He clapped. "Chop-chop. Make 'em dynamite!"

Jenna, Zoe, and Timothy immediately huddled their heads together behind their laptops.

"Mr. Walters, do you think we might be able to borrow one of the *Tribune*'s computers?" I asked.

Amne and Haru nodded eagerly too.

He looked surprised but said, "Of course," and handed over the one he was using himself to me. He told Amne and Haru he'd get them laptops from the office manager. I hugged mine to my chest. It was two inches thicker than Timothy's thin, sleek one, and had a bright yellow *Tribune* sticker on the back.

We sat at the opposite end of the conference table from Jenna, Zoe, and Timothy. Thankfully, the room was big enough, and the sound of telephones ringing outside loud enough, that we couldn't overhear each other's ideas.

"What if we did something on Chinatown?" I asked.

"Ooh!" Amne clicked open a new document, taking notes. "That's where you're staying, right?"

I nodded.

"There's this banquet this Sunday, and my friends Jason and Hank are the chefs. They've never cooked a traditional banquet before, so it's a lot of pressure. And everyone in Chinatown will be there!"

"Sounds like Little Tokyo in LA!" Haru said. "We have community events all the time. What are they going to cook?"

"That's the thing. They want to mix it up a bit, but the banquet hall owners want to keep it traditional."

Amne stopped typing and said, "That's always the struggle, isn't it? Tradition is so important to hang on to. That's why my mom's working so hard on trying to revive our native language, Chochenyo."

*Cho-chen-yo*, I repeated in my head. It sounded beautiful.

"There haven't been any fluent speakers since the 1930s," Amne explained. "But recently some old recordings were found."

"That sounds newsworthy!" Haru said.

Amne nodded. "An anthropologist named John P. Harrington

recorded one of my tribal ancestors, Jose Guzman, on a wax cylinder recorder in 1930, right before he died. But get this—Harrington was a secret pack rat. He hid his work in warehouses, attics, basements, even chicken coops!"

My jaw dropped. "How'd they finally find the cylinder?" I asked.

"When Harrington died, all his things ended up at the Smithsonian museum in Washington. Jose Guzman's voice sat in storage for like sixty years, until our tribal chairwoman paid for the first recordings of his songs! She said it was like listening to her ancestors talking directly to her."

I thought of the daily chitchat in Mandarin between my mom and dad. Every morning, I felt their love in our native tongue. I couldn't imagine not having that—at home or in Chinatown.

"I got it!" Haru declared, clapping his hands. "How about two communities in San Francisco, and their struggles and triumphs maintaining heritage?"

"I love it!" I said.

"It's perfect!" Amne agreed.

We high-fived one another, which made Timothy, Jenna, and Zoe look over with furrowed brows.

They *should* be worried. We were going to slay our pitch, and grab that seventy-five dollars!

# CHAPTER 18

Timothy, Jenna, and Zoe were first. They pitched a feel-good story about the mayor's new dog.

"We hear he's thinking of getting a puppy," Jenna said. "A rescue from the pound!"

Zoe nodded and continued, "So we could go to the pound and take pictures of the dogs, then write a profile on each one and ask readers to vote on the next First Pup!"

"I hear the mayor likes Boston terriers," Timothy said, then humble-bragged, "My mom knows his chief of staff's hairstylist."

"That could work," Mr. Walters said. "Everybody loves a good pet story!"

I had to admit, the idea *was* cute—it made me even more excited to finally meet Comma—but I still thought ours felt so much more important!

Mr. Walters turned to us. "Mia, Amne, Haru, what have you got?"

My friends and I took a deep breath, then started our pitch.

Five minutes later, Mr. Walters's lips were firmly pursed.

"I'm not quite sure I'm following . . ." he said. "What does a banquet in Chinatown have to do with language courses in the East Bay?"

"Both groups are trying to maintain community," Amne explained. "Preserving identity and heritage."

"And that's not easy, in this day and age," I added. "These banquets aren't just celebrations of food, they're celebrations of history and culture. There's even going to be lion dancing!"

"And it isn't just *any* language course," Amne said. "The lessons will revitalize the Chochenyo language, which has been *sleeping* since Jose Guzman died in 1934."

"Stories and language are how tradition gets passed down," Haru added. "It's what holds us together."

Out of the corner of my eye, I saw Mr. Miles standing in the back of the room. When did he come in? Had he been listening the whole time?

Mr. Walters looked at his boss. "What do you think?"

"Feels very . . . local to me," Mr. Miles said, pulling up a chair and unfolding a copy of the *Tribune* he'd brought. "The city section is the bread and butter of the paper. The stories we print need to be universally appealing." He pointed at the headlines—"$10,000 Spills out of Money Truck, Causing Freeway Panic," "Zoo's Crows Getting High Cholesterol on Left-Behind Burgers." "These stories feel *urgent.*"

I wanted to argue that a lost language felt more urgent than burger-chomping birds. But I bit my tongue.

"Also," he went on, leaning back in his chair and putting his hands behind his neck, "these problems you're describing, they're not new. They've been going on for decades. So why publish this *right now*? Where's the newsworthiness?"

I couldn't keep quiet anymore. "If we don't preserve these traditions, our heritage falls apart. Our communities disappear! We might not have Chinatown much longer, that's what's urgent!" I cried.

The other campers stared at me as Mr. Miles uncrossed his hands, leaned forward, and gave me a patient smile.

"Listen, Mia, I can feel your passion," he said. "But passion can cloud facts. As reporters, our duty isn't to report what *might* be true. Or what we *want* to be true. Just the *truth*. And so far, the only truth you've told me is that Chinatown is getting a couple new chefs this Sunday. And there's a weekly language class that may or may not happen in Berkeley. That's just not enough for our readers to care, I'm afraid."

*Ouch.*

My face burned as Amne, Haru, and I sat back down, our pitch officially rejected.

But passion still roared in my eardrums, louder than Mr. Miles's *no*.

# CHAPTER 19

I twirled the straw wrapper that said *Jenni's Smoothies*, still frustrated *and* hungry. I'd chugged down my entire free smoothie in seconds. I wished I could get another, but I only had eight freebies left. I wanted to conserve them for when something *good* happened.

There I went again, believing I only deserved a treat when I won. I frowned.

"Maybe next time we should pitch something safe," Amne said.

Haru and I stared at her. "Like what?" I asked.

She walked over to the corkboard next to the counter and pointed randomly at one of the flyers. "Like this lost parrot that flew away from its owner's fire escape."

Haru and I exchanged bewildered looks.

"What, you'd rather be called 'too passionate' again?" Amne put a hand on her hip.

Haru and I shook our heads.

She sighed and came back to the table. "Believe me, I get it. I didn't come here to write about parrots either. I came here to write about my people." She took a sip of her smoothie. "But we have to get there."

"Agreed," Haru said. "We've only been here for two days. Maybe we should be a little more patient."

I looked at my friends and sighed. I wished I could be more patient. But at my age, that felt like asking me to soak my hair in Listerine.

Amne and Haru started to gather their things. I was about to get up too, but some of my straw wrapper fell under the table. "I'll see you guys tomorrow," I told them, then bent to pick it up.

Then I heard Jenna and Zoe, over at the counter.

"Omg, that was so cringe," Jenna said.

"I know! She just kept arguing back!" Zoe giggled. "Mr. Miles had to practically spell it out for her: *hard pass!*"

"She's so aggressive!"

"Like, just because you get a scholarship doesn't mean you get special treatment," Zoe said. "The paper let them in *to be nice*, so the camp can be diverse or whatever. It doesn't mean they get to write whatever they want."

My whole body froze, hunched under the table. If they saw me right now, I'd be mortified!

"How does this free smoothie thing work anyway?" Zoe went on, oblivious.

"Who cares, let's just get a milkshake. It's only five bucks," Jenna said.

As the crush of ice vibrated throughout the smoothie shop, I tried to crush their words in my head.

# CHAPTER 20

Finally outside and waiting for Hank, I wrestled with a sour, vinegary feeling in my stomach. Did the *Tribune* really start the Golden Scribes program just "to be nice"? Was that why they took so many pictures of us but passed on our stories?

Or was it my passion? Or my overaggressiveness? I was so confused.

Instead of Hank, I saw Mom and Lupe turning the corner.

"Mom! I thought you were staying in Berkeley to practice doing your lesson in front of your team!"

"I was going to, but the parents wanted to sit in too," she said. "I choked! I couldn't even pronounce *coefficient*."

"You pronounced it fine just now," I pointed out.

"That's here, with you and Lupe. But for some reason, when I get up on the big stage in these massive lecture halls, I . . . I . . ." Mom shook her head, looking defeated.

Finally, something not confusing at all to solve!

"You just need practice!" I told her. "Come on, let's go home! We can use the banquet hall!"

• • •

Back at the Golden Inn, Mom stood at the banquet hall podium and Lupe and I sat at a table.

"You look great!" I said. "You just need to speak up a little!"

"I can't!" Mom hollered back, shielding her eyes from the blinding lights that Hank had turned on for us.

"Here!" I took a big stack of Mrs. Luk's feedback cards and ran up to the podium. "Flash cards!"

Mom normally got very excited by flash cards. But this time, she just stared at them.

We waited patiently while she found the words to describe what she was feeling.

"You know when you're at the grocery store and you realize that the cashier has overcharged you for artichokes, but you're afraid to tell her, because you don't know how to pronounce artichokes?" she asked. "This feels like that. But times a thousand! It's like a thousand overcharged artichokes!"

I waved my hands in the air, trying to snap her back to reality. Away from the horrifying terror of a thousand overpriced vegetables! "It's okay! We're here. No one's overcharging you, Mom!" I glanced over at Lupe.

"Let's try some facial warm-ups!" Lupe suggested, coming to the rescue as usual. "My dad fixed the cable at this acting studio, and I got to watch the students work. Let's see . . . open your mouth wide like a lion, then scrunch it small, like a mouse."

Mom tried, roaring like a lion, and Lupe cheered.

"Back and forth! Lion, mouse, lion, mouse!"

Hank walked over from the kitchen carrying a big bowl. He tipped it so I could see what he was stirring.

"Honey and soy," he whispered with a wink. He watched Mom for a minute, then turned back to me. "Hey! How'd it go at camp today?"

I glanced at Mom, but she was too busy roaring to overhear.

"Not great . . ." I murmured, then told him about our failed pitch and what happened at Jenni's. "Do you think I'm too aggressive?"

While Lupe continued to work with Mom, Hank put his marinade down on the table and took a seat. "Let me tell you a story. I remember once in algebra class, my teacher gave me back a test. He'd marked five of my answers wrong, even though they were right."

*"Really?"*

He nodded. "I should have gotten an A, but instead, I got a B. I remember going home, wondering if I should say something to the teacher."

"Did you?"

"My brother Darrius convinced me not to. He said if I did, the teacher would think I was difficult. And one day it would be Darrius's turn in that teacher's class, and he didn't want them thinking *he* was difficult too."

I frowned at the strange logic.

"He had his heart set on Stanford, so I let it go." Hank held up a finger. "But then, when it came time to choose who went to the honors classes, and who had to stay in regular, guess where I was put?"

In a tiny voice, I guessed, "Regular?"

Hank grimaced *yeah.* "The point is, never apologize for advocating for yourself. That ain't being aggressive, that's being smart. That's having self-respect. You worked your butt off to get here. Lupe too. Now's not the time to hold back."

I looked over at Mom and Lupe, who were still making all sorts of weird faces, and smiled.

"Thanks, Hank," I said. "So, have you found Darrius yet?"

"Not yet! But my poor legs." Hank heaved in exhaustion. "You know how many floors each of these firms have?"

"Wait, you actually walked through them, looking for him yourself?" I asked, confused.

"I *tried* to explain to the first firm I was looking for my brother," Hank said. "But they didn't believe me. While I was waiting, one of the lawyers asked if I was there to fix the printer, so I just said yes."

I gave Hank a funny look. "That's weird they assumed that."

"I don't care, so long as I find my brother," Hank said, picking up his marinade and heading back to the kitchen.

Mom gave an extra-loud roar, then asked Lupe, "That good?"

"You're doing great! Now stretch your tongue from side to side, it'll help you enunciate!"

"What's enunciate?" Mom asked, twisting her face.

"It means to pronounce clearly," I said.

Mom dropped her head at the podium. "See, I didn't even know that . . ." She groaned almost as loudly as she'd been roaring. "Who am I kidding? I'm just not good enough to be—"

"Hey!" I shouted, standing up from the table. "Don't you say that! You're good enough!"

Mom looked up, her face pale in the stage lights.

"You're a lion, not a mouse!" I said. "Say it with me!"

Mom gave me a small smile before muttering into the mic, "I'm a lion, not a mouse."

Lupe started clapping. Hank and Jason joined in too, from the kitchen.

"Again!"

Mom wiped at the corners of her eyes as she spoke louder into the mic, over our thundering claps. "I'm a lion, not a mouse!"

She beamed at me.

"You know, no matter how I do on Thursday," Mom said, "I feel lucky I have such a strong and fearless daughter. You're my hero, honey. You're not scared of anything."

I felt the lift of Mom's words, all her pride and hopes packed tighter than a baked BBQ pork puff.

But I also knew from Jason that overpacking a pork puff could fill it with hot air. I wondered when it would be safe to deflate in front of Mom, back to a normal kid again.

# CHAPTER 21

Mr. Walters made an announcement the next morning. "As reporters, sometimes you have to write a story as a team," he said. "Writing together can be tricky. You've got to listen. Compromise. It's not about credit. It's not about ego. Sometimes, someone else just has a better idea! And that's okay!"

With that, he told us we'd all be working on the mayor dog story.

I glanced over at Jenna and Zoe, who looked like *their* dogs had just died. But I ignored them, firing up the extra laptop Mr. Walters had gotten me.

"So what do we know about Boston terriers?" Amne asked.

Jenna typed for a minute, then said, "They're determined!"

"They like to dig," Zoe called out.

It was incredible how these little machines could spit out so much information! I typed *what dog should I get?* It led me to a personality test.

*Choose the best dog based on your lifestyle and personality traits!*

Fascinated, I clicked on the first question:

1. Which phrase best describes what you're looking for in a dog?
   A) A loyal companion who doesn't need tons of exercise

B) A sporty, high-energy dog that can keep up with your action-packed weekends

C) A guard who can help alert you to intruders

D) A distraction for a hard period in your life

I picked A.

The second question asked:

2. Describe your average weekend:
   A) Going to the beach
   B) Taking a long walk/exploring a city
   C) Eating out or going to the mall with friends
   D) Throwing a Frisbee or ball around with friends at the park

I stared at the screen. How was it possible that I hadn't done *most* of the things on this list?

My average weekend was sitting at the front desk of the motel, trying to convince a guest her pillow wasn't lumpy, while writing a column and making sure we had enough sodas in the vending machine!

I wanted to explain to the quiz: *My parents are first-generation immigrants! We're too busy making sure the sky doesn't collapse to throw a Frisbee around!*

I continued clicking until I saw *Do you feel swamped sometimes by all your responsibilities?*

Then I closed my computer.

I was done matching my life to a dog. I wanted Comma, wherever he was, to take a quiz to match *me*.

That got me thinking . . . for a busy man like the mayor, what kind of dog would be suitable?

"Hey," I said to everyone, "we should interview some people who work with the mayor and ask them which puppy they think would match his personality!"

"Actually, that's not a bad idea," Timothy said, agreeing with me for once. "If they say he's all tense and needs to relax, it could point to problems at the mayor's office."

I frowned. "Or maybe his BBQ pastry's just a little overstuffed. . . ."

Jenna and Zoe looked at me like I had two heads.

"Never mind," I said. "I'll call the mayor's office."

"No, *I* will," Timothy said, grabbing the phone from me. "It's *our* story. We pitched it."

I looked over to Amne and Haru. "Well, what are we supposed to do?"

Timothy shrugged. "You guys just chill. Maybe you can look for typos and punctuation errors when we're done."

*Ha! I'll show* him *how I "just chill"!*

. . .

For the rest of the afternoon, Amne, Haru, and I huddled at our desks.

Instead of interviewing the mayor's office workers, we called up his drivers, housekeeper, and personal trainer. Our story was warm and funny, offering an intimate, insider portrait of the mayor.

But when we presented it to Mr. Walters later that day, he grimaced. "I thought I was very clear—you are to work *together*," he said.

I started sweating. "We wanted to, but—"

"Nonsense!" Timothy interjected. "We offered to let you be the copy editor, but that wasn't good enough for you! You just *had* to write your own story."

"Mia," Mr. Walters said, "I told you, being collaborative is not about credit or ego."

Before I could get another word out, he handed us back our story.

"You're not even going to read it?" I asked.

Mr. Walters pointed to the glass window. "What do you see in this newsroom?"

I looked at the bustling office, people darting from desk to desk, pounding on computers. "Writers?"

"Exactly. Writers. Plural. All working together to ensure we got the facts. If you want to make it in the big leagues, you've got to learn to work well with others, kid."

I blinked back the tears. I wanted to say *I do work well with others. I bought a motel with others! And I collaborate great with people here too, if you'd just read our story!*

But Amne put her hand on my shoulder and guided me quietly back to our desks. The three of us tried not to look as Timothy, Jenna, and Zoe got their seventy-five dollars. I stared down at my empty hands, imagining the crunch of those hard-earned writing dollars. I knew it was only the third day. But once again, I felt like my hair was soaking in Listerine.

# CHAPTER 22

I skipped my free smoothie that day and ran all the way back to Chinatown. I was determined to uncover a story so big, so exclusive, Mr. Walters could *not* turn it down! One way or another, I was getting that seventy-five dollars!

First I went to the elders outside the wok shop.

"Who can I talk to who's got an interesting story?" I asked.

"Everyone in Chinatown," said Mrs. Chan. She pointed to the shop. "Try Mrs. Kwok, the manager. She started her business stitching empty rice bags into aprons."

"That's amazing!" I said.

Sure enough, I found Mrs. Kwok behind the counter of the wok shop wearing a rice bag apron. She told me that she got the idea of making a dress out of the sacks from her dad, who used to hand deliver hundred-pound bags of rice all over Chinatown.

"I thought, why waste these perfectly good bags?" Mrs. Kwok said. "Now after you make the rice, you can wear the bag when you cook! Look, I can even dance in it!"

She started twirling around in the shop. "Did you know you can use woks to pop popcorn, toss salads, and even bake a cake?" she said.

"Wow," I said, taking notes. "Have you gotten any orders for your wok aprons?"

"Just from the gals outside. Frank says I should sell them online. But I don't know the first thing about doing that!"

"Who's Frank?" I asked.

"Frank Wu, he owns the fortune cookie shop!" she said. "You haven't talked to him yet?"

I thanked Mrs. Kwok and skipped to the fortune cookie factory, eager to meet Emma's boss!

. . .

Frank Wu had a salt-and-pepper beard and wore a fedora, even indoors. It was the same hat he wore in the yellowed newspaper clippings hanging on the walls.

"What's it like running a cookie factory?" I asked.

"It's a pain in the butt," he said. "The other day I had someone coming in here, asking me if my fortune cookie is fat-free, sugar-free, and carb-free. I said, 'You know what's carb-free, sugar-free, and fat-free? Air!'"

I giggled. "You said that?"

"He sure did," Emma said, tossing back a grape. She was sitting next to Mr. Wu while I interviewed him.

"I put out a great product," Mr. Wu said, his chest puffing out with pride. "Made by hand, with my grandfather's recipe. What other snack gives you free advice? You think Pringles tells you what to do with your life?"

I laughed as I wrote this down.

"What's the best fortune you've ever written?" I asked Mr. Wu.

"I don't write the fortunes. I just print them," he said, pointing at his gigantic iron printing press in the back of his factory. "All the fortunes were written by my parents' friend. He wrote them all in the 1960s. Very wise man."

"Really? But that was so long ago!"

Emma turned to her boss and said, "See? Even Mia thinks it's weird. Please, Mr. Wu! Give me a chance! Times are different now. Our *needs* are different. People's *problems* are different!"

"Why fix something that's not broken? Our advice *works*. For example." Mr. Wu picked up a piece of paper and read, "'Any day aboveground is a good day!'" He beamed at me.

Emma smacked her forehead. "'Be glad you're not dead'? That's *advice*?"

"It *means* seize the day! Be happy!" Mr. Wu argued. "You know how many marriages I saved with that fortune?"

I tried not to laugh. Mr. Wu reminded me of Mr. Yao. But funnier.

As I was leaving, Emma handed me a box of chocolate-dipped cookies.

"Will you give these to Jason? He said at our picnic yesterday that he wanted to try them!"

"You guys . . . went on a picnic?" I asked, trying to hide the envy in my voice.

"Yeah! He was so sweet. He even brought a little vase and some flowers!" Emma smiled.

"Oh."

"Will you tell him I'll meet him at the same spot at Portsmouth Square tomorrow?" she asked.

I nodded, taking the box of treats, feeling my own heart dip in a vase of worry.

# CHAPTER 23

Why didn't Jason tell me that he and Emma were having lunch together? And why did my chest squeeze tight every time I thought of it?

I was so distracted walking home that I bumped straight into Auntie Lam, the short, chatty woman who ran the scarf shop. True to her vocation, she wore several bright, colorful scarves, and another tied to the strap of her tote bag.

"Mia!" she said. "The talented writer everyone's talking about! I hear you're interviewing shop owners. Come, you must interview me!"

Tucked between the flower shop and the wok shop, Auntie Lam's scarf boutique was adorned with posters of glamorous Chinese actresses. Rows upon rows of beautiful textiles hid a small salon in the back, run by Auntie Choi, who also doubled as a palm reader. All the mothers of Chinatown gathered there to gossip, get their fortunes read, swap info on discount airfare to China, and brag about their children.

"Look, everyone, it's Mia the writer!" Auntie Lam announced to the women in the salon. Turning to me, she gushed, "Your mom told me all about your accomplishments."

I flushed. Mom's overwhelming confidence in my writing made me want to buy a scarf to hide.

"You have a lucky face," Auntie Lam commented, pinching my cheeks. "Good frame too! Here! Let me get you some underwear!"

"What?" I yelped.

Apparently, Auntie Lam also sold silk underwear. Before I knew it, she'd tossed so many pairs at me, I was covered from head to toe in underwear. The other Chinese mothers swarmed around me, asking for my writing advice.

"How you write so good?" Mrs. Chu asked. "My daughter Penny, she only write two sentences, is there hope for her?"

"Of course!" I said, trying to see from underneath the underwear covering my head.

"You like red?" Auntie Lam asked. "Very lucky. Good for wearing in your zodiac year! What your zodiac year, hon?"

"Year of the pig," I called back. "Tell Penny to read more!"

"Year of the pig! Oh, very lucky, no wonder you big writer!" Auntie Doo said. "My husband also year of the pig!"

"Her husband is the Chinatown *doctor*," Auntie Lam said, giving Auntie Doo a thumbs-up.

"Not just a doctor. Dr. Doo takes the kids to movies free every summer—pay for everything! *All-you-can-eat popcorn!*" Auntie Chu told me.

I grinned. I pulled out my reporter's notebook and tugged the underwear off my head so I could write this down.

"How many kids live in Chinatown?" I asked.

"A couple hundred," Auntie Lam said. "Dr. Doo delivered most of them. Everybody go see him for everything! Even Popo!"

*Popo* meant "grandmother" in Chinese. I figured she was Auntie Lam's grandmother.

"She's doing so great, isn't she?" Auntie Choi asked, smiling. She sat me in one of her salon chairs, thrust a bowl of fruit into my hands, and began applying a curling iron to my hair.

"I can't wait till the third," Auntie Lam said. "It'll be so special for her! For all of us!"

"What's happening on the third?" I asked as I ate the tiny pieces of melon on toothpicks and watched Auntie Choi work.

"That's our monthly spa day!" Auntie Lam said.

"You should come!" Auntie Choi said, waving the curling iron over my head. "We get our nails done, our hair! You guys still gonna be here on the third?" She twirled another strand of my hair around the iron.

I nodded. "My camp ends on the second, but we could stick around another day! Can my friend Lupe come too?"

"Of course," Auntie Lam said. "All the women of Chinatown are welcome. That's the whole point of it, why we have it on the third each month—so we *remember*."

"March third was when they passed the Page Act," Auntie Chu explained.

I set aside the melon and started scribbling again. "What's the Page Act?"

"Very bad act." Auntie Lam shook her head. "It banned Chinese women from coming to this country. Passed in 1875."

"They said we were 'lewd and immoral,'" Auntie Doo said, putting a hand to her forehead, like it throbbed in pain at the very mention of it. "So we no way to come. No way to join our husband. No way to have family. No way to continue."

I gasped.

"No more children. No more Chinese," Auntie Lam whispered.

"That wasn't even the worst of it," Auntie Doo added. "*Then* they passed the Chinese Exclusion Act."

The shop got so quiet, I could hear the drip from the small oil heater.

"What's the Chinese Exclusion Act?" I asked in a small voice.

"That's when *all* the Chinese were banned," Auntie Chu said quietly. "Anyone who was Chinese or of Chinese descent. And those who were here couldn't become citizens. So they couldn't even vote to change this law. It was terrible."

I frowned. "But I thought we did all that great work on the mines and the railroads. . . ." Emma had told me that twenty thousand Chinese workers helped build the transcontinental railroad. How could they just *exclude* all those hard workers?

"By then the railroads were built," Auntie Lam replied. "And people . . . forgot our contributions."

"Anyway, after the act passed, there were many riots and massacres," Auntie Doo went on. "Many people attacked the Chinese. So many died. That's why Chinatown so important. This tiny neighborhood in San Francisco kept our people safe."

The mothers all nodded.

"So when the earthquake of 1906 happened, and the city wanted us to all move—" Auntie Lam began.

"Wait, the city wanted to *move* Chinatown?" I interrupted.

Auntie Choi put her curling iron down. "Oh sure! They complained this location too good for Chinese! Even though this was the only place our ancestors, the early Chinese immigrants, were allowed to set up their shops! We were banned from owning or leasing property anywhere else—"

"Thanks to California Alien Land Law of 1913," Auntie Doo added.

"Another terrible law." Auntie Lam shook her head. "Said Asian people cannot own or lease land. Hurt not just us, Japanese too! And other Asian Americans!"

I tensed in the salon chair, trying to imagine what would happen to the Calivista Motel if that law was still intact! We wouldn't have been able to buy the motel from Mr. Yao—because Mr. Yao wouldn't be allowed to own the motel himself. Jason and I certainly wouldn't be friends. None of us would be the same!

"That's why we have all the Chinese pagoda towers and decorations you see now. Our ancestors raced to build those after the earthquake, so this place could look decisively like Chinatown. So we couldn't get moved. So we would have a home, without worrying about what new law they threw at us."

"Wow," I said, writing every word down. "Thank you for telling me all this. I had no idea."

"Are you going to write about it?" Auntie Lam asked. She put a hand to her hair and started prancing around with her scarves. "Just imagine, my little shop in the *Tribune*!"

"Well . . . there's this whole editorial process," I started to tell her, sighing as I thought back to Mr. Walters and all my rejected pitches. "But I promise, I'll do my best."

It was getting late, so I slid off the salon chair and thanked everyone again. Auntie Lam piled eight packs of underwear into my arms, insisting I take them for free. Then Auntie Chu grabbed my hand and started studying my palm.

"It'll be quick! On the house!" she cried when I tried to pull away.

"Let's see. You have a *wonderful* money line—very prosperous future! But, what's this?" Her pupils flashed. "Your love line is . . . uh-oh!"

My stomach dropped. "What? Why *uh-oh*?"

She shook her head. "I see challenges ahead," she said. "The person you like is . . . distracted by someone else?!"

*Geez*, nothing escaped these Chinatown aunties! But this was a part of history I needed to figure out by myself.

I hid my face behind the fort of underwear and bolted out of the store.

# CHAPTER 24

"There you are!" Jason said as soon as I walked into the kitchen at the Golden Inn. He dropped a handful of radishes into a colander and pointed at me.

My curls bounced like Julia Roberts's in *Steel Magnolias*. I turned my head this way and that. *I* thought I looked sublime.

But that wasn't what Jason had noticed. "That's *a lot* of underwear," he said.

My face flushed. I tried to hide the packages behind me.

"Oh! Yeah. Auntie Lam went a little overboard. Maybe I'll regift them . . ."

"You're going to regift underwear?"

*Stop talking*, I scolded myself. I looked down at his box of chocolate fortune cookies and put them on the counter with a frown. "Here. Emma told me to give these to you. And she said you should meet her tomorrow in Portsmouth Square. *Again.*"

Jason's eyes lit up. "Oh, thanks!"

"Why didn't you tell me?" I asked, hating how jealous I sounded.

"There's nothing to tell," Jason said, shrugging. "We had lunch together while you guys were at your camps." He smiled. "She's really funny. And super nice."

My throat felt dry.

"Actually . . ." Jason suddenly looked nervous. "There's something I need to talk to you about." He drew in a sharp breath. "Maybe out by the fire escape? It's nice and quiet—and the view's spectacular!" He pointed at the stove, covered in bamboo trays of steaming dumplings. "I'll bring some food."

I smiled. That was more like it. Time for our own little picnic.

As we carried dumplings, garlic cucumbers, and dan dan noodles upstairs, I told Jason about the parrot that flew away from its owner's fire escape.

Now that our story got rejected *again*, I was beginning to think maybe Amne was right.

"My friend from camp thinks we should write a story on it," I said.

"About a missing bird?"

I nodded. "What?" I asked, registering his surprised face.

"Nothing. That just doesn't sound like a classic Mia Tang story," he said, setting the plates down on the fire escape's rusty floor. We made ourselves comfortable and he handed me chopsticks. I was starting to get used to them.

"And what's a *classic* Mia Tang story?" I asked.

Jason was right, the views up here were incredible. I could see all the way out to the Golden Gate Bridge. The clouds were the color of strawberries, melting into the deep red of the bridge, and the lights of the city had begun to sparkle in the growing dusk.

I reached for a dumpling and waited for Jason to answer, expecting him to say something funny, like "a classic Mia Tang story makes you laugh and fart at the same time."

But instead, his eyes got all dreamy.

"It's a story that if you don't read it, you're missing out," he said.

"Everyone's going to be talking about it the next day. Even kids like Stuart Dustfinger, who thinks newspapers are made out of smushed coffee beans."

I put my chopsticks down. "Jason! That is the nicest, kindest thing you've ever said to me!"

"Well, it's true," he insisted. His cheeks were as pink as the clouds.

It was moments like these that made me think, *Maybe I can get over what happened in fifth grade. Maybe I am over it.*

I told him what happened with the mayor's puppy story.

"The thing that hurt the most was when he said if I wanted to make it, I have to learn to work well with others."

"He doesn't know his ear from his elbow!" Jason cried. "You manage an *entire motel.* Does he know how many people you have to deal with? Including my *dad*?"

I chuckled. "True! I do have some strong personalities to deal with!"

I gazed out at the horizon, missing Mrs. T and Mrs. Q and everybody back home . . . even Mr. Yao. The fire escape reminded me of the back staircase in the Calivista, where I used to sit alone. Now I had tons of people.

"Don't listen to that guy," Jason went on. "If you want to write something—write it for yourself. You don't need his approval. You know how many dishes I make that I don't ever serve? I just like making 'em."

"And I like eating them," I said, popping another dumpling into my mouth. "So, what did you want to talk to me about?"

Jason put his food down and sat up straighter. Then he cleared his throat.

Whatever it was, it was knocking the breath out of him.

"Just say it!" I prodded. My heart squeezed tight. *Please let him confess his undying love to me again!*

"You have to help me," he said in a rush. "With Emma."

Now the breath was knocked out of *me*.

"What—what about Emma?"

"She's just so *amazing*. When I'm around her, I feel like . . ." He gazed at the Golden Gate Bridge for so long, I thought he'd gotten hypnotized. But then he settled on, "I feel like the version of myself I want to be."

My head felt heavy but I nodded, because I knew the feeling. That was exactly how I felt whenever Jason was down about something, and I had the honor of pepping him back up.

I *lived* for that feeling.

And now somebody else was going to have it.

I stared into my vinegar bowl and mumbled, "What do you need *my* help for?"

"Well, the last time I told a girl I liked her, it didn't exactly work out," Jason said. I looked up and our eyes locked. For the first time, I realized that the events of fifth grade weren't just weighing on me. They were weighing on Jason too. "In fact, things exploded quite spectacularly."

In the silvery moonlight, Jason looked so vulnerable and sad, I wanted to put a blanket around him.

"I remember," I said softly. "I was there."

"So I'm thinking *this* time, I need some help. Maybe some lessons or something."

I dropped my chopsticks. "You want me to *teach* you how to like Emma?"

"No! Just how to express my feelings," Jason said. "Not to be a complete doofus. Or put my foot in my mouth again. You know, the stuff I normally do."

"You're actually tolerable these days," I joked.

He smiled and rolled his eyes at the same time. "Thanks. But if I'm going to have *any chance* in my future dating life, I need to be more than 'tolerable.'" Pressing his hands together, he begged, "Please, Mia. You're the most articulate girl I know. You *know* me, and you know feelings. Better than anyone. If you can't help me, I'm hopeless."

He peered into my eyes.

I chewed my lip as a tug-of-war played out between my own heart and our friendship.

"Of course," I heard myself say. "What are friends for?"

# CHAPTER 25

"You said *what*?" Lupe stared at me from the sea of notebooks, math books, and calculators surrounding her on her bed.

"What was I supposed to do?" I flopped onto my bed and moaned. "He was so earnest. And I *am* his best friend!"

"But you're also *you*," Lupe reminded me. "A girl who has a crush on him!"

I sat up again. "I know. But don't you think the fact that he wants to work on expressing his feelings is amazing?"

"Yeah, but not for *you*." She put her pencil down and gave me a serious look. "He's doing this for Emma. You'd literally be helping him break your heart!"

*Hmmmm . . . good point.* I threw myself back down on the mattress.

"Maybe I can teach him to express his feelings all wrong?"

Lupe burst out laughing. "Like how?" She put on her best Jason voice. "Hey, Emma, your face is almost as good-looking as flourless chocolate cake."

"You're like the History Channel, but with hair," I said, giggling too.

"You're braver than the first person to try oysters." Lupe snorted.

We tossed out ridiculous compliments, one after another, until both of us got a tummy ache from laughing. Then Lupe got serious again. "But Mia, why didn't you just say no?"

I thought about it for a long while. It was dark now, and neither of us had turned on a light. The moon shone on Lupe's face when I finally turned to admit, "Because he makes me want to be the very best version of myself. And I know that version would help him."

"That version's going to get hurt . . . Take it from me, I *know*."

"Maybe. I've faced a lot worse back at the Calivista. I can handle a challenge."

Lupe reached over gently and put her hand over mine. "But this is your heart we're talking about, not a vending machine."

A gust of wind came in through the open window and blew a piece of paper from Lupe's bed over to mine. I picked it up.

*SAT Diagnostic Test—Appointment: Monday, December 30, 4 p.m.*

"What's this?" I asked.

"Just a practice test." She held out a hand and I gave the paper back. "I just want to *see*."

My jaw dropped. "Oh, no, no, no. I'm not letting our trio of keys become nothing but a rusty ring!" I said.

Last year was one thing, with Lupe taking classes in the high school, but no way was I going to let her ditch me for college while Jason ran off with Emma!

I grabbed Lupe's arm and hugged it tight. "You're not going to college. We still have so much hanging out to do! We haven't even done any of the things on the dog quiz!"

"What dog quiz?"

"This quiz that listed all the things we missed out on!"

"Because we didn't have a dog?" she asked, confused. "Or because we didn't have time?"

"Both! I don't know! Never mind. The point is—you can't go to college and leave me alone in high school!" I blurted. "I *need* you."

I covered my face with my hands.

"It's a *practice* test, Mia. You should be more worried about protecting your own heart!"

That was *exactly* what I was worried about. Tears pushed against my eyes, so I turned around and pretended the wallpaper was fascinating. Despite all of Lupe's assurances that nothing was going to change, I shivered to the tips of my toes.

*Why was everyone in such a rush to grow up?*

I wanted so badly for things to stay as they were.

# CHAPTER 26

At the *Tribune* the next day, a tall woman with long silver hair walked into the conference room.

"Good morning, I'm Erica Flemings. I'm visiting from the DC office, where I head up features," she said, smiling. "Mr. Walters is out sick, so I'll be leading your workshop today. Who's excited to learn all about features?"

Our hands shot up. Features was big. They were the department that did full-page, high-profile interviews with *very* important people.

She walked over to the door. "Well, come on then. Let's not waste another minute!"

"We're going on another field trip?" I asked excitedly.

"Oh, I never write in the newsroom," she said.

"Where are we going?" Timothy asked.

"You'll see!"

. . .

I'd never seen anyone walk so fast in four-inch heels. As Ms. Flemings clacked her way down the San Francisco streets, which she seemed to know by heart, she explained her philosophy on writing.

"To be a good writer, you need to *live*," she said. "Be one with the people! Be down here on the street. Not up there in that big steel-and-cement box." She pointed at the sky-pokers Hank admired.

I scribbled her words down. They sure sounded good to me. Talking to people, getting to know their lives was my favorite part of writing too.

"Most of all," she went on, "you need to have fun!"

Then she stopped at a corner, just as a giant double-decker bus pulled up. The doors opened and Ms. Flemings jumped inside, waving for us to follow.

My eyes lingered on the $8.45 per person sign by the driver, but Ms. Flemings shouted, "My treat!"

So I followed Amne, Haru, and the rest of the gang up to the open-air second deck, taking a seat amid all the other tourists. I giggled as the bus roared to life and the wind blew in my hair. *Riding a double-decker bus* might not officially be on the dog quiz, but it was definitely up there in terms of fun!

Ms. Flemings slid into a seat next to us. "I want you to each go up to a passenger and ask where they're from. Have a conversation. Look for the details, the kernels of truth, the tangents, the tidbits, as if you were writing a feature story on them."

"But you can't write a feature story on a random tourist!" Timothy protested. "Features are for politicians . . . movie stars . . . *important* people."

"I have news for you," Ms. Flemings said. "There's something interesting and important about everyone."

I nodded. "I run a motel down in LA with some of my friends," I told the editor. "Every day we check in interesting people. You'd be amazed at the stories I've heard!"

"I can believe it!" she said. "And I would *love* to hear them!"

Under her watchful guidance, we conducted interviews all

morning. As the bus cruised up and down the hills, I talked to an elderly Asian couple celebrating their anniversary. They'd met twenty years ago on the Hong Kong escalator, which is the longest outdoor escalator in the world, stretching from downtown Hong Kong all the way to the top of the mountain!

Ms. Flemings came over as I was talking to the couple and said, "I've been on that escalator! It goes right by the famous place that sells egg tarts!"

"Tai Cheong Bakery!" The couple nodded.

"That's the one!" Ms. Flemings smiled. She turned to me and added, "I asked the paper to send me to Hong Kong for a story. But really, it was for the egg tarts!"

My eyebrows jumped. "I'd love to go to Hong Kong!"

"Oh, it's so much fun. But you can't just stay there for a day or two. You've got to spend at least a week. . . . Go down to Thailand— the best beaches in the world are in Thailand! Visit the temples in Angkor Wat!"

"Wow, you've been everywhere!"

"When I was young, I didn't get much of a chance to travel," she explained. "I was raised by a single mom, so vacation was out of the question. I guess you could say I'm making up for lost time!"

"You can do that??" I blurted. My mind was spinning—maybe I still had plenty of time to chill!

"Of course!" She patted my hand. "You can have fun any time in your life!"

"But what about your work? All the stories and deadlines . . ." I swallowed hard and admitted, "I feel like, if I slow down for a minute, I'll lose my writing powers."

"Nonsense! You should see the groundbreaking stories I've worked on! *Work hard, play hard* is my motto," she said proudly.

I'd heard a lot of mottoes from Mom, but they were usually along the lines of *We gotta work twice as hard as everyone else!*

"Work hard . . . play hard . . ." I looked at her hesitantly. "Is that really okay?"

"More than okay! It makes me a better writer—because it makes me a happier person. Life's short."

"You're telling me! My best friend wants to run off to college!" I said.

She chuckled. "And I'm guessing you're not crazy about that?"

I shook my head.

"One thing I've learned as a features editor is you can't rush people—or slow them down. People are ready when they're ready. That goes for interviews, photo shoots, and friendships. You just gotta make the most of the time you have."

As we passed the Ferry Building, Ms. Flemings hollered at the bus driver to drop us off at Ghirardelli Square. Then she bought us all caramels and chocolates at the chocolate shop.

But it was the kernels of truth she'd given me that were even sweeter. I'd learned so much from Ms. Flemings that day. I learned the location of the best egg tarts in Hong Kong. I learned I needed to be more patient with Lupe.

Most of all, I learned I still had time to have fun.

A *lot* of time.

Standing at the pier, I bit into the most incredible white chocolate peppermint square I'd ever tasted.

*Work hard, play hard* was my new motto too, I decided.

# CHAPTER 27

We didn't have time to pitch Ms. Flemings our features stories before she had to cut out to make her flight back to DC. She told us to pitch them to Mr. Walters the next day instead.

On Friday morning, Mom paced the hallway up and down the Golden Inn at the crack of dawn looking like she was going to burst. It was the day of her big lecture at Berkeley, and to say she was nervous was putting it mildly.

"I need my hot-water bottle from home," she said. "My stomach's doing jumping jacks."

I ran back into my room. "Here, have some Ghirardelli chocolates!" I handed them to her.

She twisted the wrapper off a square and popped it in her mouth. Her eyes closed.

"These are *heavenly*," she said. Then she frowned. "How much were they?"

"Don't worry, my editor paid," I told her proudly.

Her face relaxed into a smile.

"Knowing you're doing so well at the *Tribune*, it almost doesn't matter how terrible I do this morning," she said.

I started to argue—*it's just a chocolate! For everyone!*—but she'd already gone back to her room to brush her teeth. Years of not having dental insurance had trained us all to whip out the toothpaste within seconds of eating candy.

. . .

I was excited to pitch Mr. Walters a feature on Mr. Wu. But before we even started workshop, he announced that he had two pieces of news. One, he wasn't taking pitches today—he'd approved Timothy's late last night.

"Tell 'em what you emailed me!" Mr. Walters said, practically jumping with excitement.

Timothy grinned. "I'm going to interview my grandfather's editor at Knopf about the summer he wrote *The Glass Wharf* in San Francisco!"

I jumped up from the conference table. "I don't understand—I thought pitch sessions were during Newsroom?"

"Sometimes a good idea just cannot wait!" Mr. Walters said.

"That's what email is for," Timothy said smugly.

I sank in my seat. I had my *Tribune* laptop, but they didn't let any of us take them home. And I certainly didn't have an email address.

I must have looked pretty sad, because Mr. Walters said, "You're going to like the other news!" I looked up hopefully. "I've arranged a special tour of our printers for tomorrow morning! You guys will be able to see how the Sunday edition is printed!"

"Woo-hoo!" Timothy threw his arms up.

I mustered a quiet, "Yay."

Seeing the printers did sound cool, but a fair chance to get published would be even cooler.

Mr. Walters clapped his hands. "Now! Let's talk about credible witnesses!"

I fought the urge to shake my head. I wanted to talk about credible *pitches*, specifically the chance to get published.

Amne and Haru looked similarly frustrated. We needed to strategize—pronto. I leaned over. "Meet at the smoothie shop after Newsroom?" I whispered.

They each gave me a thumbs-up.

. . .

"It's so unfair!" Haru said over his pineapple-coconut smoothie. "I had my pitch all ready to go!"

He got some papers out of his bag and handed them over.

The long, handwritten piece was titled:

### Librarian of Hope: Recounting the Atrocities of the Japanese Internment Years
### By Haru Tanaka

My eyes scanned the neatly written paragraphs under the title.

"Haru, this isn't a pitch. This is the whole story!" I said. Amne put her smoothie down and we both started reading eagerly.

On January 14, a collection of letters will be made public for the first time in history. The Japanese American National Museum will exhibit 250 letters entitled "Dear Miss Breed." The letters give us a rare glimpse into life in the Japanese internment camps during the 1940s through the eyes of Japanese children corresponding with their favorite librarian.

Miss Clara Breed loved serving the children of her San Diego Public Library. Many of her patrons were of Japanese descent. She enjoyed recommending books to them and watching them blossom as readers. So imagine her shock when 110,000 Japanese Americans living in San Diego were rounded up, in the wake of the Pearl Harbor bombing, and taken from their homes, schools, and jobs. Every man, woman, and child of Japanese descent was removed and put in internment camps. Their lives? Turned upside down. Their dignity? Robbed.

Miss Breed knew she had to do something. Amid the frenzy of fear and racial hatred, she got to work—licking penny stamps to thick stacks of self-addressed cards. Her plan? To give every child and reader leaving for the camps a postcard. "Write to us," she told the children at the train station as they were whisked away. "We'll want to know where you are and how you are getting along. And we'll send you some books to read."

For the next few years, Miss Breed corresponded with the children, sending them books, dolls, fabric for making clothes, shower caps, shoe polish, ink, and even electric clippers for cutting hair. They wrote to her candidly, pouring out their worries, doubts, haunting descriptions of their camp conditions, as well as their dreams and hopes. And she always wrote back.

With the books from Miss Breed, soon the children were able to start libraries in the camps. They made little library cards for the books, just like their favorite librarian.

Altogether, the 250 letters are a testament to the human spirit, the courage of one librarian to display kindness during a tsunami of hate, and the resilience of an entire generation of Japanese American children made to endure the unspeakable. The collection will be exhibited at the Japanese American National Museum through April.

"Haru, this is *such* a good story!" I said. "You've got to show this to Mr. Walters tomorrow! At the printers!"

"Unless Timothy beats me to the punch with another email pitch!" Haru said nervously.

"If he does, we'll *make* Mr. Walters read your story!" Amne said. "Plus, you've inspired me to write a piece on Ishi!"

"Who's Ishi?" I asked.

Amne leaned in. "Remember Kroeber?"

"The anthropologist who said your tribe was extinct?" Haru said.

She nodded. "He was also a Berkeley professor. There was a whole hall in Berkeley named after him. Anyway, he helped create a museum there, full of Native American remains. His colleagues *loved* Native American remains."

I glanced over at Haru. He looked upset, but I was confused. "Wait," I said. "Do you mean *human* remains? Like, dead bodies?"

She nodded again and I shuddered.

"That's not even the most disturbing part of the story," Amne said. "In 1911, a Native man was walking alone around in Oroville, California. He was emaciated—like, this guy hadn't eaten in who knows how long. The police arrested him for some petty food theft. And then get this. Kroeber convinced the police to release him into his custody—because he wanted him for his museum. To *be* an exhibit."

I almost dropped my smoothie. Haru sucked in a breath.

"The man refused to give Kroeber his name, so Kroeber named him 'Ishi,' meaning 'man.' Kroeber made Ishi the janitor of the museum and had him *live* there. *With* all the remains. For years, Ishi made tools and recorded songs and stories—whatever Kroeber wanted. He was totally disturbed to be there, obviously. It was incredibly creepy, on top of being completely dehumanizing. But Kroeber was thrilled. He called him a 'living exhibit.'"

"That is an outrage!" Haru erupted. "That's not what museums are for!"

Amne nodded. "My biggest hope in telling more Native stories is to let people know we're *not* an exhibit in a museum. We're *here*. We've been here all along, for thousands of years. And all our hopes and dreams, our history and our future matter."

"Yes!" I shouted, thrusting my mango smoothie into the air.

Just then Mr. Miles and Mr. Walters walked into the shop. Haru immediately poked my arm. I glanced at his Miss Breed story. I could tell he was thinking the same thing I was—if Timothy could pitch outside of camp hours, maybe we could too! This could be our chance!

But then we heard what they were talking about.

"Did you get ahold of Timothy's literary agent?" Mr. Miles asked. "I'd really like to run his feature on his grandfather's publisher for the Sunday edition—if he can file it quickly enough."

"The boy can write fast. The problem is his agent. He still thinks we're offering too little," Mr. Walters said.

Mr. Miles's eyebrows jumped. "We already agreed to come up to two hundred!"

Haru choked on his drink. *Two hundred* dollars? he mouthed to us. I shook my head, stunned. We put a giant menu in front of us, so they couldn't see us.

"He's threatening to shop it around to other publications."

"No way am I losing that story!" Mr. Miles snapped.

"Then I think we should pay," Mr. Walters said. "Unless you want it to end up in the *New Yorker*."

Mr. Miles sighed. "Fine. Make it work."

The two editors grabbed their drinks and left. Amne, Haru, and I put the menu down and let out a gasp.

"*More* than two hundred dollars??" Amne cried.

"I'm still trying to get over the fact that he has an agent!" Haru said.

"What even is that???" I asked.

"It's a manager for big-shot writers," Haru explained.

I imagined a motel manager, except instead of customers, there were famous writers in every room, typing away. *How did I get into THAT motel?*

Amne took the last sip from her smoothie and stood. "Eyes on our own papers, kids."

I nodded. I knew she was right. Still, it felt like I was in fifth grade again, getting Cs in English, staring enviously at everyone else's As and wondering when I was ever going to catch up. I closed my eyes and thought back to Lupe's wise advice that year—*You can't win if you don't play!*

Those words had gotten me all the way here. I knew in my heart that I had to keep believing. But on days like today, when it felt like some people came ready for battle with paintball blasters and all I had were pool noodles, it was hard to ignore the doubts.

I waited for Mom and Lupe to pick me up, reminding myself, *I might not have a power manager. But I am a manager manager.*

And that was no pool noodle.

# CHAPTER 28

Lupe and Mom ran excitedly toward the smoothie shop.

"Guess what??" Lupe asked. "Your mom killed! The way she taught the polar coordinates––" Lupe put her fingers to her mouth and kissed them. "Perfection!"

I squealed and hugged Mom.

"I knew you could do it!"

"I actually pronounced 'polar coordinates' right!" Mom said. "In front of so many people!!" She smiled at Lupe. "Thanks for practicing with me. All those tongue twisters really helped!"

"Unique New York!" Lupe recited, then laughed. "You know you need unique New York!"

"Maybe if I finally make it onto the committee, we can make this competition *national!*" Mom's eyes brightened. "I'll finally get to go to unique New York! See the Statue of Liberty! Wouldn't that be something?"

"Did you talk to the committee members about it?" I asked. "What'd they say?"

Mom shook her head. "I didn't have a chance today. They were all going to drinks at Chez Panisse."

"Wait," I said, confused. "Then why are you here picking me up? You didn't go with them?"

Mom looked horrified. "Chez Panisse is a *fancy* restaurant, Mia! The drinks there are twenty dollars apiece! There goes my entire pillow budget for our new house!"

"But Mom, you deserve to treat yourself! This is a big day!"

In that moment, I wished even more I'd gotten just one of my pitches accepted—the seventy-five dollars could get Mom in!

She held up a finger. "I *did* get this lovely poem from a wonderful poet, Sylvia on Shattuck, as I was heading back on the subway. Only cost me a nickel!"

She reached into her purse and produced a crumpled piece of paper. Lupe and I leaned over to read.

*Wherever you go, go with purpose.*
*Whatever you do, do with conviction.*
*Whoever you love, love with compassion.*
*Whatever you say, say with kindness.*

I sighed. It was a nice poem. But it didn't mention anything about what to do when you're up against power agents!

"You should feel very lucky, Mia. There are talented poets writing for a nickel out on the street, and you're working at the *Tribune*!" Mom puffed out her chest. "I told Sylvia I'd bring her a copy of your first story next week! You will be published by then, won't you?"

"Mom, you can't put that kind of pressure on me!" I blurted.

"Why not?" she asked. She stopped walking. "Everything all right in the newsroom?"

She searched my eyes and I quickly looked away. "Yeah, everything's fine," I said. "I just gotta get back to the inn to do some work."

"Me too!" Lupe said. "It's down to us against San Tomosa tomorrow!"

"I'm so bummed I can't come," I said. "Mr. Walters wants us back in the newsroom to tour the printers."

"That's okay! I'll give you the play-by-play after we win!" Lupe grinned.

"That reminds me, I have to call Ethan to review the formulas," Mom said. "He's still a little rusty when it comes to relating functions!"

"Can you imagine if we actually won this thing?" Lupe gushed, walking even faster. "That would look *so* good on my college applications!"

As Mom and Lupe hurried ahead, I wished writing were more like math, where it was clear who had the winning answer. No ifs, ands, or agents!

# CHAPTER 29

We'd been back for two minutes and already Lupe was at the desk in our hotel room, nose-deep in a textbook.

"You wanna go watch the elders play Chinese chess?" I asked, putting my backpack down. "In Portsmouth Square?"

She glanced at the clock on the wall. "I've always wanted to learn how to play. . . ."

"Then let's go!" I urged. "I need some fun after the day I had."

She put her textbook down. "What happened?" she asked.

With a sigh, I told her about Timothy.

"You've just got to put your blinders on," she said confidently. "We can't control other people's advantages. Some of the kids in the Math Cup have private tutors, and ex-Olympians training them in sports."

"So what do we do?"

Lupe pursed her lips. "We work *even harder*."

I blew at my bangs, thinking about Ms. Flemings. "But don't you ever get tired of working *all the time*?" I tried to pry Lupe's textbook away. "Let's go have some fun. You have all night to out-study those San Tomosa kids!"

"It's not just the Math Cup," Lupe said, wrestling her book back. "I've got that SAT mock test coming up, remember? I want to—"

She stopped, catching me mid eye roll.

"You could be a *little* more supportive!"

"I am totally supportive!" I insisted, turning beet red.

I could tell Lupe wasn't buying it. Luckily, the sound of barking jolted both our heads toward the door.

"Did you hear that?" Lupe asked.

We ran out of our room.

• • •

Three wiggly brown-and-white puppies were whimpering and pawing at Mrs. Luk's ankles in the front office.

"Puppies!!!" Lupe and I cried at the same time.

My heart melted into a puddle of silk almond tofu as I ran straight toward the tiny dogs and picked one of them up. He licked my nose and I fell on the floor, giggling.

"Are they yours?" I asked Mrs. Luk.

She shook her head. "Auntie Choi's landlord finally figured out she was keeping them in her SRO. She wanted to put 'em in her salon, but it's Christmas! I told her they'd freeze their little paws off! So here they are."

"Can we keep them?" I asked.

Mine was so warm and fuzzy in my arms, I wanted to never let him go. He looked up at me with his black eyes and wet nose, then started digging that nose into my armpit.

I was dying of giggles when Mom walked down the stairs.

"Those two are already spoken for," Mrs. Luk was telling me. "Charlie Mo's boy said he'd take one. And I convinced Dr. Doo's wife to adopt the other. But this little guy . . ." She pointed at the one I was holding. "We're still looking for a *fur*-ever home for him."

"Oh, can I have him??" I begged Mom. "This is him! This is Comma! Look, he's even a beagle, just like I've always wanted!" I kissed Comma's nose, already thinking of all the fun we'd have together. "He's perfect, Mom! Just perfect!"

Jason ran out from the kitchen. As soon as he saw me with Comma, he cooed, "Puppppy!!!"

I let Jason hold him and Comma licked our fingers.

Mom stomped her foot. "Mia Tang, you can't be adopting puppies! You should be focusing on your writing!"

"I *am* focused," I insisted.

"And what about Lupe? She's got her big championship meet tomorrow! She can't be up all night!"

"I won't be!" Lupe promised. "I'll snuggle Comma to sleep. He'll keep my toes warm!"

"We don't even know if we can keep Comma in the room!" Mom said, looking to Mrs. Luk.

"Oh, don't worry about that," Mrs. Luk said. "So long as you walk him and feed him, he can stay with you. Better than sending him to the pound." She shuddered, and I did too.

"But who's going to take care of him while we're in Berkeley and Mia's at camp?" Mom asked.

Jason shot up a hand. "I will! I am *so good* with dogs! Just call me the puppy whisperer."

I giggled and threw my arms around Jason.

Mom put her hands up in defeat.

At long last! I had gotten my Christmas wish!

# CHAPTER 30

Jason and I took my new chill buddy to my room. "Let's talk about how to train him," I said.

Mrs. Luk had kindly given us a bunch of old towels to make a warm dog bed. As we laid them in the corner, Jason said, "I got this! The key with dogs is you have to assert your authority early. It's all about tough love!"

I picked up Comma and held him away from Jason, not liking the sound of that at all. "It's not about tough love! It's about *love* love!"

"Mia, you can't just be super nice to them all the time," he said, shaking his head. "They'll chew up all your table legs! Your shoes! Even your teeth!"

"Teeth?!"

"My dog Wealthy once chewed up my wai gong's dentures!" Jason lamented, referring to his maternal grandfather. "It was *not* pretty."

Comma yelped, as if to say *Nice work, Wealthy!*

"We found a whole bunch of pearly whites on the floor. I thought it was LEGO. I nearly barfed when I smelled it," Jason said. "Wealthy got in big trouble!"

Jason gave me his meanest, scariest growl. Comma whimpered and tried to hide his head in my sleeve.

I backed away even more. "Okay, you're *not* doing that with

Comma," I said. "He's my dog and we're only using positive communication to train him."

"How's *that* going to work?" Jason asked.

"Exactly like it sounds. Be positive! Only use language that reassures, motivates, and inspires him," I said.

"What if he does something bad?"

"Then you'll be patient. You'll teach and nurture . . . you'll be honest," I brainstormed, thinking of all the things I'd want in a good relationship, with a puppy or anyone else for that matter. "You'll give lots of nice, kind feedback."

Jason put the last of the towels down and looked at me like I'd gone nuts. "Like, *thank you for eating my grandpa's teeth*?!"

I laughed. Then I cleared my throat and demonstrated, "Like, *thank you for communicating you need more appropriate dog toys*. There."

"He's a dog, not a customer!"

"He's sort of a customer, actually! He's chosen *you* to take care of his needs."

"You chose *him*," Jason corrected me.

I snuggled Comma and sighed. "Don't you want a healthy relationship built on mutual trust and respect?" Suddenly realizing that this was useful advice for Emma too, I poked Jason lightly with my elbow. "Isn't that what you wanted me to teach you?"

He nodded sheepishly.

"Then you must never, ever get mad at this perfect puppy of mine."

Jason exhaled loudly. "Fine," he finally said. "But he better behave."

I smiled, surprised. Maybe training Jason was going to be fun after all! I mean—training Comma.

# CHAPTER 31

Later that night, I set Comma down at the foot of Lupe's bed.

"Hey," I said. "I'm sorry. I totally support your college dreams. I just . . . really don't want to lose you."

"You won't," she promised, snuggling Comma. "I might not even go to Berkeley. And if I do, we can keep in touch by mail . . . maybe even by email!"

I smiled. "Yeah, maybe. And we can always still have fun on the breaks," I said. "Go to museums!"

"And Knott's Berry Farm, finally," Lupe added.

"And the beach!"

"Chase butterflies down by Dana Point!"

We went on, listing all the fun things I wished we'd already done together in Anaheim.

"Can't believe we still haven't done any of that," Lupe said, reading my mind.

I put my hand over hers. "We can still have fun, anytime we want. I learned that from an editor yesterday. So if this is what your heart wants, you should go for it. And I will support you a thousand percent."

"That means a lot to me," she said, reaching out for a hug.

Comma jumped up and down on the bed, wanting to get in on the hug too. Lupe laughed, opened her arms, and let him in. When we pulled away, I held on to Comma so I could hide my moist eyes in his fur.

. . .

I handed Jason Comma's leash on Saturday morning with a stern look.

"Remember, positive communication only," I said. Comma looked up at me and started whimpering again. All night, he'd whined whenever I made him get off the bed. But I was proud of myself for not getting mad. Instead, I'd simply curled up to sleep next to him on the floor.

So what if my back was now stiffer than a wooden plank? Big deal.

Jason produced a bag full of fresh bacon treats from his pocket. "I've got the *ultimate* reward system. Come here, boy!"

Comma perked right up.

"Maybe he and I could go for a walk with Emma!" Jason added. "After her lion dancing practice, and after I finish prepping all the mango pudding for the banquet dessert!"

I blew at my bangs, trying not to let my frustration show. It was torture getting squeezed by Berkeley on one side and Emma on the other.

"I don't know," I said, trying to keep my voice neutral. "A cookie factory? He might get totally overexcited."

Jason was kneeling down, ruffling Comma's ears. He grinned up at me and said, "Oh, she switched her shift today. She's over at the kite shop. Maybe I'll take her to the beach and fly a kite with him!" He looked back at Comma and crooned, "Won't that be fun? Yes it will!"

I thought of Jason and Emma running along with a beautiful kite flying high above them and Comma chasing behind. It sounded like the perfect multiple-choice answer on the dog quiz. So perfect I wanted to puke.

# CHAPTER 32

The printers roared inside the *Tribune* warehouse. We watched, spellbound, as row upon row of tall, steel machines printed, folded, and neatly stacked hundreds of papers before our eyes.

"Pretty incredible, isn't it?" Mr. Walters said. "This press was made in Germany, and it took a hundred and fifty tractor-trailer loads to deliver all of it!"

"Can I see my piece?" Timothy asked. "Is it above the fold?"

"It sure is!" Mr. Walters said, reaching for a paper and showing us. I exchanged a look with Haru and Amne. Guess that meant he got his two hundred dollars.

"Go on, read the first line," Mr. Walters said.

Timothy cleared his throat and said, "Genius is not made, it's born and patiently poured, according to the editor of *The Glass Wharf*."

*Oh, give me a break!* I rolled my eyes.

"Now that's a punchy lede!" Mr. Walters said. "A good lede is enticing and succinct. It's got to suck you in and keep you from turning to the next headline."

Haru nervously raised a hand. "Actually, I have a great lede example . . . Can I show you?"

Amne and I grinned, bursting with pride for our friend.

"Sure," Mr. Walters replied. "Let's go into the production

manager's office. The rest of you, I want you to practice coming up with some ledes. There's paper and pencils over on that desk!"

I grabbed a pencil, but I couldn't concentrate. I kept doodling ledes about me and Jason.

*Best friends go from wanting to barbecue each other's intestines to walking across the Golden Gate Bridge together, hand in hand.*

*Young motel owners who once fought over a pencil discover puppy love.*

Amne leaned over and burst out laughing. "Now *that's* catchy!" she said. "C'mon, give me the scoop!"

I blushed. Against the murmur of the printers, I began by telling her about our cringey start.

"I don't know why I can't just tell him how I feel," I said. "I'm the *queen* of words!"

"Memories are very powerful," Amne said sympathetically.

"Yes! How do I just forget what happened in fifth grade?"

"You can't. What happens lives inside us, in layers." Amne sighed. "The elders in my tribe are always talking about it. That's why it's so hard to let go of trauma."

It made so much sense. As much as I liked Jason now, fifth grade was *very* traumatic for me.

"I *thought* I'd been through every layer with him. But now, when I think of him and Emma together . . ." My heart lurched.

Amne leaned over and lowered her voice. "I knew this boy, Isaac, in sixth grade. He was my best friend. We did everything together. One time, we climbed to the top of Indian Rock."

"What's Indian Rock?" I asked.

"It's this giant rock in North Berkeley, where my ancestors would grind acorns and seeds into flour, along with fish and meat, with stone pestles—you can still see the depressions from their tools."

"Wait, there's a rock sitting in Berkeley named *Indian Rock*? And the government still won't recognize your people?"

"Exactly," she said. "A real estate company donated all the rock formations to the City of Berkeley. Now every year, people sit there to watch the Fourth of July fireworks."

"Unbelievable," I muttered.

"Anyway, I took Isaac to see it. It was around sunset. For a while we just sat there, looking out at the Golden Gate Bridge together. I'll never forget it." Amne's voice hitched. "The sky was so pink. The bay was peaceful and still. The water glistening."

I could practically see the romantic scene playing out again in her eyes.

"I kept wanting to say how I felt about him. But I chickened out. And the next year, he moved away." Amne looked down. "He's in Washington, DC, now."

"Awww . . ." I said, patting one of her hands.

"So don't take too long telling Jason how you feel," she said with a sad smile.

"You and Isaac, are you still in touch?" I asked.

"No," she said, turning back to her ledes. "But I know he still subscribes to the *Tribune*." Amne picked up a fresh copy. "So there's hope yet!"

I grinned.

Then we both looked up as Haru walked over.

"So?? Are you getting published?" I asked.

Haru crouched down beside the steel machines. The look on his face said everything.

# CHAPTER 33

My friends and I stared into our smoothie straws, later at Jenni's. What started off as such a mouthwatering perk had now soured in our stomachs, the concession prize for unfairness. None of us could believe that Mr. Walters had passed on Haru's wonderful article.

"What exactly did he say?" I asked.

"He said because it was about an exhibit happening in Los Angeles, it wouldn't appeal to San Francisco readers," Haru said. "Even though *just a few days ago*, he literally said that for the city section, they wanted news that would appeal to readers nationally, not just locally."

Amne pushed away her cup in frustration. "Who cares what city the exhibit's in?" she fumed. "The news is that a librarian gave hope to children suffering through one of the most horribly wrong historical decisions—and has two hundred and fifty letters' worth of proof!"

"Exactly!" Haru agreed.

I kicked the leg of the empty chair across from me. "I'm so tired of Mr. Walters and Mr. Miles! All they're interested in publishing are stories about old white men who've been dead for ages!" I fumed. "No offense to Jay Madison—his books were really good. But when are they going to give the rest of us a chance?"

Haru sank his head onto the table. "I'm too sad for smoothies," he moaned. "I just wish their process was fair and transparent." He glanced up, then pointed at the wall. "Like that bulletin board!"

I turned and looked at the community news corkboard. Haru was right. The communal space for announcements and ads was small, but it was fair. It wasn't curated by biased editors who thought that the only news worth publishing was about famous people, written by their relatives.

I looked over at Haru's article, still lying on the table. Then I picked it up and walked over to the board.

"What are you doing?" Haru asked.

Proudly, I pinned his beautiful writing to the corkboard.

"Just because Mr. Walters can't tell outstanding journalism doesn't mean other folks won't appreciate it," I declared.

Haru beamed, and the three of us gazed at his wonderful story, his words side by side with the community news, dancing with the delicious smell of sugary berries and the promise of *finally* being read.

• • •

Later, I waited outside the smoothie shop for Hank to pick me up— and hopefully deliver the good news that Lupe and Mom had won! I missed Comma so much, I imagined he could hear me in his mind.

"Hang in there, buddy," I said softly. "I'll be home real soon!"

"Mia Tang! Are you talking to yourself?" a voice hollered.

I turned around and saw Hank.

I chuckled. "Bye, Comma," I said, and hurried over. "Any news from Mom and Lupe?"

"Not yet." He pointed to a tall skyscraper. "You don't suppose law firms in this town are open on Saturdays?"

"Maybe!"

Hank and I walked over, but the revolving door didn't budge. "Dang it . . ." he said, disappointed. "I even wore my nice shoes."

I looked down at his leather loafers. "Why'd you wear those?"

"So they wouldn't think I'm here to fix the printer! You wouldn't believe how many lawyers were breathing down my neck yesterday, demanding I get them their copies. Dang printer practically ate my finger!" Hank showed me his red and scratched-up hand.

"Yikes!" I said, muffling a giggle as a woman walked out of the building.

I poked Hank with my elbow and he quickly went over to talk to her.

"Sorry to bother you, ma'am, but you wouldn't happen to work at one of the law firms in the building, do you?"

The woman gave Hank a once-over, from head to leather toe. "I'm a legal secretary for Cartwheel, Shuman, and Ottinger. Why?"

"Oh great! I'm looking for a lawyer, Darrius Caleb," Hank said, standing as straight as possible and flashing his best smile. "Is he an attorney at your firm?"

The secretary pursed her lips. "I'm afraid not," she said. "Are you looking for legal help?"

Hank shook his head. "He's actually my brother," he said. "We lost touch some time ago. I was hoping to surprise him for Christmas."

The woman put a long, manicured finger to her chin.

"Darrius Caleb," she said. "I don't know of a Darrius Caleb, but I do know of a Dean Caleb."

Hank's eyebrows jumped. *"Dean?"* he asked. He turned to me. "Did he change his name? And why Dean??"

"Maybe he really likes *Ghostbusters*," I offered.

Hank looked the secretary. "Where does Dean work?"

"At Paul, Taylor, and Harris, I believe. I used to temp there a few years ago."

"Do you happen to have an address?" Hank asked.

As the secretary reached inside her purse for a Post-it, Hank clicked his leather heels. He was going to find his brother after all!

# CHAPTER 34

Hank was so elated, he took off flying down Montgomery toward Chinatown, clutching the Post-it.

"First thing Monday morning, I'm going to surprise him!" he sang in the wind.

I giggled, running after him. I was sure I could already hear Comma's happy barks, welcoming us back to the Golden Inn. Maybe I could still play fetch with him in Portsmouth Square!

As I ran, I wrote ledes in my head for this heartwarming brotherly reunion:

*Two long-lost brothers finally experience a magical Christmas reunion after an intense downtown search!*

There were so many questions on my mind, like, What happened to make them lose touch in the first place?

But first, another big story: *Girl finally experiences coming home to a puppy of her own!*

I raced up the steps of the Golden Inn and cried, "Comma! I'm home!"

Never in a million years did I think I would find my puppy caged by an upside-down trash can in the kitchen!

I ran past Jason, yelling, "What happened?"

Before he could answer, I kneeled to free Comma. My pup

scrambled into my arms, licking my face. Every inch of him wiggled with the unmistakable message of *thank God you're back!!*

I looked up at Jason, furious and ready for answers. Silently, he held up his new silicone oven mitts.

"*This* is what happened!" he finally blurted.

Despite my fury, my jaw dropped in surprise. Jason's new mitts were completely chewed up, except for a little strip of silicon at each wrist.

He pointed at Comma, his face red. "It's all *his* fault!"

Comma hid his head in my arms, trembling.

My jaw snapped closed. "So you put him in a *trash can*??"

"These oven mitts are special! They're from Japan! My dad got them for me!" Jason stormed to the other side of kitchen and picked up his jacket. "You know what else he did? I was trying to teach him to fetch. And he tricked me!"

I rolled my eyes. "How'd he *trick* you?"

"He made *me* fetch so he could steal all the dog treats I made him! Look!" Jason held up his jacket to show me a gigantic hole where the breast pocket should have been. "Good thing the treats weren't in my *pants*!"

"He's still teething!" I cried.

"Yeah, well, thanks to his bad behavior, he lost his lunch!"

I scrambled to my feet, not letting go of Comma for a second. "Jason Yao," I growled. "Are you saying that you *starved* my *dog*?"

"He had more treats than Shamu at SeaWorld!" Jason protested. "Trust me, he's anything but starving!"

I wanted to take Jason's oven mitts and stuff them in his mouth!

"See?" I yelled. "This is why it could *never* work out between us! You're just as mean as you were in fifth grade!"

Then I turned and ran upstairs with Comma.

It was only after I locked the door to my room and slid down onto the floor that I realized what I'd said.

And Jason *heard*.

# CHAPTER 35

Five minutes later, Jason knocked on my door.

"Mia?" he asked.

I tried to stay as quiet as I could, but Comma let out a little *yip* when he heard Jason's voice. Puppies are so much more forgiving than people.

"C'mon, Mia," he tried again. "Positive communication, remember?"

Reluctantly, I got up and turned the lock.

"Look, I'm *sorry*!" Jason proclaimed as soon as he saw my face. "You're right! I shouldn't have withheld his lunch. I'm racked with guilt!"

Silently, I stepped aside, and he walked past me and sat down on the desk chair. I shut the door behind him, then turned to see that Jason had put his hands over his head.

"I don't know what got into me!" he cried. "Sometimes when I get mad, I do stupid stuff like that." He looked up at me. "Which I guess you know by now."

I set Comma down. He galloped right over to Jason, having forgotten all about his missed lunch. Jason reached and gave him a belly rub. With each scratch, I could feel my own anger melting a little. I walked over and sat on the floor next to Comma, so I could rub his belly too.

"Next time, maybe just think of one *nice* thing Comma did," I said.

Jason thought real hard. Then he smiled.

"Well . . . he did stay with me when I fell today," he said. "Emma and I were trying to fly her kite in Portsmouth Square, and I tripped over a mah-jong piece on the ground."

"Oh no, were you hurt?" I asked. He rolled up his pants slightly to show me his scraped calf.

I instantly forgot that I was mad at Jason and jumped up to get the first aid kit. Responsible motel manager that I was, I'd packed one just in case.

"Comma didn't leave my side," Jason said, still scratching him. "He stayed with me until I stood up again, even though he was off the leash. He didn't try to run away."

"See? He really cares about you," I said, coming back from the bathroom with alcohol wipes and a bandage.

"Only because he's *plotting* to steal more bacon treats, the stinker," Jason said.

Comma licked his fingers until Jason let out a soft laugh.

"Here," I said. "Hold Comma." I cleaned his leg with the alcohol, then slapped on the bandage.

As I worked, Jason asked, "What was that thing you said about us not working out earlier?"

"Nothing," I muttered. "I didn't say anything!"

"Are you sure? Because it sounded like—"

I panicked, fighting the urge to bandage my face up. Instead, I blurted, "Hey, you want to write a postcard to your dad? Tell him about the mitts before he sees them and gets mad?"

Jason looked confused. "Why would I *tell* him something bad happened?"

I reached over and grabbed a pen. "Because it's always better to communicate," I said. "Especially when something scares you."

I threw some paper at Jason, took Comma, and turned away, hoping he wouldn't realize I'd ignored my own advice.

# CHAPTER 36

Dear Dad,

I am having a lot of fun in Chinatown. Mia got a new puppy. The little guy's name is Comma. He's very cute but he did one really bad thing.

Are you ready?

(deep breath)

He ate the oven mitts you bought me. I know, I know, they're all the way from Japan and they're so nice. The silicone is so soft, yet it never burns. It's my best set of oven mitts and I'm kicking myself for not keeping them in a higher spot.

I hope you'll forgive me. Maybe sometime we can go to Japan together and buy another pair.

Love,
Jason

## P.S. Hope you're enjoying Las Vegas! Tell Celine Dion I said hi!

I looked up from the postcard.

"What do you think?" Jason asked.

"It's great!" I said. "But it needs an emotional hook."

"What's an emotional hook?"

"Something that lets the reader know why it matters to you *emotionally*," I explained. "You're not just upset because the mitts were super soft, right?"

Jason stared at the postcard, and then admitted, "No. I'm upset because my dad told his friend to buy me the *best* pair. Told him I was going to be a great chef when I grow up. Those were his words! That's a big step for my parents. They usually tell their friends I'm going to grow up to be a doctor. 'The kind who's so good, he doesn't even take insurance. All cash.'"

"See! I knew it! Those mitts *meant* something to you. *That's* what you gotta write. That's your lede!"

Jason squirmed. "I don't know . . . feels too mushy."

I crossed my arms. "You asked me to help you work on expressing your feelings!"

"With *Emma*," he argued.

"You can't just pick and choose," I said. "It's a commitment. It's a *lifestyle*."

He narrowed his eyes at me. "So I have to express my feelings with everyone?" He twirled his pen frantically. "What about the UPS guy?"

"Okay, maybe not the UPS guy," I said with a laugh. "But definitely with your parents."

Comma nudged Jason with his little wet nose. With a reluctant sigh, Jason picked up the pen and added one more line:

*Because you bought them for me to show me you believe in my dreams.*

"There," he said.

I was speechless. It was a *major* step for Jason. A year ago, I couldn't imagine him writing anything like that. He was no puppy trainer, but Jason was kicking butt at learning to express his emotions.

He must *really* like Emma.

# CHAPTER 37

A shout from below the window surprised us.

I stuck my head out and saw Lupe running toward the motel in a Berkeley sweatshirt, carrying an SAT review book in one hand and a trophy in the other.

Still running, she looked up and saw me. "WE WON!!!" she shrieked.

I grabbed Jason and we jumped up and down. "Oh my God!!!"

We raced down the stairs and I shot into my best friend's arms. "Congratulations!!!" I screamed. "You did it!"

We held hands and Mom got in too, laughing and jumping and crying tears of happiness. It felt like only yesterday when the Math Cup team could barely find a place to meet after school—now they were the reigning champions of California!

"And," Lupe said, catching her breath, "the committee wants your mom to represent us at this fundraiser ball on New Year's Eve!" She grinned at my mom. "Can't you just see her going to a big, fancy party? Getting donations from tech titans to expand Math Cup?"

The more Lupe talked, the paler Mom looked. She stopped jumping and fretted, "I don't know the first thing about balls! I don't even have anything to wear. I'll look like a duck in a museum! Probably sound like one too . . ."

I grabbed her hand again, shaking it. "Mom, you just led your team to a state victory! Who *cares* what you wear? Besides, Auntie Lam and Auntie Choi will make you look fabulous."

"That's not all." She swallowed hard. "I'd also have to make a short speech."

Mom gasped, as if the very idea made her breathless. Lupe and I exchanged a determined look.

"You've got this!" I told Mom.

"You aced your lecture, remember? That wasn't so bad!" Lupe said.

But Mom shook her head. "That was different. That was mostly kids. This is a whole bunch of adults! With big degrees and even bigger job titles! The kind of people who travel with their own special shampoo, in special little toiletry bags! Shampoo they used to leave behind and we used to collect at the motel!"

I took both her shoulders and looked Mom in the eyes.

"Okay, they have better shampoo than we do. They're still people! Just get up there and tell them how much you love math. How you shared that love with your students, and now they all love math too, and their lives are better because of it."

Mom stared back at me silently.

"C'mon, Mom," I said. "You're always telling me to shove my doubts aside. You can do that too!"

She glanced at Lupe, then back at me. Finally, she gave a terrified nod, and I hugged her, my heart doing a tap dance in my chest.

· · ·

We celebrated Mom and Lupe's big win over dinner at the Jade Empress Restaurant.

"I never had a doubt!" Hank gushed. The lazy Susan was full of glistening culinary delights. Hank and Jason were thrilled—they'd been cooking all day in preparation for the banquet the next night.

But even though our waitress set down plate after plate of delicious food, Mom was too nervous to eat.

"They say it's 'black tie.' Have you ever been to a ball?" Mom asked Hank. "What even *is* a ball?"

"A black tie ball is a lavish affair!" Hank said. "I was a waiter at one once. Everyone's in a gown or a tux. There's dancing! And a three-course dinner, maybe even four! Hors d'oeuvres. They'll serve those on little toothpicks! Unless it's escargot, of course."

Mom looked panicked. "What's that?"

"Snails!" Hank announced happily.

Mom looked like she was going to faint. "I have to eat snails?! I can't do this. . . ."

"Relax, Mom," I said, gesturing to Hank to *tone it down*. "It's just a banquet. Speaking of banquets, are you guys all ready for tomorrow?"

"Absolutely!" Jason said.

"And what's on the final menu?" I asked, sure that Jason could take over the rest of the night's conversation with talk about his cooking.

But Jason's attention was elsewhere. I followed his gaze and my appetite disappeared just like Mom's had—Emma was walking into the restaurant.

"Emma!" Jason cried. "Come join us!"

"Hey, everyone!" She bounced over and beamed at us, but I was sure she sparkled at Jason the most. "I'm just grabbing a bite with my lion dancing team," she said, but instead of leaving she sat down at our table.

Jason told her about Lupe and Mom's big win. Emma jumped up and shouted to the whole room, "Guess what, everyone?! These guys just won the Math Cup for the entire state!!!"

The restaurant exploded in applause. I clapped too, of course, but there was a tiny part of me thinking, *That was* our *news. I should be the one announcing it! Why is* she *announcing it?*

The owner, Mrs. Leung, came over and insisted that our meal was on the house—*if* Mom would look over her son's algebra?

Mom smiled. "Of course! He should join Math Cup too, maybe next year! I'm trying to get it into more districts!"

"That would be so great!" Mrs. Leung said.

"We're trying to make lion dancing into a statewide competition too!" Emma told us, sitting down again. "But it's hard. Not every high school recognizes it as an official art form."

Part of me wanted her to go to her own dinner table already. A bigger part—the journalist in me—was intrigued. I pulled out my notebook.

"Why not?" I asked Emma.

"People think it's just a Lunar New Year thing," she said, sighing. "They don't understand that there's so much teamwork to it. In order to not fall, you have to work together and trust your partner. I might be the head of the dragon, but the tail and me—we move as one."

"I'd be happy just being your elbow," Jason said.

We all turned and stared at him, watching his cheeks turn the color of plum sauce. But not Emma. She'd turned to wave at two police officers who'd just entered the restaurant.

"Officer Lim!" she called, hurrying over to the taller of the two, an Asian man with a buzz cut. "How's Popo doing?"

"Great!" he said, smiling at Emma. "I just checked on her. She appreciated all the fortune cookies you brought her!"

Auntie Lam had mentioned Popo, which meant "grandmother." She and this officer must be related, I guessed.

"Tell her my mom and I'll get her some more vegetables when we go to the food bank tomorrow!" Emma told the policeman.

A man wearing a fishing hat chimed in from the next table, "And I'll bring Popo some lotus bean pastries!"

*Wait a minute.* Did Auntie Lam, Emma, and fishing guy *all* have the same grandmother? More people from other tables started calling out.

"I'll stop by too, with some fresh cherries!"

"Ask her if she needs any more toothpaste! I can spare a couple tubes!"

Now I was thoroughly confused.

"Who's Popo?" I asked, actually grateful when Emma sat back down with us.

She gave me the same bright smile that had charmed everyone else in the restaurant, and probably in all of San Francisco. "She's the lost grandmother of Chinatown! Oh, Mia, wait till you hear *this* story!"

All my jealousy evaporated and I leaned in eagerly. Maybe this was the scoop that would turn my no-published-articles streak around!

I gripped my pen and hoped.

# CHAPTER 38

Emma leaned over the table and we all tilted toward her as she began.

"Officer Lim was out patrolling one night when he saw an unfamiliar woman wandering down the street. He stopped to check on her and discovered she was totally lost—because her family had just driven her to Chinatown and *abandoned* her here. In the middle of the night! Put all her belongings in a trash bag, then dumped her and her walker in a strange neighborhood where she didn't know anyone. Can you believe it?"

Jason shook his head like he was trying to make it make sense. "A lost grandma?"

Emma nodded soberly. "She didn't have any kind of ID on her," she went on. "And she couldn't remember where her family lived. My mama said she might have lao chi dai."

We all turned to Mom, who translated, "That means dementia. It's when elderly folks can't remember a lot of facts anymore."

I put a hand over my heart, feeling for this poor grandma.

"It's so lucky that Officer Lim found her," Emma continued. "She couldn't speak any English, so we couldn't let her go to a homeless shelter!"

"So what happened then?" I asked, jotting notes. This was it. I could feel it. This was the story I was meant to write, a story so newsworthy and riveting, not even Mr. Miles could turn it down!

"Well, we're Chinatown! We helped her, of course!" Emma said proudly.

That's when I noticed heads nodding all around the restaurant— everyone was listening to Emma's retelling, and now they put down their chopsticks to join in the conversation.

An older gentleman with a cane said, "We had a thousand volunteers working around the clock. We called up landlords, homeowners' associations—"

"Didn't stop until someone helped her secure an SRO over on Grant!" the woman sitting next to him continued. "Now she's got a home and a new family of people who care about her."

"What about her old family?" I asked, still writing. "Did you guys ever find them?"

"Nope," a man at another table said. Taro puff crumbs shifted on his lips as he frowned. "Terrible. How could they just leave her?"

"I heard they're from Lake Tahoe," yet another man said. "Or maybe Reno! Too much gambling." His passion fruit jelly drink shook in his hand.

Our waitress paused near our table to add, "They left her with only a bag of couscous. Not even rice! Couscous!" She sighed at this most unfortunate grain tragedy.

"They were rich too," a woman called from another table. "I heard she arrived with Gucci sunglasses."

Another guy was so upset he stood up to say, "But inside her wallet, no ID. No credit card. No nothing. Only thing she had was a prepaid gas card. She had no car!"

"And no money in gas card! I checked!" a woman added.

There was a collective wave of gasps.

Emma nodded. "The most heartbreaking thing was, she didn't even know she'd been abandoned. She kept asking if she could go home," she said. "Poor Popo."

My pen was flying. I couldn't get all the quotes down fast enough.

"Can I meet her?" I asked Emma.

"Sure! We can invite her to the banquet!" Emma said. "She'd love it! But I'll need another person to help me get her down the stairs of her SRO tomorrow."

Emma's eyes lingered on Jason. Before he could say anything, I blurted, "I'll go!"

A shadow of disappointment crossed Emma's face, but then her usual sunny smile reappeared. "Great!" she said.

Yes, it was great. This was going to be a *great* article, with a fantastic emotional hook!

And it would give me and Emma a chance to spend time together as opposed to . . . Emma and Jason.

# CHAPTER 39

Emma met me outside the inn the next afternoon. With just an hour until the banquet, we hurried along Grant Street toward Popo's building. Emma was wearing a baby-blue silk shirt and white silk pants. Her shirt looked like a traditional Chinese tang blouse.

"Nice outfit," I said, feeling a little underdressed in my teal cotton dress.

"Thanks. Auntie Lam made the shirt for me, after I helped her clean up her store," Emma said. She stopped at a traffic light, and added, "You should have seen how many mothballs she had in those underwear drawers."

I laughed. "My parents used to sleep with this giant suitcase underneath their bed. From China." I held out my arms to show Emma how big it was. "It was packed with mothballs and every kind of tea, socks, even Band-Aids! Like they seriously thought they wouldn't have Band-Aids in America!"

Emma laughed as we crossed the street. "I can believe it! My mom still uses a glass mercury thermometer from China! She doesn't trust the electric kind!"

"Mine either," I said. "Did your mom move to Chinatown straight from China?"

"No. She went to Wisconsin first. She was a student, studying to be a pharmacologist . . . but then I came along." Emma chewed her lip, then stopped in front of the flower shop. She hollered to Mr. Huang, "I'll stop by after the banquet to snip the stems! Don't worry, I'll close up after!"

"All right, Emma!" Mr. Huang called back.

"*After* the banquet?" I asked. "Dang, that's dedication."

She shrugged. "It'll take two seconds. If I don't do it, my mom has to. And I want her to have a good time tonight. She works so hard."

I nodded. It was why I always changed the vending machines at the Calivista. Emma and I had more in common than I'd realized.

We paused at the bakery to sniff the lemon custard cake. It reminded me of the egg tarts Ms. Flemings mentioned. "You know what this editor at my office said? She said we should work hard *and* play hard."

"That's why I like living in Chinatown! It honestly doesn't feel like work because everyone helps everyone here!" Emma smiled. "So what's it like having editors?"

"They can be . . ." I searched for the right adjective. "Stubborn."

"I can believe it. I've been trying to get Mr. Wu to let me write fortunes for *years* so he can get back in the game!"

"What do you mean?"

"We used to distribute our cookies to restaurants all around the country," she said. "But other companies have machines to make fortune cookies. They don't need people like my mom. It's faster and cheaper. And we can't compete with their prices. So now we only sell to a handful of restaurants, and to tourists."

Emma sighed.

"But I *know* we can beat them again. Not with huge machines, but with our creativity. How amazing would it be if Popo got a fortune that said, *Family isn't about blood. It's about the people in your life who want to hold your hand?*"

"That's the sweetest!" I said. "You should totally make that!"

Emma grinned, and I could see why Jason was so smitten.

"Hey, tell me about you and Jason," she said, reading my mind.

I waited until we'd crossed the street before finally saying, "Me and Jason? What do you want to know?"

"Anything," she said with a shrug. "He talks about you *all the time.*"

I blushed. *Does he?*

"We're friends," I said. "And you know, business partners. And . . . wait, what does he say about me?"

"That you're a boss queen!" Emma said. "Like how you went all over LA to find a soccer team? And you didn't stop until you found them!"

I smiled, thinking back to me, Jason, and Lupe walking into every hotel lobby in Pasadena.

"And the school dance, how you led everyone in some big flash mob?"

"Oh yeah!" I giggled. "Did he tell you he threw a bowl of fruit punch on the dance floor?"

"No!" Emma stop walking. "He *did*? Why?"

Uh-oh. I didn't want to get Jason in trouble, or tell her why he did it—because he got jealous when he saw me at the dance with Da-Shawn.

"He just . . . hated one of the songs," I lied. Then I blurted out the first song I could think of: "'The Sign.'"

"By Ace of Base?" Emma asked. "I love that song!"

She seemed bummed that Jason hated one of her favorites and I felt a little guilty.

But we'd arrived at Popo's building. As the door clicked unlocked and we stepped inside, I gasped.

*Whoa.*

I'd seen a lot of rooms in Anaheim, but *nothing* like this!

# CHAPTER 40

Door after door opened onto tiny rooms along never-ending hallways. It was a good thing I'd left Comma back at the Golden Inn. If he got off his leash and dashed away in here, I'd never be able to find him!

TVs blared from apartments packed with people and mountains of stuff—everything these families owned, wore, used, and saved. It felt like the entire building was a spaceship, ready to transport all of Chinatown to Mars!

As we walked I saw toys, pots, and pans hanging from the ceiling, and small children sitting on tiny plastic chairs while their parents stir-fried in the communal kitchens.

"Now you know why my mom works three jobs," Emma muttered, leading me upstairs. "We should have moved out in November, but with all the dot-coms driving up rent in the city . . . we gotta stay a little longer."

On the third floor, Emma knocked on Popo's door, and a moment later a younger woman I hadn't met answered.

Emma greeted her in Chinese, then called into the apartment, "Popo! We've come to take you to the banquet!"

An older lady with lustrous silver hair looked up from her bed. Unlike everyone else's SROs, Popo's was tiny and bare. She just had a few clothes hanging on a rack in one corner, and an old record player on a small table next to the bed.

"I brought someone really great for you to meet!" Emma pulled an unwrapped fortune cookie out of her pocket and placed it on Popo's table. "Her name is Mia, and she's a famous writer!"

I extended my hand. "Hi, Popo, I'd love to interview you. How do you like living in Chinatown?" I asked in Chinese.

"Oh, I love it! I'm grateful to everyone here," she said, reaching for Emma's hand. "You all make me feel so warm."

"So, Popo, are you ready to go to the banquet?" Emma asked.

"Banquet?" Popo said, suddenly looking confused. "What banquet?"

"Over at the Golden Inn!" Emma said, her voice never losing its bright cheeriness. "All of Chinatown will be there. With delicious food! Wait till you meet the chef, he's *my* age!"

Popo held out her hands, and we pulled her up to standing.

"Will there be dancing?" she asked. "I love to dance. Have I showed you my moves?" Still holding on to us, Popo started swinging her hips.

Emma and I laughed as we helped her keep her balance. Popo began to step away from us, and Emma hurried to get her walker from the other side of the room.

Then, as Popo continued to shake her butt, we led her out of her room. In an instant, five other residents appeared to guide her down the stairs.

Everyone high-fived Popo when we got out onto the street. They waved good-bye, and some called, "See you at the banquet!"

Then, inch by inch, Popo shimmied her walker down the street, ready to party!

# CHAPTER 41

A glorious red-and-gold sign awaited us at the Golden Inn. Mr. and Mrs. Luk were all dressed up in elegant silk Chinese changshans and qipaos, greeting guests. I spotted Mom and Lupe sitting up front, at the guest of honor table. They were talking to Auntie Lam and Auntie Choi.

Emma guided Popo to a table and I rushed over to Mom, Lupe, and the aunties. "Auntie Lam!" I said. "Did you hear about the fancy charity ball?"

"We were *just* talking about that! Your mom is going to need a new dress!"

"And new hair!" Auntie Choi added. She put a finger to her chin, studying Mom's head. "I'm thinking extensions, with big Diana Ross curls!"

Mom threw up her hands. "Extensions? A new dress? Isn't that going to be expensive?"

Auntie Lam waved her away. "This is Chinatown, honey," she said. "We make it work. By the time we're done with you, you're gonna look like a queen!"

"Have you thought about what you're going to say?" Auntie Choi asked.

Mom's face tensed. "Not yet," she admitted. "I'm going to work on my speech next week. Thankfully, I have the number-one writer as my daughter!"

I looked down. What if my Popo article didn't make the cut? Would she still think I was a number one daughter?

"You'll be wonderful!" Auntie Lam told Mom cheerfully. "Just remember to break in your heels." Then she leaned closer with a serious look. "You know how to walk in heels?"

Mom laughed. "Yes, that I can do. If I can afford a new pair."

Emma had joined us, and now she pointed to a man standing in the corner. "Talk to Uncle Hu. He can hook your mom up!"

"What does he do?" I asked.

She shrugged. "He's basically a walking shopping mall. Need a new car? He's your man. Lychee-scented blanket? Sure. Glow-in-the-dark chopsticks? You betcha!"

"Whoa!" I said. I didn't know about the glow-in-the-dark chopsticks, but a lychee-scented blanket sounded like something Comma might like!

"See, even Mabel Leung's hitting him up for goods," Emma said, pointing.

"Who's Mabel Leung?" I asked, studying the woman's rhinestone-studded dress. She sparkled all the way across the room.

"She's *fifth*-generation Chinatown," Emma said. "Her family owns half of Grant Street. A major landlord. But even she can't resist a good deal. C'mon, I'll introduce you!"

We walked over and I held out my hand to Uncle Hu.

"Hi, I'm Mia—"

"Tang! I know who you are! The famous writer!" he gushed. "Hey, you want pen? I got special Montblanc, just for you!"

I chuckled and shook my head. "Thanks, but I'm all good, pen-wise. I could actually use a nice pair of heels for my mom, though?"

Uncle Hu's eyes lit up, and he started rattling off options, faster than Mom could fold laundry. "You want block heel? Stiletto? Kitten heel? Cone heel? Or how about open toe? Mule? You like platform?"

I laughed—he really *was* a walking mall! I waved Mom over to let her decide.

Emma poked my elbow. "Look over there—that's Uncle Mo! He runs the YMCA, and he's the curator of the Chinese history museum!"

Uncle Mo was in the middle of talking with a younger, sad-looking boy in a basketball jersey and shorts when I walked over to introduce myself.

"I know the English questions are tricky, Jimmy," Uncle Mo was saying. "But I'm proud of how you came to the Y to do your homework. And your spelling's getting so much better!" He patted Jimmy's arm. "That's progress!"

The boy nodded, though his eyes were still glued to the floor. He held something that looked like a spelling test in his hand.

Uncle Mo turned to me, and yet again, I didn't need to introduce myself. "Mia Tang, the writer!" he cried. "Jimmy, maybe Mia has some words of advice for you!"

Jimmy immediately hid his test behind his back, clearly terrified that I was going to judge him. He stared at his shoes.

"It's okay," I said quickly. "You should have seen *my* writing when I was first getting started. Full of mistakes!"

Jimmy looked up slowly. "Really?"

I nodded. "You just gotta keep working on it. Keep practicing that muscle. It's like a sport." I pointed to his jersey. "You play basketball?"

He perked up and said, "I'm the point guard on Uncle Hu's team! We're the Chinatown Dragons!"

Uncle Mo explained, "When he's not busy sourcing glow-in-the-dark remotes, Uncle Hu is coaching the kids!"

Everyone in Chinatown seemed to have two jobs—the thing they did for income, and the thing they did for their community.

I smiled at Jimmy. "That's great," I said. "And if you keep reading, I promise, soon you'll be the point guard on English writing too!"

Jimmy grinned, then left to go back to his family's table.

"Thank you, Mia," Uncle Mo said. "Say, maybe while you're here, you can do some writing classes for the kids! I'm sure they'd all love to learn from you!"

"Classes?" I asked. "Uh, I guess I could maybe—"

"Emma could help you!" Uncle Mo said, pointing.

I turned to see where she'd gone and noticed that Officer Lim had just walked in. I watched as he and his colleagues shook everyone's hands and asked them how their day was. He seemed to know every single person in the room by name.

"Excuse me, I'll be right back," I said to Uncle Mo, hurrying over to ask for a quote. To my delight, Officer Lim was happy to answer my questions. He held out a chair for me.

"So were you the first person to find Popo?" I asked, my pen and notebook ready. "How did you feel?"

"My heart sank when I realized what had happened to her,"

Officer Lim said. "She's so sweet. The nicest grandma anyone could have. Whenever I visit her, she's always offering to cook me something."

"How often do you visit?"

"I try to stop by every day," he said. "And if I can't, one of my colleagues goes. Or someone else in the community. She's kind of everyone's grandma. We take care of each other here. I think it really speaks to the history of Chinatown."

I loved that everyone had said something similar about this neighborhood, but I especially loved that line. I scribbled it down.

"Can you say a little more about that?" I asked.

He leaned forward in his chair, giving me the same undivided attention I'd seen him give everyone else in the room. "Throughout history," he said, "there have been so many times of sudden, inexplicable pain that our people have had to live through, from the Chinese Exclusion Act to our children being denied admission to schools. Not being able to go to the hospital. Not even being able to wear our hair the way we wanted."

He let out a heavy sigh, then smiled in the direction of Popo.

"Which is why it's so important for us to protect Popo, as a community. We're protecting every person who steps through Chinatown, now and forever."

Tearfully, I wrote down every single one of Officer Lim's amazing words.

Then Mrs. Luk's voice echoed over the sound system, announcing that everyone should take their seats. Over at the kitchen doors, Jason and Hank emerged carrying large trays heavy with dishes.

Dinner was served!

# CHAPTER 42

"Thank you so much for joining us for our annual Chinatown Christmas banquet!" Mrs. Luk continued over the microphone. She stood proudly at the podium where Mom had practiced her vocal exercises, looking radiant and happy. "We're so grateful to the Chinatown YMCA, Cameron House, and the Community Development Center for once again hosting this banquet at the Golden Inn. And we're thrilled to welcome two visiting chefs from Los Angeles—Hank Caleb and Jason Yao!"

Jason and Hank set their platters down and bowed to warm applause.

"Thank you," Jason said when the room quieted. "We've cooked up all your favorites—*and* we have a few surprises for you."

Waiters with gorgeous dishes of flounder, tofu, duck, and prawns walked around the tables. Everyone peered at the colorful dishes curiously.

"Is that . . . pineapple salsa on the cod?" Mr. Luk asked, rushing over to Popo's table.

The entire room got very, very quiet as the waiter set a plate of the fish and pineapple salsa in front of Popo. No one even seemed to breathe as the older woman picked up her chopsticks and took the first bite. She chewed carefully, then smiled. In a loud, clear voice, she declared, "Best cod I've ever tasted!"

Everyone applauded, and I noticed Mr. and Mrs. Luk exchanging a look of relief across the room.

"Enjoy, friends!" Mrs. Luk said into the mic. "We've all worked a very hard year. Now it's time to celebrate!"

I beamed at Mrs. Luk, thinking about all the years my parents toiled in the motel and the restaurant, without ever having their labor recognized. How amazing it must be to grow up in a community like this, one that truly *saw* you. Turning to glance at Jason, I saw his pride as everyone picked up their chopsticks and enjoyed his work too.

. . .

It was an extraordinary night. Mom even got a chance to practice ballroom dancing with Hank. But by far the highlight was Emma's lion dancing group. As they pranced around the banquet floor to the sound of a traditional gong and Chinese drums, Jason stood next to me, admiring Emma.

"Isn't she amazing?" he asked, clapping as Emma danced.

"Yup! She is," I answered honestly. After my walk with Emma, I was even more convinced I was in big trouble.

"What's wrong?" he asked.

I looked away. "Nothing."

Jason moved closer—so close I could smell the butterscotch-and-pineapple tart on the plate in his hand. "What is it? You can tell me."

I looked into his curious eyes, torn between admitting how I felt and bolting upstairs to hide under the covers with Comma. Luckily, just then Auntie Min, the lion dancing troupe leader, grabbed the mic.

"Let's hear it for our young lion dancers!" she gushed. "And our talented musicians! It wasn't that long ago that gong percussion instruments were banned from use in performances here in the city, because they 'produced an unusual noise, disturbing the peace.'"

The audience booed.

Auntie Min nodded, then gestured back toward Emma and the other performers. "So it's all the more exciting and important that these talented young people are carrying on our traditions. Let's make some noise for our beloved lions!"

The entire room roared, and again I marveled at the love and support of this community that had fought for two hundred years to keep their heritage alive, even as the forces around them were trying to strip away their voice.

I set aside all my worries about Jason and picked up my notebook again. I told myself that right now, these were the words that mattered most to me.

# CHAPTER 43

I wrote late into the night. The words poured out of me, fueled by the community love I'd witnessed.

Lost Grandma, Abandoned by Family, Embraced by Chinatown

By Mia Tang

In early October, SFPD Officer Lim found a 62-year-old Chinese-speaking woman, lost and disoriented, apparently abandoned by her family in the Chinatown section of San Francisco.

"It was clear she needed help," he said. "I spoke to her in Mandarin, and after a few minutes of talking, could tell she didn't know where she was or how she got there. She didn't even know that she'd been abandoned. It broke my heart."

Lim knew that without English, it would be hard for Popo, which means "grandmother" in Chinese, to survive in a homeless shelter. So Lim put the word out, and the community sprang to action.

For more than a hundred and fifty years, Chinatown has prided itself on being a safe haven for all Chinese Americans. The neighborhood and its community have provided refuge for immigrants during the painful and tumultuous times of the Page Act, the Foreign Miner's Tax, the Chinese Exclusion Act, the Scott Act, and other anti-Chinese ordinances. And this time was no exception. Chinatown's residents got to work. Close to one hundred phone calls were placed in a few hours to find housing for Popo, whose only possessions when she was found were a bag of couscous and a prepaid gas card in an otherwise empty wallet.

Those efforts proved successful. Popo was offered long-term housing in a local SRO building, where she currently lives among her new "family."

This past Sunday, she attended a banquet at the Golden Inn along with three hundred other residents of Chinatown. The banquet, which was prepared by visiting chefs Jason Yao and Hank Caleb, was a celebratory dinner for the holidays.

"I'm so grateful to everyone here," Popo said at the banquet. "You all make me feel so warm."

Every day, Officer Lim and Popo's neighbors make sure to stop by her room to check on her and make sure she doesn't feel alone.

"She's kind of everyone's grandma. We take care of each other here. I think it really speaks to the history of Chinatown," Officer Lim said.

It was nearly midnight by the time I'd triple-checked my new feature for spelling mistakes. I scooped up Comma and nuzzled his ear. In her bed, Lupe stirred. She had dozed off reading her big SAT prep book. She rubbed her eyes open and looked at me.

"Did you finish?" she asked, sitting up.

"You want to read it?" I asked, too excited to wait until morning.

"Sure!" She reached to turn on her bedside lamp.

I held my breath as she read.

Lupe's enthusiastic look when she was done told me everything.

"It's brilliant! I love it!" she exclaimed.

Comma jumped out of my arms and onto Lupe's bed, making her laugh.

"You think they'll go for it? At the *Tribune*?" I asked.

"If they have any brains in their heads," Lupe replied. "Or any beat in their hearts!"

That made me think of the night a motel guest had rented *The Wizard of Oz*. Lupe and I had watched along, through the window, which we frequently did if it was a good movie and the curtains weren't drawn. We'd make Dad drive his car up to the customers' room, and we'd sit in the car with popcorn, giggling.

Now I threw my head back and burst into "If I Only Had a Brain." Lupe joined in and soon, Comma was howling with delight. It felt like old times in the Calivista again.

Finally, we flopped back on our beds, out of breath.

"I'm sure gonna miss that," Lupe said.

"Miss what?" I asked.

"Watching videos with you in your dad's car," she sighed.

"I was just thinking of the time we saw *The Wizard of Oz*!" I said.

"You should rent it tomorrow while I'm at camp—I bet they have a copy at the Y!"

"That's a great idea!" Lupe exclaimed. Then she looked down at her SAT book and her smile dissolved. "But I have to study."

"Oh, come on, one day off," I begged. "You already won the state championships! You deserve it!"

"Mia, there's a lot in here I don't get," she said, pointing to the book. "Like this question—I don't understand why the answer is A. Even your mom can't figure it out."

"Maybe it's a typo," I said.

"Maybe," Lupe said softly. "But I can't afford to shrug it off as a typo."

I nodded, understanding fully. It was the same reason I'd triple-checked my story on Popo for errors. I couldn't make mistakes if I wanted to compete with people like Timothy Madison.

"So, no movie? Maybe watch it with Jason?" I asked.

Lupe sat up and studied me. "You still haven't told him, have you?"

I shook my head and reached down to pick up Comma, bringing him up onto my bed.

"You know, before I told Allie, I didn't sleep for three whole days," Lupe said softly.

I got under the covers and turned off the light on my side of the room. I hugged Comma close and asked, "How'd you finally get the words out?"

She moved her books out of the way and turned off her light too. I waited patiently in the dark as she got settled. The shadow from the closest pagoda tower danced with the full moon on our wall.

"I pictured myself when I was little," Lupe finally said. "I knew

Little Me would want me to be brave. Which was why it hurt so much when . . ." Her voice faltered. "When she stepped all over my feelings."

I reached out and found Lupe's hand, giving it a squeeze.

"Why couldn't she have just said, *I don't feel the same way about you*? Why'd she have to try to erase my feelings?"

I got up and offered her Comma. She needed him more than I did tonight.

In the moonlight I watched her stroke his fur and smile. "Can't wait to tell her I'm skipping ahead to Berkeley—who's immature now!"

"That's not why you're doing it, is it?" I asked as I got back into my bed.

Lupe was quiet.

"You don't need to prove anything to her," I said. "Your feelings matter. *Now*, just the way you are."

"Not everyone agrees with you, Mia," she said. Then, still holding Comma, she rolled away from me and went back to sleep.

I gazed out the window and wished on the full moon that Lupe wouldn't have to move four hundred miles away from home just to prove what I already knew in my heart.

# CHAPTER 44

I got to the newsroom super early in the morning, holding my story. Mr. Walters was eating breakfast in his office when I walked in. I couldn't wait a second longer. This was *too good*!

"Hi, Mr. Walters," I said nervously. "Would you mind looking at this? I . . . I wrote something. It's newsworthy and timely, about a grandmother lost in Chinatown."

He looked up from his cherry doughnut. Then he wiped his fingers and reached for my paper.

I held my breath, even tighter than when Lupe had read it the night before. I wanted so badly to go back to tell everyone in Chinatown that the world cared about our stories.

Mr. Walters took his time reading. The other campers started to roll in. Timothy was wearing a new winter coat. Zoe was carrying a gigantic beverage, not from Jenni's Smoothies.

As Amne and Haru came in, they both stared at me curiously, but I just gave them a little wave.

After what felt like a million years, Mr. Walters looked up. "All the facts, do they check out?"

I tried not to cackle like a goose. *Did that mean he liked it?*

"Yes of course!" I promised. "I interviewed everyone personally!"

"Well, it is certainly timely," he said slowly. "And quirky, I must say."

I grinned. I'd take quirky!

He glanced at Mr. Miles's office. "I'll have to run it by the editor in chief. No promises."

I nodded enthusiastically, hoping I wouldn't faint from the adrenaline rush. "Thank you!" I squeaked, then hurried to my desk as Mr. Walters strode across the newsroom, still holding my article.

Amne and Haru huddled around to ask me a million questions. But Timothy walked over, upset.

"Whoa, whoa, whoa, did you come in early to pitch him a story?" he barked.

I stood as tall as I could. "Yes."

"You're supposed to wait your turn during Newsroom!" he said.

"Says the guy who pitched over email—"

"That was totally different!" Timothy crossed his arms.

Before I could argue, Mr. Walters walked out of Mr. Miles's office.

"And?" I asked when he reached our desks. My rib cage was practically bursting. "Did he like it?"

"We'd be delighted to run it," Mr. Walters said. "Above the fold too."

I threw my arms in the air.

"YESSSS!" Amne cried.

Haru high-fived me. I grinned, my face so warm I was sure it glistened like steaming shumai.

"Above the fold" was *major*. It meant my article would be printed on the top half of the newspaper, where all the most important stories went.

But before we could carry on celebrating, Mr. Walters motioned for us to calm down.

"There's just one minor issue," he said to me. "Let's talk in my office."

# CHAPTER 45

Closing his office door behind us, Mr. Walters gestured for me to sit down. "Here's the thing," he said, sitting behind his desk. "We can't pay you for the piece."

"Oh."

"Yeah, unfortunately, we blew through our freelancer budget this week. We had a certain amount set aside each week for your group, but we had some . . . unforeseen expenses." My heart sank. He must be talking about Timothy's pricey story. "We hope you understand. But we'd be happy to run it as an opinion piece! Of course, those aren't paid. But you'll be in print!"

"So, it'd be in the opinion section?" I asked, confused.

"No, no, we'll still put it in the city section. And again, above the fold," he promised. "But this way, we get around our budget problems."

I swallowed hard.

I thought about everyone in Chinatown. And my mom—I'd finally get her off my back about when I was getting published! This was still a win, right?

So I nodded and told him that'd be fine with me, as I tried to ignore the little voice in my head saying *Mr. Walters would* never *have this conversation with Timothy Madison.*

I looked at my shoes, wishing I could just get a straight-up win. And feeling bad for not being more grateful.

Mr. Walters didn't look like he was wrestling with any complicated feelings. He stood up and said cheerfully, "Congratulations! Tomorrow morning, everyone's going to read about Popo!"

I nodded. It *was* a big deal and I was proud.

On the walk back to my desk, I decided not to tell anybody about the money. Not my friends at the camp, not Emma or the aunties, and *especially* not my mom. I'd worked too hard and come too far to let her go back to thinking I was a bike.

And I wasn't.

I *wrote* like a car, and got *published* like a car.

(Even if I didn't get paid like a car.)

# CHAPTER 46

"Mia! Guess what?" Mrs. Luk said, putting down the phone to greet me as I walked in. "Our banquet bookings have gone way up!"

"That's great!" I smiled at Mrs. Luk. The phone rang again. As Mrs. Luk answered, I looked around for Jason and Comma.

"Look, Mia!" Jason said, bouncing over with my pup. "I taught Comma how to roll over!" He turned to Comma and sternly commanded, "Sit!"

To my delight, my puppy sat obediently at Jason's feet.

"And check it!" Jason's eyes flickered with excitement, but he kept his voice calm and commanding as he turned back to my dog and said, "Comma, *roll*."

And Comma rolled over! Jason said "Good boy!" and gave him a treat while I clapped. Then I picked Comma up and gave him a kiss.

"That was amazing," I told Jason. We walked into the kitchen together. I put Comma down as I started searching the cabinets for Choco-Pies. *Where were they?*

Choco-Pies were these delicious chocolate marshmallow cookies my dad always bought me from the Asian supermarket, and my go-to comfort snack whenever something bad happened.

I guess Jason noticed I was distracted, because as I snooped through the cabinets he asked, "What's wrong?"

"Nothing!" I said brightly. "I'm getting published tomorrow!"

"Wow, Mia, that's so great!"

"Yeah, the banquet's going to be in the paper too!" I said, still searching. "And Popo and Officer Lim!"

"So why are you looking for Choco-Pies?" he asked, retrieving them from the top shelf and handing them to me. I tried to look innocent, but Jason knew me too well. "C'mon," he said. "You know you only eat these when you're stressed."

I hopped up to sit next to Jason on the counter. As he handed me a cookie, I sighed. I told him what had happened. Not the shiny highlights version, but the unvarnished truth. The version I hoped nobody ever found out.

I'd been determined to not tell anyone the whole story, but this was *Jason*.

"I know I should be more grateful," I said as I ate a second cookie. "I mean, *clearly* I write like a car now."

"Above the fold! I'd say you're a Ferrari!" he said.

"And it's only seventy-five bucks," I said. "I can make that in tips in a week!"

"Oh, easily."

"Still. It's the principle . . ." I whispered to my cookie.

Jason hopped down and held out a hand. Comma barked.

"Come on," he said. "I have to show you something."

· · ·

Comma and I hurried to keep up as Jason zigzagged all the way through Chinatown. He finally slowed at a long, narrow alleyway leading to a redbrick building.

"It's back this way," he said. "Hurry! Before it closes!"

It wasn't until we were at the door that I realized he was taking me to the Chinese Historical Museum. Walking inside, I spotted Uncle Mo at the counter and waved.

"Hi, Uncle Mo!" Jason said. "Can we get two tickets, please?"

"For you two? It's on the house!" Uncle Mo smiled. "How's everything down at the paper, Mia?"

"Great," I lied. Well, half lied. "In fact, I'm getting published tomorrow."

The look of pride on Uncle Mo's face pushed aside my sadness. "That's wonderful! Perfect timing too, for your new class!"

"My new class?" I asked, confused.

Uncle Mo laughed. "You agreed at the banquet, remember? I already told all the Chinatown kids! They'll be so delighted to hear about your big story in the paper! First thing tomorrow, I'm buying two dozen copies to show everyone!" Uncle Mo clapped his hands. "I told your students to meet you at the Y tomorrow at two o'clock!"

"On Christmas Eve?" I asked. Tomorrow was a half day at camp, and I'd been hoping to pry Lupe away from her studying so we could *finally* get some vacation fun in! After my epic time on the double-decker bus, I was dying to ride the famous San Francisco cable cars.

"Sure! You know what happens in Chinatown on Christmas?" Uncle Mo asked.

"What?" Jason asked.

"We open for business!" he declared.

With that, Jason led me by the arm. Just a few steps inside the first gallery, he put his hands over my eyes. I chuckled as I wobbled, blind and off-balance as he kept guiding me forward.

When he finally removed his hands, a flash of bright yellow

beamed before my eyes. Slowly, America's most famous martial artist came into focus.

"It's Bruce Lee!" I said.

"Born right here in Chinatown," Jason said proudly. "First Asian American actor to ever have a lead role in a Hollywood film—*Enter the Dragon!*"

He sprinted around the room, pointing to the posters from all of Bruce Lee's movies. "Before Bruce Lee, we Asians were played by white people!" Jason told me. "They'd make us look meek and small, especially Asian men. And Bruce, he refused to do any of that. He wanted to show us kicking butt. Being strong!"

He did a little jump kick in the air and I giggled. Jason looked cute trying to be Bruce Lee.

"Eventually, Hollywood started paying attention. He got wildly popular with the TV series *The Green Hornet*, but look . . ." Jason led me to a glass case. "*This* is what I want to show you."

We walked over and looked down at the call sheet for *The Green Hornet*. It listed Bruce Lee as the second most important actor in the series. I followed Jason's finger across to where it listed the casts' salaries.

My jaw dropped.

Bruce Lee got paid less money than all the other actors, including the stuntmen.

I put my hand on the cool glass. All day, I'd been carrying around this pain alone. I thought nobody in the world could possibly understand what I was going through. Until this moment.

Now I knew I wasn't alone. Bruce Lee knew what it was like to put all of yourself into your art but still not get taken seriously. To worry that if you don't take the terrible offer, you might never get *any* offers, ever again. And the guilt of even wanting more when everyone is telling you that you should feel *so lucky* even to be given a chance at all.

They were complex feelings, and they were eating away at me.

"I thought it might help for you to see that," Jason said quietly.

I looked up at him, suddenly sure that I could get over our old chapter together. I was ready to tell him my feelings. He was the only boy who *knew* me. Who I didn't hesitate sharing my most vulnerable side with, because he always responded in the most tender, caring way. And that was worth turning a new page.

"Thanks, Jason." I looked into his eyes. "This means more to me than you'll ever know."

"I hope you'll keep fighting, just like Bruce," he said. "He proved *he* was the main draw. When Hollywood didn't want to give him any movies, he went to Hong Kong. He was scrappy. He took risks, he reinvented himself. One way or another, he kept working, making one movie after another, until finally Warner Brothers decided to finance his movie—the first ever Hong Kong–American coproduction. Changed the industry forever."

I smiled. "How'd you know all this stuff?"

"Emma told me."

*Oh yeah.* I forgot that Jason had come to this museum with her yesterday, while I was busy proofreading my Popo piece.

"One day, it's going to be you in this museum." He smiled at my shocked face. "I'm serious! Mia, you're like the Bruce Lee of writing. And when that day comes, you'll tell everyone about how the *Tribune* stiffed you seventy-five dollars, and Uncle Mo will hold up the paper and charge seven dollars a person for people to see that injustice."

My heart swelled. "Jason Yao. That's the nicest thing you've ever said to me!"

He blushed.

"Okay," he said. "You ready to go home and eat some real dinner? Or should we pick up some more Choco-Pies?"

"Some real dinner, please," I said. "Prepared by my favorite chef."

He beamed, his cheeks still pink. "Coming right up!"

I gazed at Bruce Lee's yellow jumpsuit one last time, trying to summon a little of his strength and bravery. *I can do this.*

I took a deep breath and said, "Jason, there's something I have to tell you."

Jason was already at the door, but he turned back with a smile. "Are you going to tell me I'm ready? I can finally tell Emma how I feel?"

It physically hurt to see the hope and anticipation in his eyes. I turned back to Bruce's jumpsuit and blinked hard. It was clear who Jason liked, and it was *not* me. My ears burned as I swallowed my words.

"Almost there," I said. "Just—just a few more days."

# CHAPTER 47

While Jason cooked, I sat on the stoop outside, waiting for Lupe. She'd gone to Berkeley to try to find help with the SAT math questions she was stumped on. I couldn't wait for her to come home. I needed her advice.

*Should I just tell Jason he graduated already from feelings training?* He seemed so excited about Emma. It felt wrong to drag him along any longer when he was so clearly sure about her.

Out of the corner of my eye I noticed Hank, coming out the side door to take out the trash.

"How'd it go with Darrius today?" I called. "Did you find him?"

Hank shook his head as he threw the bags in the bin, then came over to sit down next to me.

"Went to the address that receptionist gave us," he said, "but there was no law firm. Instead, it was a back office for an email company. Something called Yahoo!?"

"Weird," I said.

He shrugged. "They probably moved, but now I have a name. Don't worry, I'll find him." Hank took a closer look at my face. "What's wrong, kiddo?"

I let out a deep sigh and kicked at a pebble on the step below mine.

"You ever been in love, Hank?" I finally asked.

He chuckled. "I might have caught some feelings once or twice in my life, yes."

And then I spilled all my troubles with Jason.

"I know as his friend I should be happy for him. Emma's *great*."

"She really is," Hank agreed.

"But every time I picture the two of them together . . ." I closed my eyes. "It makes me want to grind up a fortune cookie into a powder and blow it in her face!"

"Okay, don't do that," Hank said, halfway between amused and alarmed.

I groaned. Why did I feel more shaken up than a boba tea?

"Be patient," Hank said gently. "Feelings rise and fall, just like the ocean. Jason might be obsessed with this new girl now, but that doesn't mean that it's always going to be high tide. You know what lasts a lot longer than infatuation?"

"What's infatuation?" I asked. It sounded like the name of a fancy smoothie at Jenni's.

"A romantic obsession," Hank explained. "It's when you can't stop thinking about someone. They're the coolest thing since night baseball. Since drip coffee!"

I snorted. "Since a multi-socket power plug!"

"Exactly." Hank laughed. "That kind of intense feeling usually doesn't last." He poked my knee with his finger. "You know what lasts longer?"

I shook my head.

He smiled. "Friendship. That's the real glue to any relationship." He paused for a second, gazing in the direction of the Golden Gate Bridge. "It's what my brother and I . . . I wish we had."

"What happened between you two?" I asked. "How come you fell out of touch?"

"It's kind of a sad story. You really want to know?"

"I'm a reporter, remember? I like any kind of story, sad or not sad."

He gave a wistful smile. I leaned in to listen. He finally told me the story of what had happened with him and his brother.

# CHAPTER 48

"About two years after Darrius finally moved Mama out of Detroit to Farmington Hills, she got sick," Hank said.

I hugged my knees and nodded.

"It was breast cancer," he went on. "She'd had it before, and she'd fought it off. Done the chemo, the radiation. This time, though, it came back with a vengeance. Now, my mama's a tough lady. Single mom, worked as a nurse for twenty-nine years, raised me and my brother by herself. So when she told me she was tired, I knew . . . she was *bone* tired."

"Did she . . . ?"

Hank nodded, the corners of his eyes getting wet. "I was out in LA, selling car insurance, around this time. When I went out to Michigan to see her, I just wept. She was done fighting. She just wanted to spend the rest of her days in that big Farmington house, listening to Ella Fitzgerald and eating my burgers and strawberry rhubarb pie. And that's just what we did."

I put a hand to my heart, picturing Hank cooking for his mom and making sure her last days were comfortable.

"Darrius refused to accept it. Said I was influencing her with my 'laid-back mentality.' Said it was all my fault for letting her quit chemo. When she passed, he called me a loser. Said that was why I was living a pathetic life in LA, still floating between apartments and motels."

I felt my face get hot. "That's terrible!"

"It was the grief talking," Hank said. "All Darrius wanted his whole life was to be a big shot, for Mama to be proud of him. And just when he'd gone and done that, Mama died. I told him, if he had really cared about her, he'd have spent more time with her. Love isn't just buying someone a big ol' house, it's spending time with them. Well, he didn't want to hear that from me."

A heavy silence fell over us. No wonder Hank had turned his dress shoes into confetti going up and down all the sky-pokers of San Francisco looking for Darrius. There was *so* much to mend.

He turned to me, his eyes clear again. "If you really like Jason, keep trying. Like I'm still trying to find Darrius. The right tide will come." Hank patted my shoulder. "You thought of a good Christmas present for him yet?"

"I was thinking of getting him a wok!" I said, nodding toward the wok store.

Hank hesitated. "A wok's nice. But if you ask me, the best present is always *time*."

I thought about Jason taking me to the museum. It had made my whole week. Time really was the best gift of all.

"Thanks, Hank," I said, patting him on the shoulder too. "You're surprisingly wise when it comes to love."

He chuckled. "Just promise me one thing." I noticed a twinkle in his eye. "You won't throw any cookie powder at Emma?"

I pretended to think it over. Hank burst out laughing.

"What?" I said innocently. "Could be a new makeup line! Cookie Shimmer, by Mia Tang!" Then I laughed too.

Just then I spotted Lupe coming around the corner, carrying a gigantic stalk of celery. Hank waved at her.

"That for our dinner tonight?" he called. "I can use it to make us a nice chicken soup!"

"Well here, have it!" Lupe said, walking up to us and handing him the celery. "I picked it up to go feed the animals up at Tilden Park. But it was closed already."

I clapped my hands, thrilled Lupe made it to Tilden after all.

"So that's where you were!" I said, after Hank scurried off to make soup. "You finally went!"

"Actually, I went to the library main stacks first," she said, pointing to her backpack. "But would you believe, not a single college student would look over my SAT question? They all blew me off. Said they were too busy studying or doing research for professors! Wouldn't even give me five minutes!"

"Oh, Lupe," I said as she slumped onto the stoop beside me, angry and defeated. "I'm sorry those college kids were such banana heads."

"Yeah," she huffed. "So I took the bus up to Tilden Park." Suddenly, she brightened, adding, "Did you know that they actually have a merry-go-round up there?"

"Really??" I asked. "Did you ride it??"

She shook her head and sagged her shoulders. "It was closed too."

"Hey," I said, getting an idea. "Give me your hands."

I stood up and grabbed Lupe's hands, pulling her off the hotel steps. We started spinning, right there on the sidewalk, holding on tight to each other. Lupe giggled as I started singing a Christmas carol, loud and silly and around and around.

We were our own merry-go-round, and just for a second, we got to experience what it felt like when time moved a little slower.

# CHAPTER 49

My article came out on Christmas Eve, and all of Chinatown was buzzing with holiday cheer. Elders strolled the streets, wearing their silkiest red changshans; children begged their mothers for last-minute ornaments of Santa playing the saxophone.

Over at the Golden Inn, Mr. and Mrs. Luk's phone was buzzing too—with neighbor after neighbor calling up to express their deep appreciation for Chinatown being so lovingly depicted in the *Tribune*.

I was just getting ready to leave for my half day at the paper when Uncle Mo ran over from the Y.

"Mia, your article was magnificent!" he exclaimed. "The kids are so excited for you to teach them this afternoon!"

I had to admit, it felt good knowing that my writing had helped make the folks of Chinatown feel finally seen. Finally heard! Finally represented on the page! If I could give that superpower to the kids, it'd be the *best* Christmas present.

"Sure thing, Uncle Mo!" I said, grabbing my backpack.

"Great, I'll go and tell Emma!" he said.

Emma! I'd forgotten that I'd agreed to do this class with her. I took a deep breath and reminded myself of all the things we had in common. We were both writers. We'd both had people telling us our voice wasn't important but kept going.

*I'll be fine. As long as I steer far away from the cookie powder . . .*

* * *

At the *Tribune* that morning, Mr. Walters said we wouldn't have Newsroom, since it was Christmas Eve and we didn't have a full day of camp. The morning would be more of a staff party, with hot chocolate and holiday cookies. But that didn't stop Amne from whipping out her story from her backpack.

"I was inspired by your Popo piece," she said. "So I stayed up all night writing about Ishi!"

While everyone else headed into the main conference room to grab cookies, Haru and I hung back a second to read.

> The Man with No Name
> By Amne Sullik
> To this day, the final resting place of a Native American man, taken and placed in the custody of a UC Berkeley professor, forced to work and live in the Phoebe A. Hearst Museum of Anthropology for four and a half years, remains a mystery.
>
> In August of 1911, a Native man walked into a slaughterhouse near Oroville, California. Barefoot and emaciated, he spoke a language nobody could understand. He was promptly jailed.
>
> The man was thought to be from the Yahi tribe. Once numbering in the several hundreds, the tribe's population plummeted during the Gold Rush due to a series of massacres, destruction of villages, and disease. By the late 1800s, only a

handful of survivors remained. They hid out in the Mount Lassen foothills, about 130 miles north of Sacramento, for forty years.

When the emaciated man, the presumed last lone survivor, walked into the slaughterhouse, he refused to say his name. Yahi customs required an introduction by someone from the tribe before speaking your name to outsiders. While holding the man in jail, the town officials informed the University of California Museum of Anthropology of the man's existence. Museum director Alfred Kroeber immediately went to the town. Kroeber promptly named the man "Ishi," meaning "man" in the Yahi language, and convinced the authorities to release Ishi into his custody. He intended to house Ishi at the museum, instead of having him relocated to a reservation in Oklahoma.

Within days, Ishi was brought to the museum in San Francisco, where he lived for the last four and a half years of his life, working as a janitor to earn his keep. Kroeber publicized Ishi as "the last wild Indian in California." The living exhibit became a popular attraction and Ishi spent much of his time on display for white museum audiences, making tools and recording Yahi songs and stories, which the museum still exhibits.

Kroeber even made Ishi travel with anthropologists back to the site of his family's massacre, *in the Deer Creek valley area of Tehama County, to document his culture. Kroeber told the press that Ishi was "without a doubt the most uncontaminated aborigine in the known world today."*

*According to the book Ishi in Two Worlds, written by Theodora Kroeber, Kroeber's wife, during his time at the museum, Ishi was extremely distressed to be living among the human remains of Native American ancestors, unearthed for research and scientific curiosity. He asked Kroeber to promise to cremate his body, according to Yahi tradition, when he passed. However, when Ishi succumbed to tuberculosis in 1916, his wishes were disregarded, and an autopsy was performed on his body.*

*To this day, it is unclear where all of Ishi's remains are, whether they were in fact, all cremated, and if they'll ever be returned to his native homeland. Meanwhile, Kroeber's name sits proudly on the University of California's anthropology building.*

"Oh my God, Amne!" I said to her when I was done reading. "Did you show Mr. Walters this yet??"

"Not yet," Amne replied.

I scanned the newsroom for Mr. Walters. Luckily, he wasn't in the crowded conference room yet. He was shutting down his computer in his office!

"What are you waiting for? Go show him!" Haru encouraged her. "It's groundbreaking!"

We nudged her toward Mr. Walters' office, chanting, "Go! Go! Go!"

As Amne walked over, Mr. Walters pointed to the conference room. He probably thought she was looking for the free holiday cookies. But what she had in her hand was even more precious. I just hoped he had the good sense to see it!

# CHAPTER 50

Mr. Walters didn't give Amne a decision, but he promised he'd read it over the holiday. The three of us bounced into the conference room, eager to fill up our bellies with reindeer cookies, chocolate chip waffles, and byline hope!

Emma was bouncing up and down even more than Comma when I got back to Chinatown that afternoon.

"This is going to be so great!" she said, skipping down the street to the YMCA with me while Comma tried to keep up. "What part of writing should we focus on first? The planning? Organizing? Editing?"

"I'm a big fan of write what you know," I said. "Maybe we can have the kids start off writing about something that happened to them?"

"But we gotta give them some direction!" Emma said. "Or we're gonna end up with seventy-six stories about bad bowl haircuts." Her eyes widened. "I know! How about they write a piece about the ins and outs of their SRO? Who lives there? Who takes *forever* in the bathroom? Whose chop suey is to die for?"

"Wait, did you say *seventy-six*?" I asked.

Before she could reply, Comma yelped.

"Teacher Mia!" cried the stampede of kids running toward us.

They were all holding copies of the *Tribune*. Small hands thrust pens at me for autographs, like I was a movie star. I looked to Emma with a face that screamed *help!*

But she just grinned. "Come on, Teacher Mia, let's start the class!"

. . .

It took a while to get everyone organized and into a big basement room at the Y, but eventually I was standing next to an old chalkboard and calling out nervously, "Hi, everyone! I'm Mia!"

I looked out at the sea of Chinatown kids. There were so many, all busy chatting and exchanging snacks. I wasn't sure how I was going to get their attention. Not even Comma's yelps did the trick. I looked at Emma.

This time, she put two fingers in her mouth and whistled— *loudly.*

Silence fell, at least long enough for her to shout, "This is Mia Tang. She's the real deal! So sit up and pay attention, if you want to keep getting free sample cookies from the factory! I'm looking at you, Albert!"

The boy shifted in his seat and I tossed Emma a grateful smile.

"Who here likes writing?" I asked the room.

Only about ten hands went up, including mine and Emma's.

"You know what?" I said. "That's okay. Not so long ago, I didn't like writing either. In fact, I was *terrified* of writing, because I was terrified of getting a bad grade."

"But Uncle Mo says you got published when you were *eleven!*" a voice called.

I smiled. "It's true. I wrote a letter to the editor that got published. And then I wrote columns and articles." I held up a finger. "You wanna know what they all had in common?"

"What?" the room bellowed.

"They all started with a question! For example—" I turned and said, "Emma, who's the funniest person in Chinatown?"

"Uncle Hu, of course!" she said. "He once sold me a talking toenail clipper for five dollars."

The children cackled.

"*Talking* toenail clipper? What'd it say?" I asked.

"Nothing! On the back, he wrote, 'For conversation, please call Ernie Hu. Free.'" She rolled her eyes.

I giggled along with the kids. "Did you call?"

"Of course not! I returned the nail clipper, *and* squeezed two light bulbs out of him."

Everyone clapped at Emma's superior negotiation tactics.

"See! That right there! That's a story!" I said. "I'll bet each and every one of you is sitting on a treasure trove of stories. All you have to do to uncover them is to ask questions." I turned to Emma again. "Is there anything you'd like to ask me?"

Without missing a beat, she said, "Why do you love writing?"

"Because stories connect us. They make people care. Through reading the piece on Popo, people understand a little more about Chinatown."

The kids clapped again.

"What about you, Emma? Why do you love writing?"

She thought for a while. "Because it's my chance to fly into the world," she said at last. "Even if I can't leave my little corner of our neighborhood, my words can!"

That's when I knew what the first assignment should be.

"All right, everybody!" I said, feeling more confident. "I want you to go home, interview your parents, and write a story about why they decided to settle in Chinatown." I smiled. "We're going to write *origin stories*!"

. . .

"Thanks so much for your help with the class," I said to Emma as we walked back—or tried to, as Comma sniffed everything along the way. "You were so great."

"You too! The kids loved you! It's not easy to hold that pack's attention!"

"I can't wait to read their stories," I said. I peeked at Emma and added quickly, "And yours too."

"Mine?" She shrugged, but I could tell she was flattered. "I'm just a girl who jots down random thoughts when Mr. Wu's not looking. And tries to secretly print them with his printing machine!"

I smiled. "If you could write a fortune to *anybody* in this world, and you knew they'd open it, who would it be and what would you say?" I asked.

"Could it be someone historical?"

"Absolutely!" I said.

"Then it would be for Sojourner Truth, and it would say *preach!*"

"Nice," I said. "I'd tell Mozart's sister: *You're a star too! Keep composing!*"

"Oh, you know who is *totally* overlooked in history?" she said. "Mamie Tape."

"Who's she?" I asked.

"An eight-year-old girl who *slayed*," Emma said, punching the air. "She tried to go to school in San Francisco in 1885. The principal wouldn't let her because she was Chinese. So you know what she did?"

I shook my head.

"She sued. All the way up to the California Supreme Court!"

"Really?" I handed Comma's leash to Emma so I could get out my notebook.

"And she won!" Emma said. "Well, sorta. She won the right to go to school. But the city quickly built a school just for Chinese kids, right here in Chinatown, on top of a grocery store."

Emma pointed to a bustling corner shop selling eggplants and carrots. I tried to imagine going to school right above it, trying not to get distracted by the sound of haggling customers all day.

"1885. That's seventy years before *Brown v. Board of Education*," I said.

"The newspapers were *furious*. They ran ads that said 'THAT CHINESE GIRL!'"

*"Really?"* My hands balled into fists.

"If I could write Mamie's fortune," Emma said, "I'd write, *Keep fighting, sister. You have the fire of a thousand dragons behind you.*"

*Wow*, I mouthed.

"We *seriously* need to get you behind that printing machine," I said.

She grinned. Looking down at Comma, she admitted shyly, "But if I had to pick one person to receive one of my fortunes . . . it'd be my dad."

The wind blew and Emma shivered. She bent down and picked Comma up, cuddling him.

"He broke my mom's heart before she even had a chance to tell him she was pregnant with me," she went on. "My mom never got over it. That's why she came here from Wisconsin. But I know he's out there. And I just . . . wish I could meet him, you know?"

I nodded.

"Do you think . . . maybe . . . if he read my words? He'd feel . . . a connection?"

I looked straight into Emma's eyes and held her gaze.

"Absolutely," I told her. "You know how sometimes you read a line, and you feel it, right here?" I put my hand over my heart.

She gave me a small nod.

We stopped in front of the fortune cookie factory and Emma handed Comma back to me. "Merry Christmas, Mia," she said. "I'm so happy I met you and Jason and Lupe."

"Me too," I replied.

I decided right then and there, under the pagoda towers, that I would never try to cookie powder Emma Wong.

She was a very special writer. And us writers had to stick together.

# CHAPTER 51

I skipped back to the inn and went straight to the kitchen to find Jason, but he wasn't there. Instead I found Hank and Mom standing in front of a steaming, hot pot. When I got closer I realized the delicious smell was *snails*!

Hank looked up and grinned at me. "I'm teaching your mom how to eat escargot!"

"I don't know . . ." Mom said, picking up one of the shiny critters with a small pair of tongs. She examined the little shell closely, then looked away. "I can't eat these."

"Sure you can!" Hank said. "They're just like clams!"

"Clams don't crawl over poop on the road," Mom said, putting her snail back in the pot.

Hank grabbed one with his tongs. "Don't think about that," he said as he dug out the meat with his tiny fork and put it delicately to his mouth. "Think about how they've been marinated for a whole day in parsley and butter!"

Mom watched him, then reluctantly reached out her tongs again.

"Wait!" I cried. I took off my backpack and got out my Polaroid. "I have to capture you eating your first snail!" I held up the camera. "To show Dad!"

As I snapped the picture, Mom's snail flew out of her tongs and right at me—nearly hitting me in the eye!

"Are you okay?" Mom shrieked.

I nodded. "Thank God my camera was in the way, or I'd be half blind!"

We both started laughing until tears streamed down Mom's face.

"Should we try again?" Hank asked.

"No, thanks. I almost killed my daughter!" Mom sighed. "Marinade or no marinade, I'm just going to have to go to the ball as myself."

"Good idea," I said, then picked up the escargot from the floor and pretended to crawl all over her feet with it.

• • •

After washing the parsley and butter off my hand, I finally found Jason in his room with Comma. They were sitting by the fireplace with a box of Choco-Pies. Jason had crumbs all over his fingers.

"What's wrong?" I asked him, picking up my puppy and tidying the wrappers. "You didn't feed any of those to Comma, did you? Dogs are allergic to chocolate!"

Jason shook his head. "No, they were for me," he said with a heavy sigh.

Now I was just confused. Jason almost *never* ate anything he hadn't cooked himself.

I sat down next to him and waited.

"Why'd you have to tell Emma I knocked over the punch bowl at the dance?" he finally said.

"I'm sorry," I said. "It just came out."

He frowned and reached for another pie. "Well, thanks a *lot*. Now she'll never like me!"

"Why won't she like you?"

"Because she'll *know*," Jason said, staring at his reflection in the shiny silver wrapper.

"Know what?"

"That I'm a loose cannon! That I have a short fuse!" Jason said. He covered his face with his chocolate fingers, practically in tears. "I was doing so good, trying so hard!"

I felt terrible. Reaching out a hand, I assured him, "You *are* doing really good."

"Well, now it doesn't matter. The past is like a credit score, and my credit score is *bad*," he muttered. "She'll never get over it."

"I don't think love works like credit cards," I said. "She can totally get over it!"

"You couldn't." Jason's eyes pierced into mine.

I blushed.

"Every time you look at me," he went on, "you still think of what happened in fifth grade. I can feel it. That's why it'll never work between us—you said so yourself!" Jason blinked away the tears pooling in his eyes. "It used to crush my *soul*. Did you know that I *actually* tried building a time machine in my room?"

*"What?"* My jaw dropped.

"I even got the WD-40!"

"What does WD-40 have to do with it?" I asked.

"I don't know! But mechanics always have it. I'm not some whiz smart mechanic, okay? I can make a peach flambé, but I can't go back in time. All I can do is go forward and make sure new people *never know* about my past."

"Is *that* why you like Emma? Because she's new?"

Jason didn't say anything.

"Love isn't about hiding your past," I said gently.

He shook his head at the Choco-Pies, like he wasn't fully sure.

But *I* was sure: It was now or never. My heart hammered in my chest, but I pushed the words out bravely: "And who said I would never give you another chance?"

Jason's head jolted up.

Seconds passed in complete silence.

The room got so still, I could hear the soft crackle of the fireplace. Comma stared at us, his tail swaying in the air impatiently.

In all my dreams, I imagined my confession making Jason leap for joy, or that he'd thrust his head into the sun, on top of a canyon, *Lion King* style.

But Jason was as still as a stone.

Luckily, right then Hank came in looking for a pad of paper. I scooped up Comma and ran for the door.

"Hi, Hank! Bye, Hank!" I blurted.

I flew out of the room with Comma in my arms. I was mortified. I had finally summoned the courage to tell Jason my feelings.

And he broke my heart.

# CHAPTER 52

I flopped on my bed and wished Lupe was home from Berkeley. I thought about talking to Mom, but she wouldn't understand. She and Dad were too perfect together. I could not see Mom professing her love to Dad and Dad standing there with his mouth open.

I shuddered. This was way too embarrassing to tell Mom.

Lupe took so long coming home, I thought maybe the Berkeley merry-go-round had flung her straight into the woods. But when she finally returned, there were no pine needles on her. There *were*, however, cheetah patterns on her face and arms. And glitter on her clothes.

"What happened to you?" I asked, briefly forgetting my heartache. Comma ran around her excitedly, trying to lick the bits of glitter off the floor. "Is that *foam* in your hair?"

"Don't ask," Lupe said with a groan. "I popped over to campus to try to find someone in the math department. But I walked into the wrong building."

I stared at her, still confused.

"I thought Delta Gamma Pi was a math building!" she wailed, plopping down on her bed in a poof of glitter. "Trust me, what they were doing in there had *nothing* to do with pi."

As Lupe described the over-the-top Christmas fraternity party she'd walked in on, my jaw dropped.

"Lupe Garcia! You went to a *frat* party??"

"They had a foam machine! And loud music blasting! And no one was wearing shoes! It was terrifying! Do you know how hard it is to walk on hardwood floors covered in foam?" Lupe's eyes were wide. "I'm lucky I didn't break both my legs!"

"How'd you get out?" I asked.

"Well, I couldn't tell them I was only in middle school," she said. "Who knew what they were going to do with me now that I'd witnessed their wild party? They could have captured me and made me do their math homework for the next hundred years!"

Lupe had maybe seen a few too many spy movies.

"So I pretended to be an animal rights activist and started screaming about the harmful effects of foam on our groundwater," Lupe said, pulling out a Sharpie from her bag and adding a few more cheetah prints to her arm. "They threw me out in five seconds."

"Genius," I said, laughing.

Lupe curled up in her bed, a proud but tired cheetah. In a rush, I told her what happened with Jason.

"What do you mean, he didn't say anything?" she asked.

"He just didn't! I sat there waiting for ten whole seconds before Hank walked in!"

Lupe thought for a minute. "Maybe he didn't understand what you were saying."

"I practically spelled it out for him!"

"Maybe he's the kind of guy who needs it *totally* spelled out."

I shook my head and sighed. "I got my answer. I just have to accept it. He doesn't feel the way he used to. End of story."

Comma gazed up at me with his puppy dog eyes, as if to say, *Not end of story!*

But sadly, there were some plot holes even the best writers couldn't fix.

In Jason Yao's mind, we were an item of the past.

I had to accept that and move on.

As painful as it was.

Lupe stuck her lower lip out. "What can I do to cheer you up?" she asked.

I picked Comma up, shaking my head into his fuzzy body. Then I remembered.

"Actually . . . I still haven't ridden a cable car . . ."

"Ha! Okay," Lupe said, then opened her backpack, dumped out her SAT book, and reached for her map of San Francisco.

# CHAPTER 53

Mom came with us to explore the city while Mrs. Luk watched Comma. We rode the cable car up to Lombard, the famously crooked street, then raced each other all the way down. Then at the docks of Pier 39 we snapped pictures with sea lions. We could see all the way out to Alcatraz!

There was so much to explore along the pier! Mom even found an arcade—with free admission! *Finally*, we got to just be kids. It was everything I'd imagined.

Lupe and I hopped around the arcade for hours, wolfing down kettle corn, playing pinball, arm wrestling with the mechanical muscle man, and pounding the Whac-A-Mole as fast as we could. I beat Lupe at Pac-Man, and she won a stuffed giraffe in the claw machine.

Seeing the joy on her face when she squeezed that giraffe, I thought of all the times we'd begged our parents to take us to Chuck E. Cheese when we were younger. The other kids at school went every weekend, bringing back long strips of photos from the arcade photo booths. But our parents couldn't afford to send us.

Now I looked around—and spotted a photo booth in the corner!

"Lupe! We've got to take a picture of this! We're finally chilling!" I cried.

She grinned. "We did it!"

We made silly faces while the machine flashed at us. When it came time to select the title on the strip of our photos, we both picked "Forever Friends."

It was the perfect afternoon. I wished it would never end, and not just because I wanted to keep avoiding Jason.

"Let's stop for a treat," I suggested.

We ended up at Jenni's Smoothies, where I used my credits to treat everyone. Lupe picked butterscotch toffee. As she sipped, the butterscotch smell made me think of Jason. I could barely stand the sadness.

"What's wrong?" Lupe asked.

I shook my head. My eyes drifted over to the corkboard, where Haru's piece about Miss Breed's letters was still hanging.

Underneath his article were half a dozen Post-it notes.

*People were commenting on his article!*

I dashed over to look.

# CHAPTER 54

*This was the community news I needed today!* one note said.

Someone else wrote: *Wonderful tribute of the power of one person in making a difference! Love librarians!*

*Bravo to the Japanese American National Museum for exhibiting these letters from children! I will be sure to take a road trip to look at this important exhibition! We MUST all remember this chapter in our country's history, and the treatment of Japanese Americans!*

*More please from Haru Tanaka!*

*Please keep writing!*

I started jumping up and down. I couldn't wait to tell Haru—here was proof that people wanted to read his stories!

Mom and Lupe walked over, and I unpinned the article for them.

"This is beautiful," Mom said as she read.

I grinned. "My friend wrote it," I said, putting it back up on the board. "I encouraged him to publish it here."

"Why not in the paper?" Mom asked. "Everyone should read his wonderful story."

I hesitated. Now was my chance to tell her the truth about camp. That it wasn't all equal. And that the editors weren't all fair. But I didn't want her to worry, because I knew she *would.* If writing *that* good could only find space on a smoothie shop wall, what did that say about my chances?

Could I, a girl without any legacy, literary agents, or inside connections, make it in journalism?

I didn't have the answer yet.

So I couldn't tell her yet.

. . .

On Christmas morning, Lupe and I woke up to the mouthwatering smell of bacon and Chinese egg and scallion pancakes coming from the kitchen. I smiled, thinking of Jason and Hank cooking up a storm—then felt a pang, remembering how awkward it was having dinner together at the hotel last night. I could barely look at Jason. Thank God everyone was sitting at a big banquet hall table to eat Christmas Eve dinner. The crowd made it easier to hide how embarrassed I still felt.

"Merry Christmas, Mia!" Mom said. "Get dressed so we can go downstairs to call Dad!"

I threw on a sweatshirt and some jeans.

"Merry Christmas!" Dad said over the Golden Inn's front desk phone. "How's my lucky penny?"

"Merry Christmas, Dad. I miss you so much!" I said. Comma barked, excited to meet his grandpa. I held him up to the phone.

Dad laughed and wished Comma a very merry Christmas.

"Your mom's been telling me all about your adventures in Chinatown! And you're teaching the kids there? I'm so proud!"

"Thanks." I grinned. "I wish you were here!"

"Me too. But I've been busy, getting the house all ready for you," he said. "Do me a favor, will you? Take a picture of your mom when she goes to her big fancy ball?"

"Of course!"

"I wish I were there to take her. But we'll have our own little Christmas when you come back, with Comma by our very own fireplace, just like we planned," he said.

"I can't wait, Dad," I said, and handed the phone back to Mom.

Lupe came out of the hotel office where she'd called her parents, and together we ran into the dining room.

We were in for the biggest surprise of the season!

# CHAPTER 55

Dazzling icicle lights hung from the ceiling and fake snow was sprinkled on the floor. Hank had transformed the dining room into a winter wonderland! Comma rolled all over the snow. But the biggest wonder of all?

Underneath the giant Christmas tree, there was an enormous pile of presents for us kids!

"Merry Christmas!" Hank bellowed. "From me, Billy Bob, Fred, Mrs. T, Mrs. Q, and all your parents!"

"Hank! You brought *all* these presents up? Where did you even put them?" I asked.

"I hid them in my car, of course," he said, holding out the first box for me. "Here, open this first. It's from your dad."

I grinned as I tore at the wrapping paper, revealing a beautiful leather key chain with my very own set of golden keys to our new house. I hugged them close.

Mr. and Mrs. Luk put on Christmas carols and Jason, Lupe, and I took turns opening gifts from everyone we loved back home. But it was a package wrapped in newspaper that stole my heart.

"Here, Mia," Jason said, handing me a box covered in the *Tribune.*

I gazed at the newspaper wrapping, reading the headlines.

"Jason, is that my story you're using as wrapping paper?" I asked, pretending to be outraged.

"Yes, just open it, you'll see why!"

Inside the box was a glass jar. Inside the jar were a bunch of tiny little scrolls, each individually tied with a ribbon. I pulled one out, untied it, and saw that Jason had written a quote about writing:

> Don't tell me the moon is shining; show me the glint of light on broken glass. –Anton Chekhov

I grabbed another, then another.

> Talent is cheaper than table salt. What separates the talented individual from the successful one is a lot of hard work. –Stephen King

> There is no greater agony than bearing an untold story inside you. –Maya Angelou

I looked at Jason, speechless.

"I figured they might inspire you! They're all about writing! You like 'em?" he asked, his face full of hope.

"I *love* them," I said.

Jason smiled. "Good. Took forever to choose the quotes at the library back home."

So *that's* what Jason had been doing at the Anaheim Public Library! I was so touched he put so much time and effort into his gift. Hank was right: Time was the best gift of all.

Next, it was my turn.

I handed Jason my present, which I'd picked up next to the wok store.

"Mooncake molds!" Jason exclaimed. "How'd you know I was looking for these??"

I smiled. "Thought they'd be better than Choco-Pies," I chuckled. "Maybe we can make them together sometime?"

Jason looked at me, amused. "*You* wanna cook, Mia Tang?"

I blushed. Okay, so I had a tendency to burn every dish I made. I hated just *standing* there and waiting for the food to cook—I'd start thinking of stories, and before you knew it, my toast would be charcoal. But for Jason, I could learn.

"It'll be a lesson in teamwork," I said. "Which is your last lesson in your training, by the way. If you're ready to graduate."

"Oh, I'm ready!"

His over-the-top enthusiasm made me look away, but I reminded myself it was for the best. I pulled out the recipe from the bakery shop down the street, and got out the bag of ingredients I'd hidden in the cabinets. "Let's do it, then!"

# CHAPTER 56

That afternoon, Hank took Lupe to the square to fly the kite he'd given her, and Jason gave me a cooking lesson.

"How much do I put in here again?" I asked, holding a bottle of golden syrup over a bowl.

"About half a cup," he said. "Then mix it with the lye water and the cooking oil."

The syrup was like honey, and it just refused to pour. I finally lifted the bottle high above my face, to see if the opening even had a hole in it. I squeezed with all my might.

Out came a giant dollop, right smack on my eye!

"Help!" I yelled.

"You okay? What happened?" Jason hurried over.

"I can't see!" I shrieked. "Everything looks golden!"

Jason examined me, hardly containing his laughter.

"It's not funny!" I said, tapping him on the arm to hurry up and do something.

"I'm sorry! Hold still, I'll get you some water!" He reached for a glass.

I started panicking. "You're going to pour water on my head?"

"Yes, I'm going to pour water on your head!"

Before I could protest, he dipped a towel in the water and gently dabbed it to my eye. He took care to dab it as lightly as possible, and I smiled.

"Thanks," I said, taking the towel from him.

My sight restored, we went back to work side by side, mixing and sieving. Jason taught me how to separate the egg yolk from egg white with my fingers. When I tried, I got yolk all over my hands. To my surprise, Jason didn't even get flustered. He just gave me another egg, and told me to try again.

He was getting so much better at being patient.

As we worked, Jason glanced over at me. "So about the other day . . . what you said, before Hank walked in."

I froze. I did *not* want to talk about that.

"Oh my God, look, I smushed another egg!" I said, intentionally mashing the yolk in my hand.

"Mia . . ." Jason sighed. "You said *honest communication*."

I grabbed another egg and considered cracking it on my head.

Jason persisted. "What did you mean when you said—?"

"Nothing!" I yelped. "Look, some things are best kept a secret." I grabbed the bottle of golden syrup. "Like this golden syrup! Does anyone actually know what's *in* this?"

"Yes," he said. "Inverted sugar. Basically you take regular sugar and boil it with lemon juice, and—"

"Fine, fine!" I groaned. "Bad example."

"Mia, if you have something you've been holding in, you should tell me."

"I don't!" I insisted.

He stared into my eyes, not believing me, and I stared right back.

Our intense staring contest seemed to go on forever. It was finally broken by Emma, who came bouncing into the kitchen with a stack of papers in her arms.

"Merry Christmas, everyone," she said brightly, hopping onto the kitchen counter next to us. "Mia! Wait till you see the essays we got!"

As she set down the papers, I gave Jason one last urgent plea.

"We seriously don't have to talk about it," I said. "Ever."

# CHAPTER 57

While the mooncakes baked, we huddled around Emma, taking turns reading aloud.

"Listen to this! 'I am the descendant of Tie Sing, a Chinese background cook that helped convince folks to preserve Yosemite,'" Emma read.

Jason kept peeking at me. I could tell he was eager to continue our conversation, but the word *cook* got his attention.

"What was that?" Jason asked.

Emma continued, "'In 1915, Stephen Mather hired my great-grandfather, Tie Sing, to cook for him during a wildness trip to Yosemite designed to convince congressmen and cultural leaders to start a national park system. For two weeks, my grandfather cooked trout, pork chops, fried potatoes, and apple pie.'"

"Let me see that! He made all that in the *woods*?" Jason asked.

Paper-clipped to the essay was a picture of a group of men, sitting on long tree trunks in a tall forest. In the middle was Tie Sing, the lone Chinese man, standing tall and proud in his apron.

"Wow. This ought to be in the Chinese Historical Museum. No, in *every* museum!" Jason said.

Emma handed him another essay. "This one's amazing too!"

Jason started reading.

"'My great-grandfather was a paper son,'" Jason read. "'He came over during the Chinese Exclusion Act by telling the government he was his uncle's son. It made Tai Yeye very nervous, but Uncle said it was the only way.'"

Jason looked up and Emma explained, "A paper son meant pretending to be a close blood relative of someone already here—it was one of the only ways to get past the Chinese Exclusion Act. Sons were allowed to come join their dads, for example, but nephews weren't considered close enough relatives."

We nodded. Jason continued, "'Of course it was not easy to prove. And Tai Yeye studied hundreds and hundreds of personal details that his uncle gave him about his family, like how tall his siblings were. His favorite food. Even the exact number of steps to get to the front door of his house. All this to get through his intense interview on Angel Island.'"

"Angel Island is right next to Alcatraz," I said. "Lupe and I saw it yesterday, from the pier!"

Emma nodded. "That's where they put everyone while they waited for their interrogation. Some immigrants were detained on Angel Island for *years*."

"That sounds awful," I said.

Jason continued, "'While he waited, Tai Yeye wrote poems on the walls. He ached for his past, and worried for his future. Mama and I went to Angel Island and looked all over, but we couldn't find Tai Yeye's poems. But there were many poems from other immigrants. One talked about looking out at freedom, swallowed up by fog.'"

I gazed out the window at the fog. Imagine staring at it for years straight, and not being allowed out. . . .

"'Finally, he got through the interview and he was allowed to join his aunt and uncle! At last, he was in San Francisco! The first years were hard. At age thirteen, he was put in sixth grade, but he didn't know his ABCs. He started working as a dishwasher at a Chinese restaurant. His fingers turned to prunes. But Tai Yeye worked hard. He saved up, went to night school, and got married.'"

I snuck a glance at Jason. Our eyes met for a second.

"'Now my mother and father are the proud managers of the dumpling shop Tin Fai Fok. We are fourth-generation Chinatown, from paper son to real-life grandson.'"

With glassy eyes, Jason looked at me and Emma. It was my turn to read. I reached for another story.

"'My great-grandfather made trousers for Chinese Americans in the 1800s,'" I read. "'He lived in New York City. Most of his customers were sailors and traders. But he had a very interesting customer, Wong Chin Foo. Wong Chin Foo was a crusader. He didn't believe that Chinese Americans should be treated like second-class citizens. He wanted our dreams to be taken seriously too. So he started writing about it.'"

My eyes widened at the word *writing*. I looked up at Emma, who grinned and said, "Keep reading!"

"'He started a newspaper called the *Chinese American*, in 1883, during the Chinese Exclusion Act, when anti-Chinese hate was rampant.'"

I paused to ask Emma, "Is this true?"

She nodded. "Absolutely! Wong Chin Foo was a journalist, just like you!"

"He launched his *own* newspaper?"

Emma nodded solemnly. "He wrote essays, columns, you name it! He went around the country and gave speeches, trying to get equal rights for us. I think he even testified before Congress!"

"Wow," I breathed, then went on, "'Wong distributed his newspaper for free in New York. And when they ran out of money and the paper shut down, he moved to Chicago and did it again. When the government tried to require all Chinese residents to carry around a permit just to walk around, Wong gave a speech. He said, *The politician who lords it over you today is a coward, and trims his sails to every breeze that blows.*'"

I looked up. "That's so poetic." I got out my reporter's notebook and jotted down the words, along with the name *Wong Chin Foo*—my new hero!

"Told ya he was an amazing writer," Emma said.

"Just like you," Jason offered. "Bold and daring."

I blushed as I read the final lines of the essay. "'He never let anyone take the fire from his words. It scared those in power. But it also inspired people like my grandfather to keep fighting for their dreams. And mine too.'"

I put the paper down.

"Wow," I said again. I glanced at the rest of the stack. "We have to do something with these! They're incredible!"

"Will the *Tribune* publish them?" Emma asked hopefully.

I shook my head. "I have an even better idea!"

# CHAPTER 58

We spent Christmas afternoon under the shimmery lights and red lanterns of the alley wall outside the cookie factory, hanging the stories written by the children of Chinatown. Inspired by Haru's successful "publication" at the smoothie shop, we made something called wheat paste—a thin layer of wheat glue that made the stories stick right to the brick wall.

When we were all done, we stood back to admire the stories of courage, humor, and perseverance.

"This is so beautiful!" Emma said. "We should give it a title!"

I thought very hard. "Let's call it The History of Us!"

"Perfect!" Lupe said.

Jason volunteered to get real paint from the hardware store so we could add the title, and Emma ran to tell all the kids. I went with Jason.

We picked red and gold, auspicious colors in Chinese culture. "Oh, Mia, I heard back from my dad!" Jason said as we waited in line. "He got my postcard! You were totally right, he wasn't mad at all about the oven mitt."

I smiled.

"I told him how you were helping me express my feelings," Jason added.

"And?"

"He said as long as it was free, he was cool with it."

I laughed. That sure sounded like Mr. Yao.

Jason tapped the paint cans nervously. "So did I officially pass your How to Express My Feelings course?"

I knew this moment would come. I took a deep breath and said, "You've passed every stage of the feelings course, with flying colors."

He smiled.

"Even the teamwork part?" he asked as Mr. Tam rang us up and we paid.

Before I could answer, I gasped. "Our mooncakes!" I shouted. "They're still in the oven!"

We ran all the way back to the inn. Luckily, Hank had saved the cakes from the oven. They were sitting on the counter, glowing like the perfect moon they symbolized. They'd turned out even better than I imagined.

Jason held out a hand. "We make a pretty good team, don't we?"

My heart pinched as I shook it. We sure did.

# CHAPTER 59

Over a Christmas picnic lunch of spring rolls, xiaolongbao, and noodles, everyone in Chinatown came out to celebrate the History of Us wall. Even Popo walked the full length of the alley with her walker, complimenting every single child.

"This is the best Christmas present of all. Our history, forever preserved!" Uncle Mo said. "Let's give a big round of applause to Mia and Emma!"

The adults clapped, Lupe took pictures of each child standing next to their work, and Jason passed out mooncakes. Emma and I proudly shook every writer's hand, congratulating them on being "published."

As Hank held a little boy up high to admire his work, he turned to me and said, "Speaking of family history, wanna stroll over to California Street with me? See if my brother's at his office? I got the address yesterday!"

"You think he'll be there on Christmas?" I asked, surprised.

"If he's still the Darrius I know, he'll be working," Hank said. With a twinkle in his eye, he elbowed me and smiled. "Come on. Let's go give my brother some Christmas love."

. . .

The business district streets were empty. As we stopped in front of his brother's office building, Hank looked at the little package in his hand. It had been the last present under the tree, his gift for his brother.

"This is it. Moment of truth!" Hank said.

I blocked the sun with my hand, trying to make out any workers through the windows above, but they were too small.

"How are we even going to get in?" I asked, looking around at the deserted sidewalks, shops, and offices.

Hank pointed to a side door—a janitor was walking out, so Hank hurried over. I listened as he laid out his whole story to the janitor, telling him that his brother was up on the fortieth floor and if he could just get in, they'd finally have the reunion he'd been dreaming about for years.

The janitor gazed into Hank's earnest eyes.

*Please . . . give my friend the Christmas miracle he's been waiting for*, I silently prayed.

Finally, the janitor turned back toward the building.

"Follow me," he said.

# CHAPTER 60

The kind janitor took us all the way to the fortieth floor. As we stepped into the glistening lobby of Paul, Taylor, and Harris, Hank called out, "Darrius? Brother, you in there?"

"May I help you?" asked a young woman walking into the lobby. She was wearing a headset, like an air traffic controller about to fly this building into outer space.

As Hank explained who he was, I peeked down the hall. I could hear the rustling of papers and soft murmurs of people talking on the phone. I was shocked that the firm was still working on Christmas. I thought it was just my parents who worked every holiday!

"Is Darrius or Dean Caleb here?" Hank asked the woman, extending his hand to shake. "Can I speak to him? I'd like to wish him a merry Christmas. I'm his brother."

The woman shook Hank's hand, then spoke into her headset. "Mr. Caleb, your brother is here to see you."

I grabbed Hank's hand, jumping up and down on the ivory marble floor, then stopped when the air traffic control lady looked at me funny. After another minute the woman said, "Right this way."

"Merry Christmas," Hank said as we followed her down the hall. "Hope my brother's not working you too hard."

"Oh, it's my pleasure," she said. "The end of the year is always a very busy time, especially for Mr. Caleb! He's one of our firm's top lawyers."

"I have no doubt!" Hank smiled.

As we walked down the plushy carpet, I poked my head into a big office.

"That's a corner suite," Hank said. "See how it's bigger, with more light? Darrius probably has one of those!" He turned to ask the woman, "He's got to be a partner by now, right?"

"Actually, Mr. Caleb is a senior associate. But between me and you, he's up for partnership at the end of this year!"

She stopped in front of a narrow office and opened the glass door for us. A Black man a little younger than Hank looked up from his pile of papers. His face was the spitting image of his brother's.

"Holy Toledo! Am I seeing this right?" Darrius asked, jumping up from his desk.

Hank wiped tears from his face as he walked over for a hug. I grabbed my Polaroid from my bag to capture the pure joy on Hank's face.

"Merry Christmas, Darrius," he said.

"How long's it been?" Darrius asked. "And I go by Dean now."

"Ten years," Hank told him, patting his back. "Why Dean?"

Dean shrugged. "It's easier for my clients to remember."

Hank looked confused. But I knew what Dean meant. On more than one occasion my mom had considered changing her name from Ying to Helen, so she'd "fit in" with her colleagues at school. In the end, she decided the best way to fit in was to be the best teacher she could be.

"Well, I hope the folks here appreciate you," Hank said. "I hear you're about to make partner!"

Dean smiled. "Nothing confirmed yet, but . . ." He nodded at the towering stacks of paperwork on his desk. "Working as hard as I can to make it happen."

"What'd I say, Mia? I knew we'd find you here, working on Christmas." Hank chuckled.

I stepped forward and said, "I'm Mia Tang. I work with Hank."

"You sell insurance too?" Darrius asked.

"No, I quit that years ago," Hank said, exchanging an amused glance with me. "Now I own a little motel and restaurant down in LA."

Dean gasped. "Wow!"

"Not just a little motel," I said. "It's a boutique, right outside of Disneyland! And Hank's cooking is to die for. You gotta come check it out!"

Hank shook his head. "She's a writer. So she's prone to exaggeration." He winked at me, then he turned back to Dean and said with a straight face, "But seriously, my cooking's to die for."

Dean laughed. "Hank! I'm impressed! And surprised—what are you doing up here?"

"I tried to write you and tell you," Hank said. "Didn't you get my postcards? Tell me they got forwarded to your new address."

"Oh yeah, I got 'em," Dean said. He snapped his fingers, remembering. "I've just been so swamped with work. Don't take it personally that I didn't respond." He sighed as he gazed out his window at the gray sky-pokers. "I haven't seen the Golden Gate Bridge in the daylight for so long, I can't even remember if it's red or orange!"

Apparently Dean did not subscribe to Ms. Flemings's *work hard, play hard* motto.

"That's easy enough to fix! Let's go!" Hank said.

His brother looked at him, confused. "Now?"

Hank glanced at his watch. "If we leave now, we can catch the bus to Golden Gate Park!"

Dean's face went all dreamy. "Forget the park. If we really want to see the bridge, let's go to Murray Circle in Sausalito! Best burger in San Francisco," he said. He glanced down at his paperwork again. "But . . . maybe some other time."

Hank put a hand on his brother's shoulder. "It's Christmas," he said gently. "You should take some time. Enjoy yourself. It's what Mama would have wanted."

A minute later, Dean had grabbed his jacket and told the air traffic control lady that he'd be back. We hurried to the elevators and I threw my arms up in triumph.

# CHAPTER 61

We rode the ferry over to Sausalito, just on the other side of the Golden Gate Bridge. As the wind blew in my hair, I pictured myself walking across the bridge with Jason.

Maybe then I could whisper to him *my* favorite author quote:

*I believe you are one of the people that can lift the corners of the universe. -Ann M. Martin*

I looked over at Hank and Dean, deep in conversation, and smiled.

The two brothers talked the whole way as we passed Alcatraz and Angel Island. I put a hand over my heart, remembering all the hopes and dreams detained there.

When the ferry landed, Dean grabbed a taxi to Murray Circle, a former military fort that was now a hotel and restaurant. As promised, it had an incredible view of the Golden Gate Bridge.

As we dined on crab cakes and gourmet burgers, Dean told us how the managing partner of his firm had brought him here when he first joined the firm, years ago.

"It was me and five other associates," he said. "Everyone besides me was white. We hung on to the partner's every word. Mr. Paul has this real *presence*. I remember being so nervous, just sitting next to him." Dean winked at me, just like Hank, and added, "I accidentally ordered lobster bisque."

"But you're allergic to shellfish!" Hank said.

"I know! I'd pointed to the next soup on the menu, but the waiter got confused. I didn't know what to do!"

"What happened?" I asked.

"I ate it anyway!"

Hank and I both gasped.

"You're kidding," Hank cried.

"It was the managing partner of the firm! I didn't want his first impression of me to be the idiot who ordered what he was allergic to!" Dean shook his head. "So I chugged it down, and crossed my heart and hoped for the best. Then when lunch was over I ran to the nearest urgent care."

Hank covered one eye with his hand, cringing.

"The things I've had to do over the years," Dean said, sighing. "But if they give this to me, I'll be the first Black partner of our law firm."

Hank held up his sparkling water and toasted his brother. "To the first Black partner!"

Dean grinned as we all clinked glasses.

"What do you think of the burger?" he asked me.

"Honestly?" I said. "It's great, but doesn't compare to Hank's."

Dean smiled at his brother. "Mama always said your burgers were something else."

Then Dean's jacket started ringing. He reached inside and pulled out a mobile phone. Hank and I stared as he answered the call.

"Dean Caleb speaking," he said. His face tensed when he heard who it was. "Hi, Matt, merry Christmas. No, I just . . . I stepped out for a minute." He flushed. "Of course, I was just working on that. I'll have it done by tonight. I'm headed back to the office now."

He pushed a button and tucked the phone back in his pocket.

"Everything okay?" Hank asked.

Dean nodded, though his face was tense. "My boss. Wanted to know where I was."

"But it's a holiday!"

"Holidays are like stomach ulcers to this guy. They're annoying and you have to work past them," Dean said.

*Whoa.* My eyebrows shot up at *that* motto.

"He lives and breathes the firm. Speaking of which . . ."

The maître d' walked over, and Dean jumped up.

"Hey there, any chance you guys can accommodate a private event on Saturday? A hundred people?" he asked. "The restaurant my firm uses for our annual dinner had to cancel."

The maître d' shook her head. "I'm sorry, we're fully booked."

Dean sat back down, looking dismayed. "Oh well. It was worth a shot . . ." He shook his head.

Hank clapped his hands together. "If y'all looking for a restaurant, I could help you out! I'm running a huge kitchen in a hotel, just a few blocks from your office!"

I nodded excitedly. "The food is perfection!"

Dean looked up hopefully. "Really?" He reached for his phone. "You sure?"

"Positive. You should see the banquet hall! Plenty of room!" Hank said.

"Oh my God, you have no idea the favor you'd be doing me! I'm going to call my boss. No, better yet, I'm going to call up *his* boss, the managing partner, Jonathan Paul! This will score me major points!"

Hank chuckled at his brother's glee. "It'd be my honor!" With a pen, Hank scribbled down the Golden Inn's address on a piece of paper and handed it to Dean. "Oh, before I forget . . ." He reached into his jacket and pulled out a small gift-wrapped package.

Dean put his phone down and gently picked up the present. Inside the paper, a tiny box held a wine cork.

"From the champagne when you graduated from Stanford," Hank explained.

"Mama kept it all those years?" Dean asked, smiling.

"No, *I* kept it," Hank said, his voice catching. "I kept it with me, from motel to motel."

Dean might not have understood the enormity of the gesture, but I did. The last few years hadn't been easy for Hank. There were times when he was chased out of his motel room with barely a suitcase. The fact that he'd hung on to his brother's celebration cork spoke volumes.

"Merry Christmas." Hank smiled.

Dean opened his arms. "Merry Christmas, brother. I'm so glad you came up."

I could hardly contain my tears as the brothers hugged. It was a Christmas miracle I'd be thinking about for a long time. And I knew Hank would too.

# CHAPTER 62

Mr. and Mrs. Luk were overjoyed to be throwing another banquet. As Hank set about making it the grandest holiday party Paul, Taylor, and Harris had ever seen, I skipped to the *Tribune*.

I was excited to tell my friends about Haru's admirers and the History of Us wall. But when I neared our desks, I heard sniffling coming from the snack room.

It was Amne. She was sitting in the corner, alone. I hurried over.

"Did Mr. Walters say anything about your story?" I asked. I'd been keeping my fingers crossed about her Ishi piece all Christmas. "What's wrong?"

She pushed a piece of paper across the table. It was her article, covered in red ink.

"They want to make all these changes," Amne said, glancing at Mr. Walters, who was in Mr. Miles's office as usual.

My eyes jumped from one red strike-out after another. Everything about Ishi being made to work at the museum was taken out. Kroeber making him visit the site of his tribe's massacre was crossed out too.

"Mr. Miles said it sounded too much like an opinion piece. But it's not my *opinion* when a *human* gets objectified as a living exhibit! It's not my *opinion* when he said he wanted to be cremated and not dissected but no one knows where his remains are!"

She was absolutely right.

I wanted to talk to our editor, but Timothy Madison was already pacing outside Mr. Miles's office like an overeager rooster.

"Did you tell him those changes aren't okay?" I asked. "We can't let him run it like that!"

"Mr. Walters said if I want a career in journalism, I have to be willing to take feedback," Amne said. "I can't be *precious* with my words. I have to be *collaborative*."

"Yeah, collaborative, as in bringing your ideas to the table! Your passion! Your *truth*!" I said. "Not having it gutted *out*!"

In that moment, I knew what we needed to do. We couldn't just keep banging our heads and our words against the same stubborn, ancient wall.

We needed to do something bold!

Something daring!

Something totally groundbreaking!

We needed to Wong Chin Foo this thing!

. . .

"Hear me out," I said to my friends as they followed me down Montgomery after camp. Haru smiled as we passed the smoothie shop, where we'd gone for lunch so he could see his article. The reader comments had made his whole day!

"Wong Chin Foo was a journalist!" I continued. "He published his own paper in the 1800s, actually multiple papers! At a time when Chinese Americans were being told to get out—he somehow found the courage to *speak* out. And that's what we need to do!"

Haru and Amne stared at me. "Are you suggesting . . . ?" Haru began.

"We have the stories! The talent! Why can't we be our own publishers?" I asked. "If Wong Chin Foo can do it in the 1800s, surely we can find a way to do it now!"

"A real newspaper?" Haru asked. "Not just some stories stapled together?"

"A *real* newspaper!" I insisted.

"Why not?" Amne nodded excitedly. "What do we have to lose— our stories aren't getting published anyway. Well, except Mia's."

I stopped walking for a second. As embarrassing as it was, I finally told my friends the truth about my Popo article, and how I never got paid.

"*What?*" Amne's jaw dropped.

"They said they ran out of money," I mumbled. "They'd blown through their budget. . . ."

My friends gasped. "How could they?" Amne cried.

"Those sneaky cold sores!" Haru snarled.

I nodded. "That's why we gotta shake things up, just like Wong! We can't keep pouring our hearts out for dust," I said. "We have to try something new. Maybe it'll work, maybe it won't. But we'll never know unless we try!"

Amne and Haru looked at each other for a long moment. Then they turned to me and extended their hands. We all shook firmly on it. Our first agreement as editors.

No—as *publishers*!

"Wait, where are we going to print this?" Amne asked. "We can't go to Germany and get a hundred and fifty tractors!"

I smiled. "Luckily, we don't have to!"

# CHAPTER 63

"Emma, we need your help!" I said, bursting into the cookie factory with Amne and Haru right behind me.

Emma was in the middle of mixing a new batch of cookie dough. She climbed down from the step stool and said, "What's up?"

I took a moment to gather myself, then announced, "I want to be Wong Chin Foo!"

Emma looked confused until Amne added, "We want to print our own newspaper! And fill it with stories and important issues about every community! A paper by the people, for the people!"

I showed Emma Amne's brilliant Ishi article and Haru's heart-warming piece about Miss Breed. As her eyes danced across the page, I said, "All we need is to use the cookie factory's printing press—we can even pay for the paper!"

"Okay, but what about Mr. Wu?" Emma asked. "He's real protective when it comes to the press. It's kind of his baby. . . ." Her eyes darted over to Mr. Wu sitting in his office, carefully inspecting a cookie with a magnifying glass.

Slowly we walked over.

"Absolutely not," Mr. Wu said when we asked. "I have enough trouble as it is, trying not to lose money printing all the fortunes!"

He pointed to a gigantic bucket of chocolate-dipped fortune cookies with red and green sprinkles that no one had bought for Christmas.

"You know how hard we worked on those cookies? I stayed here all night hand-dipping them—I was covered in chocolate! You should have seen all the sprinkles on me!" he said, screwing up his face.

It was pretty funny imagining Mr. Wu covered in Christmas sprinkles, but I kept a straight face.

"Still, nobody came by!" he wailed.

"Because you don't have any publicity!" I told him. "If you let us print our newspaper here, we'll put Dragon Fortune Cookie Factory front and center in our ads section."

"Ads section?" Mr. Wu said, then added grudgingly, "I like the sound of that."

I nodded, glancing at my partners. "We'll share the ad revenue with you, fifty-fifty. Right, guys?"

Amne and Haru nodded eagerly.

"Revenue?" Mr. Wu put down his magnifying glass.

Now we *really* had his attention.

"Yeah! Newspapers are a business!" Haru informed him.

When Haru told him how much the *Tribune* charged for a quarter-page ad, Mr. Wu's eyes boggled.

"You wouldn't even have to risk anything! You already have the printer," I reminded him. "It's just sitting there!"

I pointed to the back room with the printing press that churned out all the fortunes.

"And we've got all that recycled paper in the back too," Emma pointed out. "You said we couldn't use it because the paper's too thin for the cookies?"

Mr. Wu considered our proposal.

Tense seconds went by. Finally, with the smack of his desk, Mr. Wu announced, "I'm in!"

# CHAPTER 64

Amne, Haru, Emma, and I took a box of Christmas fortune cookies from the factory and went out for celebratory boba. We toasted to Mr. Wu agreeing to let us print an initial run of two hundred copies of our four-page newspaper on recycled fortune cookie paper.

Emma offered to help, since she knew how to work the old printing press. We immediately divided up all the stories of the first issue: the Ishi article, the Miss Breed letters, and the most moving pieces from The History of Us. In addition, Amne wanted to write a piece about the shell mounds in the Bay Area, and how developers were putting up buildings and even malls over the ancestral burial sites of her people, for the next issue.

"We absolutely have to write about that," I agreed. "Haru, what about you?"

"I want to interview Japantown shop owners about how they kept them going during the internment years," he said.

"Great idea!" I said. "And I'll write a feature on Wong Chin Foo, and how his legacy inspired the newspaper!"

We made a pact to not tell anyone at camp about our plans. After all, we didn't know how Mr. Walters would feel about us publishing the stories the *Tribune* had passed on.

"But wait, what do we call it?" Amne asked.

Everyone started tossing out ideas.

"How about the *Bay Voice*?" I asked.

"But Haru and you will both be going back to LA soon," Amne pointed out. "You'll want to keep working on the paper from there, right, Mia?"

"Absolutely!"

"How about *You Read It Here First*?" Haru suggested.

"It's a little long," Emma said. "On this old machine, a shorter title will be much easier."

"How about *Scoop Unfolded*?" Amne said.

"Or just *The Scoop*?" I said.

"Perfect!" my friends all agreed.

We toasted our boba teas again and ate more cookies. My heart pounded with adrenaline. We were really doing this!

# CHAPTER 65

Friday morning, I packed my draft of the Wong Chin Foo profile into my backpack, planning to finish it up at camp. Putting on my nicest shirt, I looked in the mirror.

"Do I look like a publisher?" I asked Lupe.

She rolled over sleepily and gave me a thumbs-up, then glanced at the clock. "I'll be late tutoring my students!" she cried, jumping out of bed.

"You're tutoring?" I asked.

She nodded. "Some of the Chinatown kids—Johnny and Katie," she said. "I met them the other day at the wall! They're only nine but they want to learn algebra!"

"Good for you!"

"I'm going to teach them equations with the Chinatown lanterns." Lupe beamed. "Maybe we can do math *and* have fun walking around!"

I smiled. "Work hard and play hard!"

"Oh, by the way, I finally figured out that SAT question—by myself! The one I was stuck on!"

"No way! When?" I asked.

"The other day, when we were riding on the cable cars and I had my head stuck out the window!"

"Lupe, you were doing *math* with your head stuck out the window?"

She chuckled. "Yep! And the answer came to me, like a blast of wind. Guess my brain just needed a rest."

"So you're still going to take the mock test on Monday?" I held my breath, hoping maybe she'd reconsidered.

But she nodded. "I think so!"

I glanced over at the picture of the two of us on my desk. *Forever Friends.*

My eyes focused on the word *forever.* I hoped it was made of superglue. But even if it wasn't, I knew the first word was even more important.

I smiled at Lupe. "Good for you."

. . .

I found Mom in the banquet room, practicing her speech at the podium. She was able to get through most of it without any mistakes, but she still struggled with making eye contact while she spoke.

"Maybe try reading a little less from your flash cards," I told her as I quickly ate my breakfast congee and fed Comma.

"I can't," she said. "I'll lose my place!"

I walked up to the podium and looked at her cards. She had every single word of her speech written down.

"Why don't you try bullet points?" I suggested.

She shook her head. "What if I freeze?"

I put a warm hand over Mom's cold one.

"You won't," I promised her. "Everything on this card, you've lived. Don't you want to look out at the audience and see everyone clap for you?"

"Nope, I'm good," she said, clinging to her cards.

I didn't have time to argue with her because I needed to get to camp—I had a paper to publish! As I ran to the kitchen to drop off Comma and put my congee dish in the sink, I hollered back to her, "You can do this! Believe in yourself!"

"Believe in my flash cards!" she hollered back.

# CHAPTER 66

Amne, Haru, and I huddled over our desks at camp, writing furiously straight through to lunchtime. Then Haru hurried off to do the interview he'd scored over the phone that morning with a mochi shop—the oldest storefront in Japantown! He returned with a brand-new article.

Mochi Holds a Community Together
By Haru Tanaka
Mochi is very important to the Japanese community, especially around the holidays. Filled with red or white bean paste and other creative fillings, it's the perfect gift for visiting friends and family. Take it from the owners of Benkyodo; the 115-year-old mochi shop is Japantown's oldest business.
Suyeichi Okamura first opened the storefront in 1906. He decided to name it Benkyodo, which means "affordable," because he wanted to make sure the community always had a place where they could shop comfortably. He believed that desserts meant much more

than just snacks. They conveyed affection, history, and stories. Everyone deserved access to authentic desserts.

After the attack on Pearl Harbor in 1942, Suyeichi and his family were sent to an internment camp in Amache, Colorado. Desperate to keep his beloved dessert shop going, Suyeichi asked his Chinese neighbor to watch over his store while he was gone—and he did.

For three years, the Okamura family lived in harsh and bare conditions far from home, while Suyeichi's neighbor ran the shop. When they got out, the neighbor returned the shop to Suyeichi.

Now, Suyeichi's grandsons run the shop. Ricky and Bobby Okamura make about 1,000 pieces per day. They do everything by hand. "We could use a machine," Bobby said. "But all the pieces would look exactly the same. Ours have a unique taste, texture, and look."

The brothers have worked together in the back room of the pastry shop since childhood. And though it is not always easy getting to work before the rest of Japantown wakes up, the history, tradition, and stories embedded in each mochi makes it all worth it.

"This is so good!" Amne and I said in unison.

"Thanks!" Haru said. "I was so inspired, I wrote it right there in the café! The owners were so nice. When I told them about our paper, they said they'd take out a small ad."

"Seriously?" I asked. "Our first real advertiser!"

Amne gave me a high five and we squealed—I guess a little too loudly, because Mr. Walters came walking over.

"What's going on?" he asked. "You guys get a good scoop?"

I almost choked. Haru immediately threw a bunch of pens over his article so Mr. Walters couldn't read the headline.

"Nope!" we said, smiling sweetly.

We waited until Mr. Walters left, then resumed our publishers' meeting.

"You know who else we should hit up for an ad?" I said, glancing at my staff card.

Amne and Haru grinned.

"The smoothie shop!" we said at the same time.

# CHAPTER 67

Nervously, we showed the manager of Jenni's Smoothies our ad rates leaflet. Unlike the *Tribune*, which charged $200 for an ad, we were only charging $20. Still, we weren't sure if we'd get any takers.

But the manager smiled and said, "We'd be glad to support you! Count us in for a regular spot!"

"Oh, thank you! You're not going to regret it!" I said.

"I know we won't!" He pointed at the bulletin board. "Your wonderful story has already brought in a lot of business! Everyone loves it!"

Haru's jaw dropped when he saw all the new Post-its that had appeared under his story. There were twice as many since Christmas!

I gave him a high five and Amne cried, "Let's go publish our paper!"

· · ·

Back in Chinatown, Emma and I got to work on layout. The cookie factory printer was this big, clunky iron machine Emma nicknamed "Sir Jams-A-Lot," tucked away in the windowless back room of the factory. It was even older than the ones at the *Tribune*. We had to do everything by hand, including setting the type and all the spacing.

Emma demonstrated by printing a bunch of new cookie fortunes she'd just written. They were hilarious, and I giggled as the printer spat each one out.

"Your turn!" she said.

I took my time picking out all the fonts.

"I know it's frustrating to do everything by hand," Emma said. "But you get used to it."

"No, it's cool!" I said.

"Once the type's all set, it's actually really easy!" Emma rolled the paper in and secured it into the pin locks. "All right, Jamsy, do your thing!"

To my surprise, Jamsy didn't jam at all! I stared, mesmerized, as the words *The Scoop* came out in black ink.

My hands shook as I held my first front page.

It didn't even have any of our articles on it yet, but it felt miraculous! All this time, I'd been trying to prove to a national paper that I mattered, that my stories mattered. Now I was taking my own future by the reins!

"How's it feel?" Emma asked.

"Amazing!" I said. "Have you ever used it for anything besides fortunes before?"

Emma nodded shyly. "Once." She walked around to the back of the machine and retrieved something a little larger than a postcard. I realized it was an invitation, printed on very fancy paper.

For a second, I thought it must be for Jason. My mind immediately flashed to an image of them ferrying over to Sausalito for her next birthday. I tried to swallow the envy in my throat.

But then I read the card.

Dear Dad,
　　You're invited to meet me. In San Francisco, or a location of your choice. I just know you'll enjoy getting to know me, especially if you are the type of person who likes history, lion dancing, kites, noodles, and writing. Even if you are not, I know I will enjoy getting to know you.
　　　　　　　　　　Sincerely,
　　　　　　　　　Your daughter,
　　　　　　　　　　Emma Wong

My eyes misted as I handed back the card. It made me miss my own dad in LA even more. "It's beautiful. Are you going to send it?"

Emma shook her head. "I don't know his address," she said sadly. "Just that he likes kung pao chicken."

I thought about Emma's dream to get Mr. Wu's cookies back in every Chinese restaurant in the country, so she could get her writing into her dad's hands. Then I glanced over at the neatly stacked, official fortunes.

With a mischievous grin, I reached for one of Emma's original fortunes, then stuck it in the middle of the others.

She gasped. "Mia!"

"Oops," I said. "I made a mistake." I grinned. "But as my dad once said, sometimes a mistake isn't a mistake. It's an opportunity!"

# CHAPTER 68

It was nearly 8:00 p.m. when I got back to the Golden Inn. I found Hank giving his brother a tour of the banquet hall he'd lovingly decorated for the law firm dinner.

But Dean's face was clouded with worry. "You didn't say you were cooking in Chinatown."

Hank looked at his brother, confused. "This hotel is one of the oldest in the city!"

Dean pointed at the red leather chairs and the gold chandeliers. "You can't be serious with this furniture. We're a white-shoe firm!" He squinted at the stage. "Is that a dragon?"

"Hey, dragons are very auspicious in Chinese culture!" I shouted from the doorway.

"Well, it's not auspicious to me making partner!" Dean said. He turned to Hank. "How could you not have warned me?"

Hank crossed his arms and retorted, "Warned you what? That I was working at an authentic, premier establishment? One that has been a tentpole in the community since the Gold Rush?"

Dean put his hands up. I could tell he was getting flustered and trying very hard to remain calm. "Nothing against Chinatown," he said. "But I've got a lot riding on this party. I've got to prove that I *belong* in the corner suite." He pointed at the floor.

"You know what they're going to think if I bring them here?"

"No, Dean, what are they going to think?" Hank's voice had an edge that I wasn't used to hearing.

"That I'm not serious! It's bad enough I let you talk me into slacking off!"

"Slacking off?!" Hank shouted. "Is that what you call having Christmas dinner with the brother you haven't seen in ten years?"

Dean covered his eyes. "I should *not* have agreed to this. I should have known better."

"Oh, because I couldn't possibly work in a place good enough for you and your fancy firm? A pathetic guy like me." Hank stared at him, daring him to deny it. "Isn't that what you think I am? Go ahead. Say it."

The room fell silent.

Dean looked away, refusing to speak. Then the mobile phone in his jacket started ringing. When he answered it was set to speaker, so we all heard a booming man ask, "Are we all set for tomorrow?"

"Actually, Mr. Paul—"

The man barreled on. I poked Hank and whispered, "That's the managing partner, right?" Hank just shrugged.

"I gotta hand it to you," Mr. Paul went on, "when you said you found us a spot at the last minute, I thought, *There's a guy who can get things done.* My wife, Helen, and I are so excited. She *lives* for the annual firm dinner!" He chuckled. "We'll see you at the restaurant!"

Dean didn't get a word out before the *beep* of Mr. Paul hanging up. Dean stared at his phone, then sheepishly at his big brother.

"I'll give your partner his party," Hank said. Then with some serious side-eye, he added, "I might be pathetic, but I always keep my promises."

Hank turned and walked back to the kitchen. I hoped his words sank in. Because Dean wasn't the only one who had a lot riding on this party. Hank had poured himself into mending their relationship . . . but he couldn't do it all by himself.

# CHAPTER 69

Saturday flew by. I spent hours helping Emma find all the fonts for our first paper. With each word, my heart did a somersault. I couldn't wait to hold the final product in my hands!

That evening, I put on my sequined red dress with a black collar. I'd been saving it for a special occasion, like maybe a fancy journalism event. But tonight's banquet was special enough!

Jason walked out of his room in a suit with a bow tie, stopping in his tracks when he saw me.

"You look . . ." He shook his head and mouthed *wow*.

I blushed. "Thanks," I said. "You don't look so bad yourself."

He stood up a little taller, beaming.

"Have you seen Hank? Are the guests starting to arrive?" I asked. I was sure that once Dean saw the delicious hors d'oeuvres and sparkling silverware, he'd change his tune.

"Yes! Hank's in the hall," Jason said.

He grabbed my hand and I felt sparks fly inside me, even as we hurried downstairs.

Mom wore a ruffled peach gown, looking absolutely radiant as she greeted the guests. "Mom!" I cried, and she twirled, smiling at me.

"You like it?" she asked. "Auntie Lam made it for me using a *thousand* pieces of silk scarves!"

"It's stunning!" I gasped, rushing over and gently touching the silky fabric. It felt like touching a cloud.

Hank walked over in a black tuxedo and handed Mom a single long-stemmed red rose. "From Li," he said.

Mom breathed in the flower while I cooed "Aww." It was so sweet of Dad to be there, even from four hundred miles away.

Hank started passing around mini mushroom turnovers and Mom went back to welcoming people.

"Hi, I'm Ying," she said to one of the lawyers. "I teach math at Anaheim High School. Do you like math?"

I knew that to Mom, making small talk with fancy people was as scary as climbing Mount Everest. But she was doing great! In no time at all, the guests were smiling and laughing.

Jason went to the kitchen and I stayed in the entry, watching the door. Finally, Dean walked in. He wore a pressed tux and handed Hank his coat nervously, scanning the crowd for his boss. Mr. Paul was walking in right behind him.

Dean turned awkwardly and said, "Jonathan, Helen, this is, uh—my brother, Hank."

"Thank you so much for having us," Mr. Paul said, shaking Hank's hand earnestly. "I remember coming to Chinatown every weekend with our kids! Our two girls were adopted from China. It was the highlight of our week, wasn't it, Helen?"

Mrs. Paul nodded, smiling warmly. "Every weekend."

"Wow," Dean said, his face relaxing. "I love coming to Chinatown too."

Mr. Paul's smile shifted to Dean. "Well done, Caleb. Couldn't have thought of a better place to celebrate."

Dean looked like he was about to pass out from the relief and shock, while Hank just calmly led everyone into the banquet room.

. . .

That night, under the shimmery lights of the banquet hall, Mr. Paul led the attorneys of Paul, Taylor, and Harris in doing the Macarena.

As the rest of the firm danced, Dean walked slowly to the back table. Hank was setting down the last of the chocolate mousses that Jason had whipped up. I stood nearby, waiting to help clear dishes.

"Hank, I owe you an apology," Dean said.

Hank handed me some plates to take back to the kitchen, but I didn't move.

Dean slid into a chair. "You don't know what it's like to give up *everything*, just to be invited into a room. To question whether you're good enough, day in and day out, because no one who looks like you ever got this far before."

I found myself nodding silently. I knew the crushing weight of being the first. And the fear that if you didn't sacrifice every ounce of your life, you might be the last.

Hank sat too, and Dean looked him in the eye. "I'm not doing it for the corner office. I want the *acknowledgment*. That the blood, sweat, and tears I've put in is irreplaceable."

Hank nodded. "I get that."

"See these folks? Also vying for partner?" Dean asked, nodding at the dance floor. "Some of their dads know Mr. Paul. A few are our clients. They've been running in the same circles for generations. And I'm just a kid from Detroit."

My eyes misted, listening to Dean. It was exactly how I felt every day in the newsroom, like I'd gotten in—but I was still outside.

Hank put a hand on Dean's shoulder.

"You're gonna get it," Hank assured him. "Because ain't nobody else sacrificed as much as you. That's a fact."

Dean swallowed hard. "That's what I want to apologize for. I've been so *obsessed* with making partner, I let everything else go. I gave up every weekend! I even gave up my name! I should never have said what I said last night. I was angry at myself, for not being there for Mama. All I ever wanted was to make her proud." Tears streamed down his face.

Hank pulled him in for a hug. "You did, my brother. Her face bloomed like peach meringue whenever she talked about you."

As they pulled away, Dean rubbed at his cheek, smiling a little. "If I was the peach meringue, you were the amaretti."

Hank chuckled. "Haven't tried that yet."

"Oh, you have to. It's an Italian cookie. Exquisite."

Hank smiled.

Dean stuck out his hand. "Will you forgive me?"

"I'm here, aren't I?" Hank took his brother's hand and added softly, "You know what cooking and family have in common? You can forget the dishes that didn't work out so great, as long as you're willing to get back in the kitchen."

As the brothers reached for flutes of champagne to toast, I looked around for my Polaroid—then remembered it was in my room. I set down the dishes I'd never cleared and hurried out of the banquet hall.

I was surprised to find Emma standing in the lobby. "Mia!" She held something up. "Look!"

I squealed, and joy flooded my veins—it was the very first copy of my very own newspaper! Our very first issue was done! I hugged issue one of *The Scoop* to my chest and breathed in the wonderful inky smell of freedom.

"Did you print all two hundred?" I asked.

"Yep!" she said, pointing to the box at her feet.

I squealed. I couldn't wait to distribute it to every restaurant, bus stop, library, and park my feet could carry me to!

But first, I invited Emma in for some chocolate mousse, whipped by her favorite chef. She'd earned it!

# CHAPTER 70

First thing the next morning, Jason, Lupe, Emma, Amne, Haru, and I ran all around San Francisco distributing *The Scoop*. I told Mom that the paper was a homework assignment for camp, but my heart pattered faster than Comma's feet.

We gave copies to mothers, baristas, brides taking wedding photos, street musicians, poets, marine biologists, dog walkers, and anyone else we could find.

Jason went inside every restaurant and talked to every manager. To our surprise, almost all of them let us leave a few at their restaurant, and some took our ad rate card too!

Emma made sure to give a copy to each of the kids in Chinatown whose stories we'd published. They all asked us editors to autograph their papers, but we explained to them that actually, *they* ought to be autographing them for *us*.

I never thought anything could make me happier than seeing my own story get published. But seeing the joy on those kids' faces warmed me to my toes.

That night, I smiled into my dreams. We had done it! Just like Wong Chin Foo, we'd taken back our voices, and done it in style! I had so many ideas for the next issue—a letters to the editor section, a help wanted section so Mr. and Mrs. Luk could find a new chef, even a recipes section! My mind raced while my body was bone tired from hitting the pavement all day. I finally drifted to sleep, snuggling Comma and dreaming about butterscotch.

Then the morning came.

. . .

"MIA!"

I wriggled out of bed. Opening the window, I stuck my head into the biting morning air. Emma looked up from the sidewalk, her usual smile gone.

"What's wrong?" I asked. "Is it the paper?"

A sudden terror jolted through me that Mr. Wu had changed his mind and wouldn't let us keep printing, but Emma shook her head.

"It's the History of Us wall!" she cried. "Someone painted all over the stories!"

"What?"

Jason's head shot out of his window too. He looked as livid as I felt.

"We'll be right there!" he said.

# CHAPTER 71

All of Chinatown was gathered in front of the History of Us wall. Someone had spray-painted the words *Yo mama!* over and over, in gigantic silver letters, right on top of our students' wonderful stories. They'd added rude smiley faces with straight lines for eyes and buck teeth.

"This is such an insult!" Uncle Hu shouted. "They're making fun of us and our history!"

Everyone looked heartbroken, especially the kids.

I was boiling inside. "Who did this?" I cried, but of course no one knew. I could not stop staring at the infuriating smiley faces.

Auntie Choi tried desperately to scrub out the graffiti with a towel, but it was no use. The words permanently shook the kids' writing confidence too, as they took their stories off the wall and held them to their chests.

Uncle Mo turned to the kids. "We don't give in to terror! We're gonna rewrite those stories, every single one of them, and put them back up!"

The moms in the crowd cheered. Lupe hugged Johnny and Katie and promised she'd help them.

"We won't be bullied into silence!" Uncle Mo went on. "Not a hundred years ago, and not now!"

"Yeah!" the crowd cried.

"I have paint at the hardware store," Mr. Tam said. "We can repaint the wall today! Who's ready?"

A hundred hands went up.

"Great! Starting tonight, we'll have a community patrol too!" Uncle Mo said. "Mia!" he called. "Will you let the *Tribune* know this happened? Maybe they can print something on this outrageous act!"

"I'm on it," I said. Anger fired me up as I raced back to the hotel to grab my Polaroid. The more eyeballs we had on this crime, the more likely we were to find the person responsible.

• • •

Mr. Walters frowned as he looked at my photos. "Kids these days, with their graffiti. So unfortunate."

"It's a lot more than unfortunate," I snapped. "It's straight-up racism."

"Racism?" Mr. Walters looked shocked. "There's nothing derogatory here. It just says *yo mama*."

I pointed to the smiley faces. "These eyes are derogatory!"

"I think that's just how some people draw smiley faces, Mia." Mr. Walters shrugged. "Personally, I like to draw mine with two vertical lines, but horizontal is popular too."

I couldn't believe Mr. Walters was turning a hate crime into a cartoon lesson!

"So you're not going to cover the story?"

"I think we're good on Chinatown. We already did the lost grandma story last week, remember?"

I'd had enough of his illogical thinking. "Fine, if you think we're 'good on Chinatown,' I'll offer it to another publication that's *actually* interested in covering the news."

Mr. Walters looked flabbergasted. "Which one?"

"*The Scoop.*"

"Never heard of them," Mr. Walters said.

"They're new. But trust me, they're gonna give you a run for your money!"

I stomped out of Mr. Walters's office and back to my desk, where Haru let out a giggle and Amne gave me a high five under my desk.

. . .

After camp I headed straight for the cookie factory, eager to lay out the next issue of *The Scoop.*

On my way there I found Lupe at the wall, patiently helping some kids tape up their rewritten essays.

I smiled at Lupe. "Thanks for doing this."

"Of course!" she said. "Oh, and Emma was looking for you. You guys are getting more calls for ads!"

"Wow, really?" I asked. Take *that*, Mr. Walters! Then I remembered. "Lupe, it's Monday! Aren't you supposed to be taking your practice test?"

"Yeah . . ." She shrugged. "This was so much more important."

Katie put her hand to the wall and looked sad for a second. "Why do you think they drew on our writing, Lupe?" she asked.

Lupe thought for a long while. "Not everything is as logical as math. Sometimes terrible things happen for no reason at all. But you know what makes it better? Having someone to talk to." She smiled at me. "And going for a walk together."

"Or a cable car ride," I chimed in.

"And letting all your feelings out," she said, "because you know you're supported."

I reached over and gave my best friend a hug.

For the next hour, Lupe and I got to work helping the kids rewrite their stories until the wall was covered with our community's voices again.

# CHAPTER 72

A community patrol, led by Uncle Mo and Uncle Hu, kept the wall safe all night. On New Year's Eve, Emma, Jason, Lupe, and I got up at the crack of dawn to deliver issue two of *The Scoop*. The front page headline?

*Chinatown Won't Be Bullied into Silence*
*Community Cleanup after the History of Us Wall Is Defaced*

Walking into the *Tribune* newsroom, I was shocked to see Mr. Walters and Mr. Miles each holding a copy.

"What is this thing?" Mr. Miles demanded, rattling it.

"It appears to be a newspaper, sir," Mr. Walters muttered.

Mr. Miles rubbed his forehead, irritated. "I *know* it's a newspaper, but where did it come from? Who's behind it?"

"Well, some of our campers are contributors," Mr. Walters admitted. "But in terms of who's publishing it? No idea."

The other editors and campers starting crowding around.

"Look at that flimsy paper. That's one step above a napkin," Timothy mocked.

I glared at him but kept my mouth shut.

"I saw three people chuckling over it in the elevator," Mr. Miles grumbled. "Made me want to take the stairs!"

I stifled a giggle. It took every ounce of self-discipline for me, Amne, and Haru not to blurt out, "It's us! We're the publishers of your competition!"

Instead, we put our heads down and got to work on our next issue. Haru wanted to interview taxi drivers about the most interesting nooks and crannies of the Bay Area. Amne wanted to cover the Novato New Year's Eve tradition up in Marin, where twenty thousand small bouncy balls were dropped onto the street from forty feet in the air and kids got a souvenir "hard hat" to catch as many as they could.

And I was excited to do a little field reporting—at Mom's black tie charity ball!

. . .

Mom clung to her flash cards while Auntie Choi and Auntie Lam did her hair and makeup. They gave her an Audrey Hepburn updo, adorned with jewels from Auntie Yan's jade shop.

"How do I look?" Mom asked, spinning around in her silk scarf dress, putting a satin-gloved hand to her sophisticated hair. I took a picture for Dad and wished he could be here.

"Like the leading lady in a Bruce Lee movie," Jason said.

I flashed Mom a smile. "No, like the lead *star* in *any* movie!"

Hank clapped. "*Now* you're talking!"

Jason handed me a small take-out box. "What's this?" I asked.

"A little something in case you get hungry," he said. Leave it to Jason to know I was already hungry. All that getting ready was exhausting. In addition to Mom's hair, it had taken Auntie Choi an hour to tame my wild mane into a neat bun, and another thirty minutes to steam out the wrinkles in my blue jumpsuit.

"Thanks." I smiled at Jason.

"Report back to me about everything!" he said for the millionth time. "The color of the plates, the way they folded all the napkins on the tables, most of all—whether they have any dishes better than mine!" He walked us to the taxi waiting outside.

"I can tell you right now, they won't!" I promised. Only one chef in the world knew the way to my heart.

Lupe held Comma up, and I gave my pup a final snuggle as Mom and I got into the taxi. As the driver stepped on the gas, Mom patted my hand. "I'm so glad you're coming with me, honey! Good for the *Tribune*, picking you to cover the ball!"

I took a deep breath. "Actually, I'm not writing it for the *Tribune*, I'm writing it for *The Scoop*."

Mom's brow wrinkled. "What do you mean?"

"This isn't a camp assignment. I want to cover the ball for the newspaper I started with my friends. Our articles kept getting rejected, so we're publishing ourselves."

It felt good to tell the truth. But I'd wanted so badly to give Mom the beautiful story that she believed in, the one where her daughter had made it at a national newspaper.

It hurt, but I couldn't keep pretending.

She still hadn't said anything, so in a small voice I made myself ask, "Are you disappointed?"

The city lights glistened in Mom's eyes. "Oh, honey, I don't care what paper you write in, as long as you keep writing. As long as you keep fighting for your dream and you keep using your voice."

"But Mom, I didn't kick the door down," I whispered.

"But you created a *new* door." She put a satin-gloved hand to my chin. "And you did it on your terms. I'm so proud of you. You'll succeed—"

"And if I don't?" I interrupted. "Will you still be proud of me?"

It took all my courage to squeeze out the words. I needed her to accept me even if I failed.

"With every beat of my heart," she said.

As she wrapped me in a hug, I felt all the pressure that had been pushing on my chest lift. I could finally raise my wings and fly *for myself.*

I mouthed *thank you* to the immigrant gods as Mom and I sat up straight again in the back seat.

"I think this calls for a snack!" I said, unwrapping the box from Jason. Inside were two mooncakes. I gave one to Mom. "Cheers!"

We giggled and toasted them.

As the taxicab pulled up to the Four Seasons Hotel, I bit into the mooncake. Instead of lotus paste, Jason had filled it with a new flavor . . .

I smiled.

*Butterscotch.*

# CHAPTER 73

The San Francisco New Year's Eve Charity Ball was the most decked-out, exclusive, lavish affair I'd ever seen. They had a red carpet, a chocolate fountain, a river of floating candles, and black and gold balloons bobbing on the ceiling.

But Mom was barely enjoying it. She looked like she was about to pass out as a woman in a bright red gown walked up to the podium with a clicker. The woman's presentation about her charity came up on a screen. As she clicked, talking about her charity's statistics in creative text art, the tech titans in attendance applauded, impressed.

"What am I going to do??" Mom asked, panicking. "I didn't prepare fancy slides!"

"You don't need them," I promised her. I held both her hands. "Listen to me. I freaked out at camp too. But you gotta believe in the power of a story. Nothing else matters. Trust me."

"Next up, we have Ying Tang, from Math Cup!" the announcer said. "Ying, are you ready?"

Mom looked down at her flash cards, then at me.

"Nobody else has a story like yours. *Believe*," I whispered.

Then a miraculous thing happened. Mom handed me the flash cards. "I believe you," she said, then walked up to the podium with nothing but her passion.

"Good evening," she said into the mic. "My name is Ying Tang. I am an immigrant. I used to be an engineer in China."

Big applause from the audience. Mom smiled, relaxing.

"Then I moved to this country. Like many immigrants, I had to change my profession. First, I worked as a waitress, then as a motel manager. I cleaned the toilets. Many, many toilets. But I did a thorough job, because, you know, I'm an engineer." She smiled again and paused.

I couldn't believe it. Mom was making a joke! And everyone laughed! I snapped a photo.

"One day," she went on, "I started thinking. There's gotta be more for me in this country. I didn't know what, but I knew one thing. I knew math! So I worked really hard, and eventually I got a job at my local high school. I am proud to say, this year I led my team to win the state championships of the Math Cup! The first time ever in the history of my high school!"

"Go, Mom!" I shouted. Others joined me in clapping.

"I want to give the gift of math confidence to as many kids as possible, especially kids in underprivileged districts," she continued. "Because knowing your true worth—not being afraid to ask for better terms because you understand your value—is what changed my life."

Her eyes met mine as the whole room erupted in applause.

She did it! She delivered her speech, straight from her heart! And judging by the long line of people walking over to talk to her, she'd captured their hearts too! Just by being herself and telling her story.

"Ying!" a voice called.

Mom and I both turned—and got the surprise of our lives.

"Dad!" I screamed, running over and jumping into his arm.

"Li!" Mom exclaimed, laughing as she leaned in and gave him a kiss. "What are you doing here?"

"You really thought I'd miss your speech? Not a chance!" Dad grinned. As the orchestra started to play "I Swear," Dad held out a hand. "Now, may I have this dance?"

*Dad . . . dance??*

I reached for my camera as Mom handed me her purse.

Under the black and gold balloons, my whole family welcomed the New Year together. I snapped pictures of my parents dancing with the elites of San Francisco. Or rather, Mom danced. Dad . . . kind of looked like a limp noodle twisting in the wind. But it didn't matter; he was having fun. I smiled, thinking of Ms. Flemings. I was *so* glad Dad had taken some time off.

My parents kept their eyes on each other as they twirled. It was like they were in their own little cocoon. I guess that's what happens when you marry your best friend and you're still madly in love, years later. The world disappears and you're a mooncake of two.

# CHAPTER 74

On New Year's Day, we woke up to the sound of firecrackers and drums. Everyone was out celebrating!

I threw on a sweatshirt and ran out to find Dad. There was so much to show him: *The Scoop*! The cookie factory! Portsmouth Square! The Ferry Building!

He was downstairs making breakfast with Hank and Jason. Lupe was with Katie and Johnny, stirring rice.

"Happy New Year!" Hank exclaimed.

"Happy New Year, Hank!" I walked over and gave him a hug. He handed me a plate with pancakes, steamed buns, and a glutinous rice pyramid wrapped in bamboo leaves. "Is that zongzi?" I asked.

I hadn't seen zongzi since we were in Beijing last Christmas! I picked up the sticky leafy pyramid and breathed in deep.

"I found bamboo leaves at the grocery store and couldn't resist," Jason said, handing some more Chinese sausage to Lupe, who was helping Katie and Johnny wrap the zongzi.

"*My* favorite filling is pork belly," Hank said, grabbing a piece and putting it in his mouth. "Don't forget to save some for me and Dean. He's coming over later!"

"He is?" I asked, impressed.

Hank grinned. "He finally made partner—you should have heard him on the phone! Thought we'd celebrate by making some zongzi together!"

"That's a wonderful idea!" I said. "We should have a zongzi party!" I got excited, thinking the community event would make a fantastic piece for *The Scoop*!

Mom came running in. "I just got off the phone!" she said, out of breath. "The committee heard about my speech, and guess what?"

I glanced at Dad, who was beaming like he already knew—but I still screamed when Mom said, "I got it! You're looking at the newest member of the Math Cup steering committee!"

"YESSSSS!!!"

Jason threw bamboo leaves in the air, and Lupe and I ran over to hug Mom.

"I never doubted it for a minute," I told her.

"I did," Mom confessed, hugging me back. "But you were right. All I had to do was believe in the power of my story."

"Now *that*'s something I want to stuff into every zongzi!" I grinned.

• • •

Dad and I stood next to each other by the sink, preparing the leaves for the zongzi party that was underway at the inn. Dad washed them while I added a tablespoon of oil to prevent the glutinous rice from sticking. Then we boiled them. As we waited, Dad caught me up on the latest at the Calivista. Then I showed him my newspaper.

"*The Scoop*, that's a great name!" he said. "You could distribute it in Anaheim too when we get back! Bet it would be hugely popular!"

"Say, I have a friend in New York who prints menus for Chinese restaurants," Uncle Hu hollered from the zongzi filling table. "Maybe he'd be interested in distributing it on the East Coast!"

My eyes boggled. "You mean we could go *national*??"

I'd never thought of that! It would take a lot of hard work and *a lot* more stories, but if there was one thing I'd learned, stories were everywhere. From the tree trunks of Yosemite to the rock formations of Berkeley to the discarded library books of the San Diego Library to the poems carved onto the walls of Angel Island . . . you just had to take the time to find them.

When the last of the zongzi was wrapped, I asked Dad if he wanted to help me distribute *The Scoop*.

"I'd love that!"

"We could take the streetcar, see all the sights!" I said. The vintage streetcars, with the trolley pole connected to an overhead wire, ran all over the city. They were the only local transportation I hadn't taken yet!

"Sounds perfect."

As Dad went to get his jacket, I walked over to Jason. "Thanks so much for the mooncakes last night," I said. "They were delicious."

"Glad you liked them. I tried a new flavor, butterscotch!" Jason said proudly. "I was a little scared it'd be overpowering."

"It wasn't," I said. With a shy smile, I added, "It's actually my favorite flavor."

"Mine too!"

"I know. You always smell like butterscotch." I laughed.

Jason blushed and sniffed his hand. "I do? Well, in that case . . ."

He stuck his hand all the way out to my nose, and I almost choked from laughing.

I glanced over at Emma, digging into her a freshly steamed zongzi with her mom. Jason followed my gaze.

"Have you told her how you feel yet?" I asked.

He took his time replying, and my pulse quickened with hope.

"Tomorrow," he finally said.

# CHAPTER 75

As we rode the streetcar up and down Powell Street, Dad tried to get it out of me why I looked so blue. I finally told him about me and Jason.

"Ahhhh, young love," Dad said, bumping his shoulder into mine. "My little girl's growing up! I suppose it was bound to happen."

"Don't get too excited. I'm in *no* rush to grow up." I told him all about my plan to get better at chilling. "I want to enjoy being a kid," I said. "Instead of working all the time, I want to make more time for fun!"

"I like that *a lot*!" he said.

"But still . . . Jason doesn't even like me back."

"Because you won't tell the poor guy how you feel!"

"It's not that easy, okay?" I shook my head in frustration. "What if he rejects me?"

"So what if he does? You know how many times your mom turned me down before we finally went to the movies?"

My jaw dropped to the streetcar floor. "Mom turned you down? I thought you guys were soul mates!"

"We are!" Dad said. "That doesn't mean it was automatic from the start, though." He patted my hand. "Your mom was a very special swan. And she was admired by a lot of people."

"So how'd you get your chance?" I asked.

Dad gazed out the window toward Fisherman's Wharf. As the streetcar carried us through the mist, he said, "I painted her a picture of our future. A picture so full of heart and brightness, she couldn't get it out of her mind."

I smiled. "So you told her a story."

"I sure did," Dad said, looking into my eyes. "And even though I got some parts wrong—okay, a *lot* of parts—I got one part right: We're still very, very happy together. And we have you." He patted my hand again.

I cozied up to Dad as Karl the Fog hugged us.

"Don't be so scared by the conclusion that you don't even find out what happens," he said. "You owe it to yourself to experience the story."

I thought about Dad's words long after the last of the fog had lifted.

. . .

It took me a full day's tour of San Francisco, but I finally realized Dad was right. I'd been so terrified of this story's ending, I'd forgotten to enjoy the middle.

I thought about all my favorite books. The journey was always the best part of every story! Not who Jo March or Claudia Kishi or Francie Nolan ended up with, but the laughs they had. The adventures they went on. *That's* what kept me reading late into the night.

I had to tell Jason how I felt.

The next morning, I scrambled down the stairs to find him. But he wasn't in the kitchen. Instead, I found Dean with Hank.

"Mia!" Dean greeted me. "Happy New Year!"

"Happy New Year, Dean." I smiled. "And congratulations! I heard the great news!"

"Thank you," he said, beaming. He handed me a freshly steamed zongzi. "Here, try one! We stayed up late last night making these."

"You stayed over?" I asked, surprised.

"Thankfully Mrs. Luk had an extra room for me. The fireplaces here are classy!"

I smiled, glad to hear he'd come around about the Golden Inn. Turning to Hank, I asked, "Have you seen Jason?"

"I think he went to the store," he said. "Heard him say he wanted to get some more vanilla and dark brown sugar. But I'll tell him you're looking for him!"

I thanked Hank and breathed in the zongzi, smiling. I thought I detected the faint scent of strawberry in the delicate sticky rice.

"What's in the filling?" I asked.

"Strawberry rhubarb," Dean informed me. He put a hand on his brother's shoulder. "Just like the pies our mama used to make."

I took a delicious bite as I headed out for my last day of camp. I was so glad Hank and his brother were whipping up new memories in Mrs. Luk's kitchen.

Stepping inside the newsroom, I found Mr. Walters and Mr. Miles waiting for me at my desk. The way they were glaring at me, I knew something was wrong.

Then I saw that my desk was covered in paper—issues of *The Scoop*.

*Uh-oh.*

# CHAPTER 76

"When were you guys going to tell us about your little project?" Mr. Miles asked me, Amne, and Haru.

"How'd you figure out that it was us?" I asked.

Mr. Walters frowned. "Very funny. You've made your point. You've pulled an impressive prank on your editors—"

"This isn't a prank," I protested. "We're serious about *The Scoop*. We're going to keep publishing it, even after camp!"

Amne nodded.

Mr. Miles balked. "They're kidding, right?" he asked Mr. Walters.

"Oh, we're totally not kidding!" Haru said. "You know how profitable advertising can be if you have great stories? It's a *lot* more than seventy-five dollars!"

Haru reached over to high-five me and Amne.

I smiled sweetly. "Funny how the articles you turned down for being 'unnewsworthy' turned out to be such a hit! In fact, we have plans to go national!"

"Unbelievable," Mr. Miles said. He looked like he wanted to kick us out of his newsroom, but then he tried another tactic—negotiating. "Look, if you really want to get published, we'll find a space in the paper. But this isn't the way."

"Is that space a once-a-year Chinatown spot?" I asked.

"Or real facts slotted in the *opinion* section?" Amne crossed her arms.

"I think he means the can't-pay-you section," Haru said. He covered his mouth with his hand and whispered, "Because we're not related to someone famous."

We shook our heads. "Nope. That's not gonna work for us," I said. "But thank you for the opportunity. And thank you for reminding us what we can do with our passion."

As Mr. Miles flushed a deep red and stomped back to his office, we looked up. To our surprise, a few of the other editors and writers in the newsroom came over to congratulate us on *The Scoop*.

"Sick layout!" the production editor complimented us. "If you have a minute, I can show you some layout tricks that have helped me."

"You kids these days. If I had the courage to start off on my own ten years ago," a Latinx photo editor said, shaking our hands, "I can't even imagine the possibilities!"

Several other writers nodded.

I smiled. That gave me an idea!

"We're always looking for freelancers and contributors!" I said, handing out our contacts.

That day, we handed out cards with our phone numbers to everybody at the *Tribune* who was also sick of being overworked, overlooked, and underpaid. It truly felt like we were starting a revolution.

Before I raced home to find Jason, I put an issue of *The Scoop* in the mail for Ms. Flemings, with a note:

Work hard, play hard, and always know your worth. :)

—Mia Tang

I smiled, thinking of Mom's words. She was right; there really wasn't anything more powerful than knowing your worth.

# CHAPTER 77

"Emma!" I called, walking into the cookie factory with the new ad I'd made to find Mr. and Mrs. Luk a permanent chef. We were ready to start running a jobs section in *The Scoop*.

Emma was in the printer room, talking to someone. As I strolled inside, I saw it was Jason. I froze. Shrinking into the shadowy wall, I held my breath and listened.

"Will you meet me there?" Jason asked. "I'll tell you tomorrow. Just don't be late. It's kind of important." He inhaled deeply. "I've been waiting forever to ask you that. Like *a really really* long time!"

My heart dropped to my stomach.

"Must be pretty special if you want to meet me at—"

A loud bang on the printer cut out the last part. As the machine purred back into motion, my overactive imagination filled in the missing words. Jason was meeting Emma at the Golden Gate Bridge. I knew it! I was too late! I'd blown my chance!

Now my beloved butterscotch was going to walk hand in hand across the bridge with my publishing partner! Who I couldn't even get mad at because only she knew how to work the printer!

Hot tears dripped down my cheeks as I heard Emma coo, "Great, see you there tomorrow!"

Just like that, their date was set.

I hunched behind the printing press, trying to imagine a different headline—the one my heart deserved—if I'd only found the courage to tell Jason how I felt.

. . .

It was impossible to focus on writing and proofreading articles for *The Scoop* the next day. I stress ate Choco-Pies in my room, jumping up and glancing out the window every two seconds. *Were Jason and Emma back yet?*

I twirled my pen faster and faster as I imagined them skipping across the bridge and ending up at Murray Circle. Ordering curly fries and Shirley Temples. With the cute little cherries. I loved those little cherries! The thought depressed me so much, my pen flew straight into the air, squirting ink all over my cheeks.

"What's wrong??" Lupe asked, walking in. She reached for a tissue and handed it to me.

"I'm sorry!" I wailed. "I was thinking about Jason and Emma. And Shirley Temples!"

I buried my face in my arms.

Lupe walked over and pulled me up by one elbow. "You know what you need? A spa day! C'mon, let's go have fun."

She threw me a robe. I'd forgotten it was the third! Auntie Choi and Auntie Lam's monthly spa day!

Together, we walked down the street toward Auntie Choi's salon. Women all over Chinatown were headed there in robes. Mom was already inside, helping Auntie Choi and Auntie Lam set up. The salon smelled like coconut, honey, and lavender. As the women of Chinatown escorted Popo inside, helped her get settled, and made themselves at home, Auntie Lam handed out jade rollers and put on old Chinese love songs.

"Welcome to Chinatown Spa Day, ladies." Auntie Choi smiled. "Absolutely no worrying allowed. This is *our* time. A time for us to unwind, reflect, and be present with each other."

Lupe and I sat back, closing our eyes as we moved the jade rollers over our faces.

"Speaking of being present," Lupe said with a sigh, "I decided maybe I should hold off on taking the SATs for a little while. Maybe give high school a chance."

I stopped rolling. Forget the Shirley Temples, this was music to my ears! "That's *great*! What made you change your mind?"

Lupe thought for a long time.

"I realized bad things can happen anywhere. In high school, college, or even on the wall of a beloved neighborhood. But it's the people I'm around who make it better. Like you and Jason and my mom."

I smiled. "Yes, it is," I said, leaning my shoulder over to touch hers.

"Maybe instead of hurrying to move on, we can support each other right here, right now."

I put my jade roller down and threw my arms around her. "You can count on me, here and now and always!"

The ladies in the salon dabbed their eyes as we hugged, until Lupe pulled away and gave me a playful poke.

"Besides, I can't let you beat me at Pac-Man," Lupe joked. "We need a do-over!"

"We totally need a do-over!"

As we made plans to hit Chuck E. Cheese as soon as we got back, the door swung open and Emma came in. I jumped up from my salon chair.

"Emma!" I cried.

"Hey, Mia!" she said. "I've got your new issue right here, with the help wanted section! It looks brilliant!"

I was sure it did, but I was more interested in hearing about her big date with Jason! As she sat down on a salon chair, I hopped into the one next to her and started interviewing her.

"So tell me!" I urged. "Did you meet Jason at the south side of the bridge? Was it windy?"

"What are you talking about?" Emma asked, confused.

"The Golden Gate Bridge. You and Jason. Isn't that where you were today? Were there lots of cars? Did you see any dolphins or—"

Emma held up a hand to stop me. "Mia. I didn't go on the Golden Gate Bridge with Jason."

I stared back at her. "You didn't?"

She shook her head.

"Did you go on *any* kind of special date with him today?"

"No. Mia, what—"

My heart pounded. *Did Jason chicken out? Was he going to tell her tomorrow?* I jumped out of the salon chair. *I still had a chance!*

"I have to go!" I said. I had to find Jason *right now*. I glanced in the mirror. Okay, maybe I should first wipe the huge ink stain off my face. I sniffed my armpit. And maybe take a shower.

"Where you going?" Lupe asked.

"To tell Jason!" I said.

Mom smiled. "Wait, wait, wait!" She reached for a flower nearby and pinned it up in my hair. She put a hand to my cheek. "Your dad told me," she said when she saw the confused look on my face. "Whatever happens, know that you are worth every bit of happiness in this life. And nothing less."

I gave her a hug.

"Tell Jason what?" Emma asked.

"Let's talk on the way over! Is the cookie factory still open?" I had a great idea about *how* to tell Jason, but it was going to involve Emma's help. I put my hands together. "Will you help me?"

Emma hesitated, then handed her jade roller back to Auntie Choi. As I ran out onto the street, she gazed at me like my hair was on fire. But I didn't care. *I was finally going to tell Jason!*

# CHAPTER 78

As we zigzagged down alleyways toward the factory, I told Emma my true feelings about Jason. She didn't seem surprised. As she struggled with the cookie factory lock, I finally asked the other question I'd been worried about.

"Now that you know, are you sure you still want to help me? I know you and Jason were close. *Are* close . . ." I looked down hesitantly. "If you feel weird about it . . ."

Emma unlocked the door and turned to look at me.

"I don't feel weird," she said, walking inside and propping herself beside the printer. She mustered a smile. "Besides, even if I did, would that stop you from writing the most epic love story of our generation? Would it have stopped Louisa May Alcott? Or Jane Austen?"

"Good point," I said, immensely flattered she was comparing me to the writer of *Little Women*.

"Besides," she said, throwing a package of fortune cookies at me. I reached inside and pulled one out. I broke it in half and read the fortune inside.

*Sometimes you have to take a chance in order to find what you lost. In my case, it's writing this fortune . . . hoping YOU might write back.*

"Emma!" I cried.

"Printed a hundred more sheets this morning." She beamed

proudly, pointing at the thick stack of paper sitting beside me. "Thank you for inspiring me to put my words out there."

That afternoon, with Emma's help, I printed my own fortune on the printing press. Something so special, there was only one place in the world to open it.

Fingers trembling, I slipped a note under Jason's door that night:

Meet me at the Golden Gate Bridge (Vista Point South) tomorrow at 10 a.m.!

—Mia

# CHAPTER 79

The wind blew wildly in my hair as I waited at the entrance of the Golden Gate Bridge. My hands were frigid. Mom and Dad had dropped me off in a taxi. They said they'd be back in an hour to pick us up. My fingers clutched my special fortune cookie in my pocket as I looked to my left and to my right. *Where was he?*

Finally, I heard his voice.

"Mia!"

My heart pounded as I turned around. There was Jason, running up to the bridge sidewalk.

"Jason!" I called.

He ran as fast as he could, with one arm behind his back. We finally met on the bridge. "I have to tell you something!"

"Me first! I have to get this off my chest or I'm going to pop! I like you, Jason Yao! I've liked you since the second moment I met you! And I know I should have told you this sooner, but I'm telling you now—I can't imagine you not being a part of my story! No matter how it turns out. I'd rather turn the page and get my heart broken than not turn it at all."

The sound of rushing cars and roaring wind filled my ears as I waited for Jason to respond. He didn't say anything at first, just moved his arm to reveal what he'd been carrying behind his back:

the finest-looking bouquet of flowers I'd ever seen in my life. I gasped.

"You don't know how long I've waited to hear those words!" he said.

I took the flowers from him.

"Emma helped me pick them out," Jason said. "Better than the dandelions I gave you the first time?"

I chuckled. "Definitely better," I agreed. Then nervously, I asked, "So you and Emma . . . ?"

"We're just friends," he told me. "I thought I liked her, but when we started training Comma together, I realized . . . there's no other person in the world I'd rather train a puppy with. Even when they chew up my oven mitts!" He chuckled. "A thousand mitts, so long as you give me a chance. I promise I am not going to break your heart."

I reached into my pocket and presented the fortune cookie.

Carefully, he opened it up and read the fortune.

*You are the ink in my pen, Jason Yao. And I hope our story never ends. Love, Mia*

Jason leaned in and hugged me. It felt like the wind and the fog was hugging us too, holding us together.

"And just so you know," I said, "I'm not ready for anything more than just being friends who like each other."

"Absolutely," he agreed.

"No funny business," I told him.

"No way."

"I still cover my eyes when I'm watching *Little Women*," I added.

"I do too," he said. "Aunt March scares me."

I laughed. With that settled, I slowly held out my hand. As Jason took it, I felt the music in my head soar.

Hand in hand, we started walking down the bridge. Jason gave me his jacket when I shivered. "Thanks." I smiled at him and asked, one last time, just to be safe, "But seriously, though, you're not going to stomp all over my feelings, right?" My face turned stern and I joked, "If you do, I'll write a thousand books about you!"

Jason grinned. "And I'll buy every single copy and build a first-edition *I'm So Sorry* apology kitchen."

"Filled with butterscotch mooncakes," I added.

Jason stopped and dug inside his own pocket. To my surprise, he pulled out a mooncake. This one was shaped like a heart.

"Mia, it's always been you," Jason whispered as he handed it to me.

As I took in the warm smell of butterscotch, I felt my own heart melt.

# CHAPTER 80

Mom and Dad packed up the cars the next day. I couldn't believe it was our last day in Chinatown. I was going to miss this place so much! Auntie Lam and Auntie Choi were there to say farewell, plus Uncle Mo and six of my History of Us students. Auntie Lam put a hand-knitted sweater on Comma. Lupe was in the corner saying good-bye to little Katie and Johnny, who promised they would do all the math equations she assigned them and keep her updated on everything going on in Chinatown.

I turned to Emma, Amne, and Haru, who had come too. As we hugged good-bye, we made plans to keep publishing the paper even after we all went home. We were going to expand it to LA and New York.

"Maybe even DC?" Amne added, with a smile.

"For sure!" Haru said. "There's a computer at the museum. I can email you guys my stories!"

"Great! I can borrow the computer at the YMCA!" Emma said, glancing over at Uncle Mo, who nodded. He wrote down the email address for the museum and handed it to me, Haru, and Amne.

Amne wrote down her uncle's email, and I jotted down my fax number at the Calivista. I felt a little sad to be the only one who still didn't have an email address. But I reminded myself of the fortune

I'd written on my very first day in Chinatown. *It wasn't the tools that mattered, it was my courage and character.*

Mom and Dad walked back in. "Well, that's everything," Dad said.

As Mr. and Mrs. Luk thanked Hank and Jason for their extraordinary cooking and pitching in to help save the Golden Inn, I threw my arms around Emma. "I can't believe this is good-bye."

"It's not," Emma said. "Just go to your local Chinese restaurant when you miss me." She grinned. "Chances are, my words will be there. I have a plan to go nationwide, too!"

I grinned back at her. "I'm sure you do. And you will. You have the fire of a thousand dragons behind you."

Emma smiled at the line, then gasped. "The résumés!" She ran over and grabbed a big stack of paper from her tote bag. "I totally forgot! We received all these yesterday! They're for the chef's position!"

Mr. and Mrs. Luk couldn't believe their eyes. "My goodness! There must be a hundred résumés here!"

"That's more than we've ever had!" Mr. Luk said. "With any luck, we can fill the position this week!"

We all cheered. Then Mrs. Luk turned to me. "You must always keep writing, Mia. Your words *matter.*"

"Oh, she will," Uncle Hu said, coming in carrying another surprise. It was an old Macintosh computer, with a keyboard and a mouse! He set it down right in front of me on the table in a cloud of dust. "For you."

I started screaming, I was so excited. Comma jumped up and down at my feet. I picked him up and showed him my dream come true. "Look, Comma!" I squealed. "A computer!"

Lupe ran over with her students to admire it. It was old and dusty, but the keys felt like soft pillows under my fingers.

"Now you can keep editing the paper, even from down south," Uncle Hu smiled.

"How much is it?" Dad asked, opening his wallet. He looked worried.

"Oh, no, no, no," Uncle Hu said, waving Dad away. His eyes twinkled at me. "You just keep writing your paper. Then one day, when you famous author, you give this computer back to me. And I sell it for *ten times!*"

I laughed. What a businessman! "It's a deal!" I said, shaking his hand.

As Hank helped Uncle Hu get the big computer into the car, Dad turned toward us.

"You know, we have a bit of time. Maybe we can take the long way!"

"Oh, I like the idea!" Hank seconded. "Stop somewhere fun!"

"Where?" Mom asked.

"I have an idea!" Jason said.

. . .

Four hours later, we were in Yosemite National Park, climbing the long and twisty trail up to Sing Peak. It was icy cold and we shivered in our winter coats, even Comma in his special sweater. But we kept pushing, inspired by Tie Sing, the backcountry cook.

All the way up the trail, Jason told us about Tie Sing.

"He was an amazing cook. Everybody loved his food," Jason said. "He made trout and pork chops and fried potatoes and apple pie— right here in the woods!"

"Apple pie," Lupe said, rubbing her belly as she hiked. "That sounds good right about now."

"Fried potatoes too," I agreed.

"He'd start cooking at the crack of dawn! He'd make steaming hot coffee in the morning, along with sausage, hotcakes—you name it!" Jason went on.

The more he described the delicious food, the faster we marched. Up, up, up the hill.

"The trip was a success because of him! Let's face it, food is the best route to the heart," Jason said, flashing me a smile. When at last we came around the final bend, he pointed at the gorgeous snowy mountain peaks. "Look!"

"We did it!" Lupe yelled, throwing her hands up in the air. "We made it to Sing Peak!"

I gasped, taking in the view. Standing on top of Sing Peak, I breathed in deep and felt my soul expand. The sun kissed the mountaintops as far as I could see, melting the snow into majestic waterfalls.

"Wow . . . this place is *exquisite*," Dad whispered. Turning to Jason, he added, "Sounds like Sing made a lot more than apple pie. He made history."

I smiled. "Just like we are . . . in our own little way."

Mom squeezed my hand. As we all looked out toward the horizon at Sing Peak, I thought of how far we'd come, each and every one of us . . . and all the wonderous possibilities that lay ahead.

# AUTHOR'S NOTE

Copies of my newspaper, the *Pen Times*

When I was fifteen, I started a newspaper called the *Pen Times*. Like Mia, I was frustrated by the reporting in the big newspapers in my town. I was living in the San Gabriel Valley, Los Angeles, a heavily Asian American community, and I rarely saw feature articles about people who looked like me and my neighbors.

So I decided to start my own free newspaper for the community, by the community. I recruited other kid writers to help. Together, we published breaking news, stories, poems, recipes, an advice column, a *lengthy* movie review section, and much more.

I remember going to Office Depot with my mom for the first time, asking if they had newspaper stock to print my paper on. They chuckled. I told them I was serious. I intended to publish my newspaper every month at their store, and distribute it all over town.

And that's just what I did. For two solid years, the *Pen Times* showcased the hope and joy of a small community. A community much like Chinatown, San Francisco, wrestling with change; trying to reinvent itself while staying authentic; honoring the role it played, historically and today, in providing refuge to so many.

I am so proud to bring to life Chinatown's rich, beautiful history in Mia's *Top Story* adventure. I hope after reading these pages, children are inspired to learn more about the Chinese Exclusion Act, the Page Act, the Alien Land Act, the Foreign Miners Tax, and all the other *real* and pivotal moments of Asian American history that Mia learns about—because Asian American history *is* American history.

In doing research for this book, I went to Chinatown and interviewed community leaders, small business owners, historians, journalists, and police officers. I'll never forget walking through the Chinese Historical Society of America museum, and seeing the pen that President Roosevelt used to sign the Chinese Exclusion Act into federal law. I'd known about this act, but seeing the actual pen made my stomach drop to my knees.

But then I turned a corner, and there was the Bruce Lee exhibit, reminding me of all that we can achieve, the *mountains* we can move when we replace the hate with love. With kindness. With possibility. My eyes welled with tears of hope. Hope is the vital ingredient that

The pen with which President Roosevelt signed the Chinese Exclusion Act

has made Chinatown survive and thrive, all these years. Popping in and out of banquet halls and noodle shops, I saw smiling aunties and uncles extending that hope to every child in the community. My heart swelled. That's the power of a place where you feel seen and safe.

Sadly, just like in the story, the future of Chinatowns all over the United States is in peril. The Covid-19 pandemic, coupled with soaring anti-Asian hate, have taken a toll on so many small businesses in Chinatown. The vandalism of the mural wall that the residents in the story encountered is just one of the many senseless acts of hate that residents in Chinatown have endured in recent years.

Ultimately, it is up to each and every one of us to protect the communities that we love. All of us have so much power to affect change, with our voices, our pens, and our courage to shape a brighter future! As can be seen in the true inspiring story of Clara Breed, the actions of one individual can have such a profound impact on so many people.

Finally, I hope through reading *Top Story*, more children will be inspired to learn more about the history of Indigenous Peoples of this country, including the Muwekma Ohlone Tribe's struggle for federal recognition. I want to thank the Muwekma Ohlone Tribe of the San Francisco Bay Area for sharing with me the story of the first people of the San Francisco Bay Area, for naming Amne Sullik, and reviewing my pages. For more information on the Muwekma Ohlone Tribe's efforts to restore federal recognition, please visit: http://www.muwekma.org.

As complex and fraught as our history is, I believe in the future. I believe in the next generation, their capacity for empathy, and their excitement to *be* the change they want to see in the world. It all starts with a bold, brave voice. So, get out there and tell your stories, far and wide! The world is waiting. The world is listening.

# ACKNOWLEDGMENTS

Believe it or not, some of the scenes in this book have been in my head for six years, ever since I wrote the first draft of *Front Desk*! That's how long I have been rooting for Mia and Jason in my head! I am so proud that we finally got here, and it wouldn't be possible without the following people:

My incredible team at Scholastic, starting with my amazing editor Amanda Maciel—it is my great luck in life to have you as my editor! Thank you to Ellie Berger, David Levithan, Lerina Velazquez, Elizabeth Whiting, Erin Berger, Rachel Feld, Seale Ballenger, Elisabeth Ferrari, Lizette Serrano, Emily Heddleson, Maeve Norton, Maithili Joshi, Melissa Schirmer, and the supremely talented Maike Plenzke, who truly blew me away with this cover!

A million thanks to Tina Dubois, who cheered me on with every step; Sylvie Rabineau; Joel McKuin; Paul Sennott; my team at Curtis Brown, including Enrichetta Frezzato, Roxane Edouard, and Isobel Gahan; Shelby Renjifo for her help with the research for this book; my dear friends Paul Cummins, Bill Isacoff, Jeff Kinney, Stuart Gibbs, Victoria Piontek, Mae Respicio, Jerry Craft, Varian Johnson, Stacy McAnulty, Jennie Urman, and Lindsey Moore; my family, Stephen, Eliot, Tilden, Nina, my amazing parents—Mom and Dad, I love you; and Anna Cummins and Marcus Eriksen for their insight on farming and WWOOFing.

I owe a huge amount of gratitude to the Muwekma Ohlone Tribe of the San Francisco Bay Area, including Gloria E. Gómez for your help with naming Amne, and Alan Leventhal, tribal ethno-historian, for your help with reviewing the pages for sensitivity and historical accuracy. I would like to thank Catherine Herrera as well as Jonathan Cordero for speaking with me and answering my questions.

Huge shout-out to my friends in San Francisco's Chinatown, starting with my dear friend Christine Ni! Thank you to Myron Lee, Justin Hoover, executive director of the Chinese Historical Society of America Museum, Max Leung, Jonathan Sit, and Will Ma—all of you are heroes of Chinatown. Thank you for sharing your stories and love for the community with me. Many thanks to Kevin Chan, owner of the Golden Gate Fortune Cookie Factory, for letting me visit the factory and being so patient with me while I (hilariously) tried to make fortune cookies! Readers, if you're ever in San Francisco, I hope you stop by Chinatown and visit the museums, restaurants, shops, and Golden Gate Fortune Cookie Factory!

Finally, my heartfelt thanks to all my readers. It's because of YOU that I get to keep writing. It's because of YOU that we got this fifth book! It's because of YOU that kids all over the world see themselves in these pages and now have the courage to headline their own top stories! Thank you for giving me this tremendous honor and I hope I did you proud with this book!